Salem's Vengeance

Vengeance Trilogy: Book One

Aaron Galvin

Aames & Abernathy Publishing

Salem's Vengeance
Vengeance Trilogy: Book One

Published by Aames & Abernathy Publishing,
Chino Hills, CA USA

Edited by Annetta Ribken.
You can find her at *www.wordwebbing.com*
Copy Edits by Jennifer Wingard.
www.theindependentpen.com
Cover Design by Greg Sidelnik.
www.gregsidelnik.com
Book formatting by Valerie Bellamy.
www.dog-earbookdesign.com

ISBN-10: 150037525X
ISBN-13: 978-1500375256

Printed in the USA

for those who love the night and the countless secrets
She holds.

&

for Karen, who still prefers the safety of day.

&

to my hometown
Lebanon Public Library
Hope you enjoy the read!

Facts

In 1976, psychologist Linnda R. Caporael published an article linking the behaviors of Salem accusers to that of ergotism, or ergot poisoning, caused by the fungus *Claviceps purpurea.*

According to the American Phytopathological Society:

> "*Claviceps purpurea* infects the ovary of cereal and grass plants. In the early stages of disease development, a sticky exudate (honeydew) often appears. The infected ovary is replaced by a purplish-black sclerotium, commonly referred to as an ergot.
>
> Before this disease (ergotism) was understood, the ergots were ground up along with rye grains and ingested when the flour was used for baking. In the Middle Ages, this led to a frightening disease of humans known as 'holy fire' or 'St. Anthony's fire'.
>
> People under the influence of ergot alkaloids may have convulsions, become manic, appear dazed, be unable to speak or have other forms of paralysis or tremors, and suffer from hallucinations and other

distorted perceptions. These strange behaviors have been linked to ergotism during the French Revolution and witchcraft in Europe and the U.S. (Salem, MA, in particular).

Common symptoms included strange mental aberrations, hallucinations, a feeling of burning skin or insects crawling under the skin."

Modern toxicology reports reveal alkaloids present in ergot include lysergic acid, of which the psychedelic drug LSD is created.

Sources
Caporael's article in *Science*, issue 192
http://goo.gl/Dw27F0

American Phytopathological Society
Ergot of rye
Schumann, G.L. 2000. Ergot. *The Plant Health Instructor*.
DOI: 10.1094/PHI-I-2000-1016-01
http://goo.gl/R1uwZx

-one-

- October, 1712 -

Winford, Carolina Territory

My freedom comes with the moonlight. A dim ray, broken and scattered by my wooden shutters, spreads over the pine floor of my room. My toes tingle with anticipation beneath the heavy checkered quilt Mother sewed for Rebecca and me. The time for dancing draws nigh.

Clink!

The rock striking our window ledge quickens my heartbeat.

Something is wrong. The moonlight should be spread over four boards, not one, ere it would be the proper time to leave.

A quiet voice floats through my window. "Sarah!"

"Shh!" Another hushes.

Rebecca stirs beside me on the straw pallet we share.

I stroke her flaxen hair ere she awakens further. "All is well, sweet sister," I soothe. "Go back to sleep."

She rubs her tired eyes with balled fists. "But I wish to join you and the others," she says.

Clink!

My limbs tense anew. Father will surely wake to their voices soon. I wait, listening. He can be silent as a barn owl in flight when he chooses. Still, even he cannot rise from his rickety bed without it creaking under the movement.

I hear nothing but my own heart pounding.

"Sarah!" the quiet voice calls again.

It must be Emma. An ever-present fear has clouded her since she heard tell of the Tuscarora Indians who raided and slaughtered throughout the Carolina territory. I suppose it hardly matters to her most of the savages were put down a year ago September past.

Rebecca tugs at the sleeves of my lace nightgown. "Please, Sarah," she whispers. "Please, take me."

I kiss the top of her forehead. "You are much too young for the dance."

Rebecca wrenches away from me to pout.

I sweep our quilt of muted blue and white over her head. The breeze from the open window tickles my bare feet and drifts up my thighs like a feather tracing against my skin.

I shudder, and revel in its chill; the same feelings I hope to continue at the moon dance. I gather my thin leather shoes in hand. Turn toward my escape. Though my windowsill is but three quick steps away, my path holds creaky floorboards that will betray my otherwise silent movements. I step over the first of them, and leap sideways to avoid the next two.

Rebecca giggles quietly. It must seem to her I play scotch-hopper.

The fresh scent of strung, dried lilacs from my room dissipates the moment I poke my head out our window. Odors of farm life—sweet-smelling heifers, excrement-sowing swine, and the like—blend together in the night air. Fifty yards away, our four-storied barn is a hulking gravestone casting its long shadow over our homestead.

The nearly full moon is perfect to dance beneath. Not so, however, for one seeking to flee without being seen. To reach the barn will be only a quick sprint. But my friends are not as fast as I, nor as cautious. I wish I had the sliver moon and less light to escape beneath.

Across the yard, Mother's dogwood shrub shakes. A slender, trembling girl in a dull blue dress emerges from behind it, her narrow face accentuated only by the roundness of her eyes. This eve, they are near the size of tea saucers.

"Sarah!" Emma says.

I raise a finger to my lips.

Another girl leaps from the shrub and yanks Emma into hiding. "Be silent!" she hisses.

Ruth...At least she has the good sense to know they stand before Paul Kelly's household.

Father is quick with the strap. I harbor no misgivings he would whip the daylights from both my friends if roused by their noise.

Carefully, I swing my leg wide over the window ledge to not snag my gown. I lean forward to jump when there comes a rustling from our corn shuck mattress.

"I shall tell..."

I wheel to face my sister. "You shall not!"

Rebecca raises a rebellious eyebrow.

"Sarah..." Emma calls.

I glance over my shoulder and out the window. Emma again emerges from the shrubbery. The fool stands in plain view of Mother and Father's window.

I wave her away to hide.

Emma nervously clutches her apron with one hand. She points to our barn with the other. "Ruth leaves us!"

At times, I wonder if Emma were born daft. When Ruth

once told her keeping chicken bones in our aprons would ward off evil spirits, Emma carried them for nigh on a year. And when I warned her mythical snipes lived in our barn beneath the hay, she never again ventured inside. How has Emma not yet realized Ruth's favorite custom is to hide amidst the corn to scare her?

It next occurs to me, for all Ruth's many virtues, patience is most lacking. She is ever the one who misses dancing most. Mayhap she means to make good on her threat of going alone. I imagine her running down the rows of corn, off into the woods without me.

I snort the thought away. It would not stand for her to share the night whilst I remain here, thwarted by the threat of an eight-year-old.

I turn to face my sister again. "Rebecca..."

Her arms cross, like Mother oft does when in a foul temper. "Take me," she says. "Or work my chores."

I dig my fingernails into the windowsill. "No!"

Rebecca dangles her tiny bare feet inches from the floor in warning. "Then I shall wake Father and tell."

"Saaaarah..." Emma whines.

My sister's smile is evident in the dim light. Even at such a tender age, she knows time is on her side this night.

"I will do *one* of your chores," I reply.

"You will milk the cows?" She says it so quickly I wonder how long she has planned to force this upon me.

I grit my teeth. "Agreed."

My sister yawns in victory and happily scratches her head, content in her victory.

I pull my gown up past my knees, and drop below ere Rebecca

coerces me further. I pause to listen for any stirrings inside my home. Spreading my toes, I take the dewy grass between them to cool my nerves.

A minute passes with no noise; Father sleeps soundly.

I slip my shoes on as fast as possible and hurry to join Emma. She makes a tiny yelp at my sudden pull of her hand. Hand-in-hand, we run toward the barn. Her clumsiness slows my pace, but I will not let go. If she falls, it would not happen silently.

When she does eventually stumble on the cold and slippery grass, I slip my arm under her armpit to keep her afoot. Emma tugs away as we near the barn. No doubt she desires to give it a wider berth ere a snipe emerges to drag her within.

Cornfields lie before us. The stalks stand only six feet tall, yet the dark makes them appear larger. Like a foreboding wall of spears, we must pass into their protection to reach our destination.

I release my grip on Emma. Plunge ahead, five rows deep.

The dry leaves scratch at my skin; a small sacrifice for the joyous reunion to come. A few stalks lie broken near their shafts. I shall need to scold Ruth later. Father will know neither deer nor Indians bent them in such a way.

Emma whimpers behind me. I watch her gently push the stalks aside as if the mere touch of them will taint her perfect skin. "Why did you not come sooner?" she asks. "With Ruth gone, I feared you abandoned me to journey alone."

"Alone?" I ask. "But where is Charlotte?"

Emma shakes her head. "Her father suspects she has danced." Her voice trembles. "I fear mine does also."

I frown. It is not like Charlotte to miss a gathering. Especially not when the last occurred three months past.

The corn crackles three rows over like teeth chattering in the grip of a January nor'easter. Emma draws closer to me.

I step forward. "Who comes?"

"One who has no fear of the darkness."

An apparition brushes the stalks aside. Ruth's skin, pale even in daylight, is luminous by night. She has discarded her white bonnet and scandalously tied back her raven hair with a scarlet ribbon. Ruth closes her eyes, tilts her head back to inhale the night air. "Art thou ready to dance, sisters?"

Emma releases her hold on my dress. "You should not have left me!"

"You should not have remained behind," Ruth replies curtly. "The moon dance waits for no one—nor do I."

A cold wind harrows through the corn, confirming Ruth's claims, ushering us ahead. I step in the earthen path between the rows. The hard dirt warns of a frost soon to come. I am glad of it. The solidity will not reveal our tracks so easily as in the wet spring or dry summer.

"Come," I say to my friends. "We should not tarry."

We walk for nigh half an hour to our destination. Emma is a constant shadow at my side. Holding my hand all the way, she frequently glances skywards as if she fears witches on broomsticks will fly over us. Ruth tromps in the next row. Her fingers run over the corn ears as she quietly hums a tune I have never heard.

"Emma," I say. "What shall you wish for tonight?"

"A safe journey home," she replies, casting another furtive glance at the moon.

"I shall wish for a night that never ends!" Ruth shouts.

I laugh with her. Even Father cannot hear from this far away.

The sound makes Emma jump with fright. Her grip stiffens. "You should not speak so loud. My father would—"

"Your father sleeps at home." Ruth lazily swats at the corn.

"A-aye. H-H-He would be very displeased to find me here," Emma shakes her head like a horse with flies at its ears.

"What if he knew you journeyed to a gathering of *witches!*" Ruth says.

A shudder runs through me. "Enough, Ruth. You should not jest of such things," I say. "You beckon the darkness upon yourself."

Ruth grins. "As well I should. I am sister to the moon. A lover of night!" She loosens her ribbon. Her dark hair spills about her shoulders as she lifts her arms. "For why dance if not to beckon the darkness into our hearts?"

Emma looks at me as one betrayed. "Y-you said dancing was innocent. N-not a sin."

"Dancing *is* innocent," I reply. "I said naught of what Ruth speaks to."

Ruth scoffs. "I thought you were a fellow lover of the night, Sarah."

"I am."

"Then why do you come this eve?" Ruth asks. "Dancing can be done by the light of day."

"A-aye," says Emma. "I think it best we only dance by day henceforth. My father—"

"Why, Sarah?" Ruth asks. "Why do you come?"

"Only at night am I truly free," I say. "Free to do as I will with no one to speak otherwise, or—"

"Listen!" Emma says.

I hear it too; the quiet beginnings of a measured symphony

wandering over the night sky. The gay pipes call to the wood spirits of Pan. Each hypnotic beating of drums beckons us to venture further.

The gathering starts without us.

Ruth and I grin at one another.

"Race you to the woods!" She runs ahead without waiting for me.

Nor do I pause for Emma. The sprint to catch Ruth is longer than first I guessed. I fear my lungs will give out ere we reach the end of the field. The drums beat as one with my heart to lend me strength. I pass her at the last, bursting from the field and into a clearing of dandelions.

The wind in the corn follows us out. It blows the hundreds of translucent florets away from their stems. Like wisps, they create a rippling blanket of nature to lead us.

A dim glow rises inside the woods. It grows brighter with each passing moment. Shadows from the flames climb the trees as if to escape from Hell and sneak into Heaven.

Emma thrashes behind us, her once beautiful gown now mottled with stains, and her bonnet askew. Even so, she cannot help but smile at the sight of rising fire.

We sisters of the moon clasp hands. Together, we cross the meadow and enter the woods. I have oft visited this same hallowed place to escape my chores and dream of what lay beyond its borders.

Tonight, the woods feel foreign. A place no goodly person ought be.

Tiny, thin bones from some unfortunate forest creatures hang in the trees, strung together as one by thick horsehair to form relics. I see feathers tied to them—crow, falcon, and eagle. There are freshly cut saplings also, interwoven to form odd, twisted dreamcatchers.

I shake whilst walking beneath the jangling bones. Their invisible power is palpable. It seeps through my skin and twins with my soul.

We exit the underbrush into a clearing, seventy feet across. Nine cut elms have been leaned against one another; a towering teepee set alight. A ring of girls surrounds its blaze. Some wear bracelets of silver serpents with rubies for eyes. Others have adorned themselves with necklace reliefs of the moon in all its stages.

Emma gasps beside me. "Ne'er have I seen so many before..."

I watch the unknown girls approach the fire. They tempt its flames to sear their skin and dance away ere it licks them.

Ruth points to a sharp-jawed girl in a forest green gown. "Charlotte!"

Charlotte turns at hearing her name called. She releases hands with the other girls. I watch the circle instantly shrink to fill the void she leaves. Charlotte prances toward us, hugging Ruth first.

"We feared you would not come!" Ruth says.

"I thought the same of you," Charlotte replies.

A naked girl, dancing in the circle, motions us closer. Her body is a canvas of tattoos. Trained ivy and dragons snake around her limbs. Raven feathers litter her belly and chest. A pentagram covers the space between her breasts.

"Wh-who are these girls?" Emma asks. "They are not from Winford."

Charlotte looks upon the strangers. "Aye. I gather many come from the north. All wish to share the night with us. They bring..."

Several girls pull their gowns over their heads. They toss them aside with little care. I see their bodies decorated in similar, tattooed fashion.

"*Strange* customs," Charlotte says. "They claim there is nothing like a sister's kiss." Her face flushes red. "I-I must admit. I wish to try."

"Yes!" Ruth says. "We shall try together!"

My gaze sweeps over the gathering. I take special notice of a tall, slender woman at the center. A dark veil, lined with scarlet silk, covers the top of her head and trains down her back. Her emerald eyes stare at me from behind a mask of raven feathers that glistens in the firelight.

I look away from her piercing gaze.

Ruth does not. "Who is that woman?"

Charlotte chuckles. "The others name her Hecate, the Devil's daughter." She waves at the woman and receives a bow in answer. Charlotte turns back to us. "They say she comes to lead us." She whispers. "Have you ever seen a woman so beautiful as she?"

I caution another glance.

Hecate approaches us. Her violet robe clings and moves so smoothly it seems painted.

"Good eve to you all." Hecate purrs. "Charlotte has told me much and more of you...Ruth...Emma."

I watch her give a nod to each of my friends in turn, then linger on me. She reaches out, gently lifts my chin that I might look her full in the face.

"I find your face even more familiar, child..." Hecate grants me a smile to elicit a marriage proposal from any young man. "You must be Sarah Kelly."

A lump forms in my throat. "I am, Madam."

Hecate laughs. "I am no madam. Call me sister, for we are all but daughters held in sway to our Moon Mother, yes?"

"Aye," Ruth says. "We come to dance in Her light!"

"And you are most welcome." Hecate bows away and opens her arms to permit us entry to the dance.

Charlotte tugs at my hand. "Come. Let us join!"

Emma falters. "Perhaps we should not...not dance with those we know nothing of. I feel...odd. Ne'er have I felt so at the dance before."

Ruth and Charlotte will not heed her. They pull Emma and me to join them.

I glance over my shoulder, see Hecate's glittering gaze trained on me. *Why does she watch me so?*

Any nervousness I held is lost upon entering the circle. I surrender myself to the melodic tune. The moon dance and my sisters are all that exist. Unknown faces stand before me whenever I chance to open my eyes. I recall Emma's words. I am among strangers, yet these outsiders seem friendly. I put any question of their intentions out of mind. Tonight we all are moon sisters.

A girl holding my hand lifts it to her mouth. Kisses the back of my hand. When she smiles, I see her teeth have a touch of black stain to them. I shyly pull my hand away. The girl shrugs and is gone, replaced by a new one who only laughs at my discomfort. Her teeth are normal.

I put away the idea I witnessed a demon amidst us, and lose myself to the music's rhythm again. Only later, when it stops, do I question whether I danced for a few minutes or several hours.

Embers from the fire pop and spark brilliant shades of orange into the air. As if signaled, the drums begin anew in a slow, measured tempo I fear will lull me to sleep.

Hecate elegantly enters the middle of the circle. She has donned a thin, black cloak and stands so near the fire I fear it will catch aflame. She lifts her arms to the night sky, unbothered by the heat. Her light, silky voice commands my attention. "Sisters, sisters, one and all. Your Maiden's beauty held in thrall."

The other girls repeat her chant.

I feel the circle of oneness enveloping me into the fold.

I must join them. I think. *Or be outcast.*

A shadow moves outside the circle. Snaps me from the reverie. I search for its owner, but now there is only dark where the shadow existed not a moment ago.

The drums beat faster, yet they no longer hold me to their cadence.

Not so for the other girls. They continue to sway and tug at my arms, willing me to rejoin them.

The invisible feather returns to drift down the nape of my neck. Now awakened from the music's spell, I shudder at the oneness the others experience.

These are strangers here. Emma's earlier fear catches within me. *Their customs odd.*

I search the circle for my friends.

Emma is easiest to find. She sits across from me—the only other girl not content with the oneness. Her eyes are two deep wells of tears. *Save me,* they plead. *End this nightmare.*

My gaze sweeps over the unknown faces. I see more than I first supposed. Were there so many all along? I cannot recall the circle being so large when first I entered.

Ruth sits nearest Hecate, still entranced with the tune. Blissfully swaying beside her, Charlotte, too, remains in the music's grip.

Hecate thrusts her arms out. The fire at her back makes her appear liken to a bat with the cloak she wears now tightly drawn. An assortment of leather pouches dangle from twine cords inside it. She jerks one free of its binding. "Mother, Mother," she cries. "Let these who would serve never tire!"

The drums quicken. The circle follows.

My body aches to join. My mind rejects the notion.

Hecate's escorts slip silently forward. They carry a silver platelet—long and thin like Mother's griddle—and hold it before her chest.

Hecate unties the binding round the bag and sweeps it over the platelet. A dusky snow of fine, purplish-black powder falls across its surface. "Father, Father. Hear my plea!" Her voice heightens. "Let these who would call spirits, come unto thee!"

I see Ruth rise in a stupor. She strides into the circle's midst, never stopping until she stands before Hecate.

Hecate places her right hand upon Ruth's shoulder. With her left, she motions her escort to raise the platelet.

My conscience screams to stop her, but my body seems racked with molasses. I cannot move. Not even when I see Hecate gently push Ruth's face toward the powder.

Ruth opens her eyes at the last.

I see doubt in them. "No..." I hear myself whisper.

Hecate tilts her head, places a skeletal finger on Ruth's cheek to draw her attention. Then she swoops low. Dragging her nose across the plate, she snorts the powder in example.

The drums grow louder.

The girls chant as one. "*Hama shelabedi—hama shelabedi—hama shelabedi—hama shelabedi!*"

Hecate pulls away from the plate, moaning in satisfaction.

A thin trace of powder lingers beneath her nostrils. She sweeps it away with a quick flick of her finger. Fixated on Ruth, Hecate points to the plate.

Ruth takes a hesitant breath...and plunges into the powder.

I stand without meaning to, the spell over me broken.

Ruth pulls away quickly, gasping. Her fingers clasp into fists. Her eyes go wide.

Hecate lifts her arms in praise.

The gleeful pipe music begins anew. The circle of oneness is over. Some of the girls dance. Most hurry to have their turn at the platelet. They do not notice Ruth collapse like I do. The others crowd over and around her, each more desperate than the next. All while Ruth's hands claw at her nose and throat.

Hecate glances over her shoulder. She nods.

A pair of masked and hooded figures emerges from the clearing line. I cannot tell if they be women or men. Unlike Hecate, their bulky garb is not royal—deerskin and beaver pelts. They cross the distance in short manner. Each roughly grabs hold beneath Ruth's arms. They drag her limp body back the way they came.

I start forward. A bird's whistle distracts me.

Far outside the circle of light, the shadow has returned. A weatherworn pastor's hat shields the wearer's face, but I feel their cold gaze upon me.

A new figure steps into my line of sight.

"Why do you not join us, Sarah?" Hecate asks. "We have come so far to share in the night with you and your friends. You do us grievous wrong by leaving now."

I take a step back. There is naught but trees where the shadow stood moments ago.

"I-I..."

She reaches for me. Her fingers massage my shoulder blade.

I gather the massage will become a vice if I run. My breath is ragged, and this she seems to find amusing.

"Rest easy, sister," Hecate says. "Your secret is safe with me."

"But I have no—"

"We all keep secrets, even our Moon Mother. It's why She only comes at night, when things are best kept hidden. Would you like to know that which She guards closest of all?"

I nod.

"She *hates*." Hecate relishes. "At night She is beautiful and free, all Her mysteries kept. But Her master, the sun, reveals them in the light of day, for nothing is hidden from His sight... just as nothing is hidden from mine."

I fight off a shudder.

"I *see* others for who they are." Her voice holds me. "You are different, Sarah."

"H-how?"

"Your friends lust after forbidden things, as children are wont to do. Thrills and conjures, magic and wonder." She shrugs gaily. "But our Moon Mother did not bring you here this night for such works alone."

I shake my head, even as I am unsure of what she presumes to know of my intentions.

"Night is the time for secrets. Truth is best left to the light of day." Hecate draws me close.

I feel a weight fall into the front pocket of my apron.

"Learn your truth, Sarah," Hecate whispers in my ear. "As I did."

She releases me.

Despite the fire's warmth, I feel cloaked in ice. I stumble out of the circle, and run to the brush where I witnessed Ruth taken.

I fight through the limbs and shrubbery barring my path.

My shin hits something hard. It occurs to me this be the same direction from which I saw the shadow appear. I turn to see if a person wishes harm upon me. Release a sigh when I see only a small stump.

Someone moans not far from me.

I climb to my feet, and hurry to follow the sound to its owner. Twenty feet away, I discover Ruth lying in a pile of dried leaves.

I kneel beside her. "Ruth, we must leave."

Her head lolls to the side. The veins in her neck pulse feverously. Beads of sweat train down her face. Ruth opens her eyes. She stares at me like I am unknown to her. "I can see..." she says. "Sp-spirits. They call...call me to dance."

I hear the underbrush trampled. Mayhap it is those who brought Ruth here! I stand and lift a fallen branch to ward off whoever comes. It is only Emma, aiding the frightful mess Charlotte has become.

Charlotte laughs hysterically. She swings her arm off Emma's shoulder and collapses beside me. A touch of powdery residue remains under her nostrils. She crawls forward. "I wish to dance with you, Ruth!"

"And I with you!" Ruth answers.

Charlotte attempts to stand. I keep her from falling. "Yes!" she says. "Come...come, sister. Let us dance together with the spirits of the night!"

"You cannot mean to stay," I protest. "The dawn approaches. We must leave—"

Ruth leans upon a tree to help her stand. "The night lingers on!" she snarls. "And the spirits...they need us!"

She is not in her right mind. I think. *The powder stole away her wits.*

"We are sisters, borne of shadow," Ruth says to Charlotte. "We—we dance until the dawn!"

Charlotte pitches forward, barely catching hold of a tree to stay upright. "Come, sister!"

Giggling, Ruth stumbles to Charlotte.

What sort of devilry did the powder possess? I wonder. *We were only to have danced...*

"I like this not at all, Sarah," Emma sulks. "I wish to go home. Can we not leave?"

I go to her. The weight Hecate gifted me shifts in my apron. I feel a sharp prick dig into my inner thigh. I cast a final glance toward the fire. See Hecate welcome my friends back into her fold. Her eyes find me; hold me in sway to their beauty.

Emma breaks me of it. "Sarah! Please let us go!"

I put my back to the dance, and escort my friend away, out of the woods.

Even so, the music echoes in my ears when we reach the cornfield. And, despite my fearful misgivings, all I desire is to return and welcome the dawn with my sisters of the night.

-two-

"Be still, Lila." I pat the old cow's haunch. Skittish of nigh everything, a better name for her would be Emma. I chuckle at the thought, even as I rub sleep from my eyes.

The fault lies with Emma, I slept not at all. She refused to leave my side until the pair of us reached her homestead. I hardly made it back to my own ere Father left for a morning hunt with George. If either saw me enter the barn, they made no mention of it.

I clench Lila's teat with all my strength and pull down. She rewards me with but a few drops of milk in the pail. I release my grip to flex the stiffness from my fingers. I wish Father would sell the old cow or slaughter her. Her udders are nearly dried up as it is.

I yawn.

Lila jumps at the sound, nearly knocking my pail over.

"Easy, old girl," I calm her again.

Both my pails full and the chore finished, I hurry to the barn door to learn if Father and George may be returning. I look out across the fields, but there be no sign of them. I rush back to my stool, and take the gift Hecate gave me last eve from inside my apron.

The black leather cover feels oddly cold. The page edges shine gold, liken to Father's Bible. They glitter as I flip through them, promising secrets if I have the courage to read them.

What manner of book is this? One filled with spells? Fortune-telling, perhaps? Finding new books to read has ever been a chore, let alone those of any interest to me. Something about this book frightens me. I turn it over in my hand, feeling the cover for any sort of design. I find nothing. *Why did Hecate gift me this?*

The only way to know is to open it. I do so hurriedly, shrinking as if some malevolent spirits trapped within wait for their release. There are no spirits, only a few words written in a neat, legible hand.

Journal: Sgt. Thomas Putnam, Jr.

A thrill passes through me as I idly flip through to weaken its stiff binding. I notice rough, torn edges at the beginning where many pages have been ripped out. I stop upon finding the first entry.

I begin to read.

~

16th day of October, 1691

Perchance, I crossed paths with Dr. Simon Campbell this afternoon. The lad mentioned he considers taking up residency in Billerica. For now, he plans to travel abroad and determine where his best prospects lie.

I did not tell him I had already heard of his rumored brilliance from our own Dr. Griggs. Indeed, Griggs so loudly proclaims his fervent support for this young man, I've begun to question his sincerity. It has not been so long ago since I learned Griggs sent his great-niece to both serve his competitor and spy on his practice dealings. Mayhap he seeks to spy on this new doctor as well and flatters the young man in the waiting time.

A clever plot, that, and I find no fault in Griggs's using the girl. She should count herself fortunate enough Griggs took her in after the Indian wars made her an orphan. I see no reason he should not profit from sheltering her.

I am more intrigued by this Dr. Campbell, however. After our introduction, he immediately expressed condolences for the legal ills he heard I have suffered at the thieving hands of my brothers.

I did not inquire as to where he heard tale of my misfortunes, but I assume the damnable Bridget Bishop told the tale. The wench's proclivities to wag her tongue for those fair in face be little secret around the village. I accepted Dr. Campbell's words courteously, however, and hid my true outrage for a stranger to speak in so familiar a manner.

He then shared with me a bit of news he overheard of our troubled Reverend Parris. Aye, an interesting bit of news. Apparently, the faction vowed to drive Parris from Salem are now also vowed to quit his wages.

'Tis little wonder why. A more avaricious man I have never met, though I like him slightly more than our former three reverends. In truth, I fear his position cursed. Parris be already the fourth reverend appointed in Salem these past eighteen years. The previous two did not last more than four years; why then should he?

Damned fool. I warned Parris those in the village were a shifty flock, and said as much to Dr. Campbell.

The young doctor smiled at the mention, a knowing smile that irks me still. He next claimed my foresight made him eager to meet me and named my pulse of Salem's society as hallmark to a great mind.

I gave my farewell then, but not ere Dr. Campbell suggested we meet again soon to further our friendship. I must needs learn more of this new doctor and why he takes up residency in the countryside when Boston would seem a sounder choice for a young man of his ambition.

⁂

My conscience warns I should not be privy to a stranger's secrets, but I cannot help myself.

Hecate could have given this book to anyone, but ensured it came to me. Why? What truth did she hope I might find in its pages? I know naught of this Sergeant Putnam, nor any of the men he mentioned in his entry. Still, the mere mention of Salem bids me read on.

⁂

16TH DAY OF NOVEMBER, 1691

God be praised, and bless Dr. Campbell.

A knock came at my door late this eve, and he behind it. My daughter Ann stood with him. So, too, did my servant Mercy.

What cause did they have to be out so late at night? I asked them both. And alone with a young man too?

Dr. Campbell requested to speak with me outside. I consented, but first promised both girls a thrashing upon my return for her disobedience. God help me. My daughter knew my act all for show and exhibited little fear in front of my guest. I shall need to remedy her of that. The child should at least pretend to obey me, as Mercy does.

Dr. Campbell and I rode off together with he leading me toward the nearby wood. There, I saw two torches burning inside a glade. I should have turned back then had I not heard my name called and beckoned come hither by Dr. Griggs. I soon learned Reverend Parris there also.

What secret council is this, I demanded of them. And why must it be held in the black of night?

Dr. Campbell mentioned then he discovered not only both my daughter and my servant in the woods that night, but with several friends also. Griggs's niece, Elizabeth Hubbard, and both Reverend Parris's daughter, Betty, and his niece, Abigail Williams.

Dr. Campbell mentioned he saw others also, but made especial note of these five. He next claimed he watched the girls pretend at witchcraft.

Parris and I nearly came to blows with him for such a remark.

Thank Heaven we did not.

Dr. Campbell mentioned he will say naught to anyone of his findings in the woods, he not wishing trouble upon us. We each thanked him for his silence, yet questioned why bring us together now. Dr. Campbell next asked if we could be trusted.

An ignorant question, to my mind. Why should we answer anything but aye? Only after we agreed did he inquire if ever we had heard tell of Goody Glover.

Aye, I said. Three years ago they hanged her for a witch in Boston for afflicting children.

Dr. Campbell then inquired if we believed in witchcraft and Goody Glover guilty of being one.

The hailed Reverend Cotton Mather said she were, I recall Parris saying. And those four children afflicted too. What else could she be, but a witch?

Dr. Campbell smiled at us in an arrogant manner. Then he revealed the plan he has devised. A more dastardly one I have ne'er heard.

Indeed, though he affronted we three at the first, now I have determined this Dr. Campbell speaks with a silver tongue.

Each of us have trouble with our neighbors. We have done naught but squabble until now...

This newcomer brings a dark solution.

When we asked of him why his plan required our girls to unfold, Dr. Campbell quoted Psalms, chapter eight, verse two: Out of the mouth of babes and sucklings hast thou ordained strength because of thine enemies, that thou mightest still the enemy and the avenger.

I see now, Griggs spoke true when first he mentioned Dr. Campbell; a brilliant mind this young man truly has. A grim plan he brings, I admit it freely, yet one that could finally deliver the vengeance I have longed for.

Aye. And that which rightly belongs to me but were stolen.

❧

The sound of mewing bids me look up from the journal. Cats throng about the milk pails, lapping at the treasure I have neglected. I slide the journal back into my apron and shoo them away. All but one—a fluffy orange tabby—scatter before me. I kick at it.

The tabby dodges then turns to growl at me.

Its defiance takes me aback. I have oft heard tell of familiars, those who can send their spirits into animals. The thought makes me hesitant to kick at the beast again. Something leery in its green eyes reminds me too much of Hecate.

"What's this? My daughter, frightened by a cat?"

Father stands in the doorway, his gaze steady upon me. Several pheasants and two doves are slung over his shoulder. Day-old whiskers darken his cheeks with more than a bit of silver spiced amidst the brown.

My brother, George, is with him; a miniature version of Father in all ways, but he lacks the years of seriousness to burden him.

Father hands his flintlock to George. He strides ahead. His grin belies the stern demeanor typically reserved for my brother. Father reaches for the cat without hesitation.

The tabby hisses and swipes at him.

Father does not shrink away. He grabs it by the nape. Lifts it like a mother would her kitten. The tabby's body goes limp with its paws draped over its belly. A low growl escapes from deep within it. Father flings it high and away. I hear it land amongst the straw pallets meant for our cows. Then, the quick patter of feet as it scurries away.

"You mustn't show fear to any of God's creatures, Sarah," Father says.

My sight lowers to the four scratches down his forearm where the cat drew blood. Father seems oblivious to them.

"Sarah," he says.

I look up into his leathery face. "Aye, Father."

"And why not?"

"Satan has many tools to beguile us." I give the answer he seeks. "Yet no one with God on their side has cause to fear."

Father nods. His deeply set brown eyes drift to the milk pails. "What brings you to work your sister's chore?"

"A small kindness." I lie. "The pails are nigh too heavy for me to lift, let alone for one so young as she."

Father lifts the pails with two fingers, never once sloshing the milk. "Only by carrying them will she grow stronger." His brow wrinkles as if weighting my words. "If it be as you say, perhaps we should find another chore for her. Henceforth, you will milk the cows until she is strong enough to do so."

"Aye, Father," I say humbly, shutting out the sound of my brother's immediate snort.

Father squeezes my shoulder. He unslings his quarry and hands them over to me. "Come then. We must break our fast, and then to church."

Even now, laden by the pails he carries for me, his gait is quick and sure. Mother oft says Father has never been one for idle walks. Doing so saps the time he might better spend elsewhere.

George tries to match him step-for-step. He has not yet come of an age to have the growth in his limbs, though, and falls behind with me.

I take in the sight of our home as we walk. My friends oft reiterate how fortunate I am. Our diamond-paned casement windows especially keep out the cold. So many others in Winford rely only on wooden shutters.

Emma's family is poorer still. They have naught to cover their windows.

I frown at the thought.

Father would be angry with me for pitying her. It be little secret he harbors no love for Emma's father. Indeed, Father says any man who cannot provide for his family is no man at all.

I think an unfair comparison; Emma's father to my own. Hers is but a spindly scarecrow. Father is strong as our prized bull, Samson.

I wonder if that is why she is ever afeared of Indian raids. She knows her father could do naught to keep the savages at bay if they came. I have never shared such fears. It would take five braves to come for me with Father around. Of those, at least three would not live to try again.

I close my eyes and breathe deeply of the fall air. October is my favorite month. I love the mixings of cold and warm and watching the summer bounty harvested and tucked away. It is also the time for butchery. Even now, outside in the yard, I can smell fresh bacon and roasting ham over the hearth waft its way toward me. The scents spur me faster.

I see Rebecca's frame through the windows as she busies about the table in placing dishes for our meal. George pauses at the doorstep to remove his hat and hang it. He unslings his flintlock, and places it barrel-up beside Father's.

I catch Rebecca watching me as I wait for him to move. She yawns in amusement, knowing full well I must be tired for I never did return to bed. I scrape clean any filth upon my shoes onto the stone ledge of the doorway. Continuing to the table, I drop one of the dead pheasants over Rebecca's shoulder when Mother is not watching.

She screams as the bird lands in her lap.

"Oh, Rebecca!" I cry. "Forgive me."

Mother swoops in to take it from her. Thrusting the bird back into my hands, she then sits to calm my sister.

George chuckles.

Father does not. He had not been there a moment ago. Gone to wash up, I had wrongly supposed. He stands there now though. Watches me in the way he often looks at George, one speaking of a strapping to come. Father clears his throat as he takes his seat at the head of our table. "Do that again, Sarah, and you shall eat the bird whole, feathers and all."

"Aye, Father," I answer quietly. I string his quarry near the hearth to clean and boil later. Then I take my seat beside Rebecca.

Father bows his head. "Bless us, O Lord, and this food of which we are about to partake. We thank You for this bounty and ask You let it nourish our bodies."

I open my eyes.

George grins at me from the opposite side of the table. He quickly checks to ensure Father is not watching him.

Silly. If Father's eyes were open, George would have been clapped upside the head by now.

"Help us to be mindful of the many gifts you have provided—"

George imitates milking a cow. He grins wider.

"—to give willingly, and be an example unto others of how those in your service should act," Father continues. "All these things, dear Lord, we ask in Christ's name. Amen."

I kick George's left shin under the table. "Amen," I say upon connecting.

My brother winces, but does not cry out. He knows the pain I gave him is nothing liken to what Father would, especially if he found us sporting at prayer.

Father motions us to give him our plates, and spoons the corn mash upon them.

George leans down. No doubt to rub at the bruise I hopefully left upon his shin. "We saw a queer sight this morn, did we not, Father?"

"Aye," Father answers.

Mother takes a few strips of bacon to drape across Rebecca's plate. "Pray, what sight?"

"There be a small clearing deep in the woods not there before," Father says. "Formed in a circle with a fire pit in the middle and the ashes still warm. Small footprints went round it, then vanished into the forest."

"Oh..." Mother sets the plate upon the table harder than I believe she aimed.

"I believe it were witches!"

"*George!*" Mother scolds. "You should not speak of such—"

George stabs a slab of ham. "I have oft heard tell of witches hiding in the woods. Some say those who escaped the gallows of Salem ventured south to our territory and yet lurk about."

Mother shakes her head and passes me the meat. "The trials were nineteen years ago, George. And Salem near five hundred miles away too! What makes you take up such stories?"

Father, chewing his mash quietly throughout their exchange, swallows before he speaks. "I will hear no more talk of witchcraft in this home. Nor the evils of Salem." He takes George in with his eyes. "And you will speak nothing of what we discovered to your friends at church. I'll not hear it said my son spread rumors."

"Aye, Father," George says.

I watch disgustedly as he shoves a bit of ham in his greedy mouth. He even swallows without chewing.

"What do you fear it might be, husband?" Mother asks.

I hear a touch of fear in her voice, though she does her best to quell it. Her tone suggests savages. Mother is a hard woman, but any mention of Indians makes her prone to fits.

Father sits back in his chair. He strokes his whiskers. "It would not be the first time someone has ventured near our homestead. The circle aligned in such a way it might well have been they danced around the fire. A tribal gathering, mayhap."

"We found stalks broken in the field also," George adds.

"No Indian braves did such a thing," Father says quickly. He gazes across the table at me.

I meet it. Fearful he will know me for a liar if I do not.

"Children, mayhap," Father says to avoid frightening Mother further. "But no braves, nor squaws. They do not leave trails so easily followed."

"Then whom?" Mother asks.

Father shrugs. "I know not. They have departed for now, and I am glad of it. Let them stay gone. They are of no nuisance to me yet." He looks at me again before forking his meat. "But henceforth, I shall be more vigilant."

-three-

THE CRISP IN THE AIR IS GONE AS WE RIDE TO CHURCH, BANISHED by the sun's rays. A reminder the late summer has not yet abandoned us. I had thought to read more of Thomas Putnam's journal along the way.

Father's speech of vigilance put a quick end to any notion of it. It would be difficult even so to concentrate with our wagon rattling along the dirt path plagued with rocks. Every so often, Father hits one and we jolt upward.

Rebecca seems to think it a game. She laughs at every bounce.

We pass others walking along the road. A reminder I should be thankful we have a wagon to ride in.

Rebecca asks Father several times to stop and offer those less fortunate a ride.

He will not do it. Not even for her.

I, too, asked him when younger in years, but he claimed it would wound their pride to take favors such as he would offer. Perhaps I am too young, but I cannot understand this. I would gladly accept a ride if made to walk.

Ahead, I see a golden crucifix catch the light on our approach. Placed high atop the white-washed steeple for all to see, by no coincidence is the church nearly as tall as our barn. Father directed the planning and raising of both. My legs tingle at the thought of him dangling off the side to hang the crucifix.

Other wagons arrive as we do. Most decided to take in the

bright, clear day without their coverings to shield them from the elements. Always one prepared, Father has tucked and folded ours under his seat in case the day gives way to rain. He pulls gently on the reins, slowing our draft horses, and our wagon comes to a halt.

George immediately leaps over the edge to take the reins from Father and tie off the horses. I am surprised he is not scolded for doing so. Two Sundays past he did not land so well and dirtied his best clothing.

Father climbs down from the wagon as easily as he might descend a flight of steps. I gather from his stern gaze George will receive his scolding later, in private, rather than here for all the church to witness. His anger gives way when Rebecca jumps into his arms.

Both George and I know Father has always favored her most. Perhaps because she looks so much like Mother. Both have the same high cheekbones, equally straight noses, and hardy physique. It is plain for all to see Rebecca will be far prettier than I when she is older.

Like George, my features favor Father more; brown hair with tints of yellow when dyed by the sun, a round face that often bears an accusing frown, and a squat nose. The only small portion of Mother I share is the cloudy grey color of her eyes. I remind myself to envy is to sin before continuing with my family toward church.

The double doors have been swung open to let in the air more than to welcome us. Indeed, even as I step through the entryway, my pores sweat rivers. Not for fear of the Almighty, but rather that Mother and the ladies of Winford insist we dress in our best woolen skirts. I oft wonder if it be God's will we are made to suffer so, another unjust punishment for Eve's transgressions, to my mind. The heat on such a day is unbearable, let alone we be dressed in such attire. Is it any wonder my friends and I prefer the cool air of the moon dance rather than the heated sermons of day?

Father leads us toward the front, as befits his high esteem in our community. I see Emma near the back. Even now, at sixteen years of age, her mother still coddles her. I search out my other friends, and think it odd when I find neither Ruth nor Charlotte amidst the crowd.

We reach the front pews. Father and George turn to take their seats at the left side of the pulpit. We women do so on the right.

I watch Reverend Corwin displace himself from the pew. When our previous reverend, old and ragged as a worn-out nag, passed on, our community desired someone more experienced, but younger; one to lead us in these dark times with furious vigor.

Father says they failed at both.

Reverend Corwin speaks when he should listen, Father oft says, and the only thing Corwin will lead us to is starvation, both spiritually and physically. Indeed, I think he looks as one who eats the fatted calf whole rather than preaches of it.

Reverend Corwin takes the pulpit to lead us in a hymn of *The Lord Is My Shepherd*. His high tenor voice rings out above all the rest. Even louder than the woman seated behind me, Mrs. Bradbury, she who believes singing is the same as shouting.

I glance to the men's section. Two rows back from Father sits Wesley Greene. Most other girls in Winford claim if God made Adam in his own image, He markedly improved His draft with Wesley. His shoulders seem to widen every week, and I swear he has grown two feet since last year.

Charlotte told my fortunes once and deemed Wesley and I should be married. Ruth claimed she did not hold with such nonsense and scattered the runes. The next week after, I saw her cozy up to him. To his credit, Wesley kindly turned away Ruth's advances. He has ever been one of the more dutiful young men in Winford. Gazing at him now, I see more than a little of why my friends fawn over him so.

Wesley catches me watching him. He smiles, and turns his attention back to Reverend Corwin and singing.

I wish that I could be so compliant. Staying in tune is a near impossible task with Mrs. Bradbury staining the melody. I mouth the words rather than add to the ruin of what little harmony remains.

Finishing the hymn, Reverend Corwin bids us take our seats.

I sit between Mother and Rebecca. The hard-backed pew reminds me to sit straight and not slouch. I raise my hand to fan myself of the sweat.

Mother halts me. She gives me a reproachful look ere returning her gaze to Reverend Corwin.

"Brothers and sisters," he begins, his voice booming from the deepest recesses of his giant belly. "I welcome you on this glorious day the Lord has seen fit to bestow upon us. I heard tell of troubling news that seeps into our good community from our neighbors to the north. Rumors of—I hesitate to say—*witchcraft.*"

I believe the gusto with which he speaks belies his early words.

Reverend Corwin, however, seems pleased to hear the discomfort among some of his flock. I too hear the sounds of shifting pews. Reverend Corwin may believe many do so under the threat of Satan's minions working their dark magic amongst us.

I think the heat is more likely to blame.

"And evil that need not be further mentioned. In such times as these, we need only turn to the Lord." He lifts his Bible in the air, and points to it ere he licks a stubby finger to open it. "And the Lord gives us an example in Deuteronomy, chapter eighteen, verses ten through thirteen. It reads: There shall not be found among you anyone that maketh his son or his daughter to pass through the fire, or that useth divination, or an observer of times, or an enchanter, or a witch—"

I hear a pew creak far to the back. Emma, I warrant, wrestling with her conscience.

"Or a charmer," the Reverend's voice rises to keep us engaged. "Or a consulter with familiar spirits, or a wizard, or a necromancer. For all that do these things are an abomination unto the Lord! And because of these abominations, the Lord thy God doth drive them out before thee!"

Reverend Corwin pauses to catch his breath. "You understand then, brethren," he says in a softer tone. "These...*witches*...these necromancers, they are an *abomination* our Lord will drive out with a furious vengeance as He did far away in Salem those nineteen years ago. That scripture and knowledge alone we should take solace in—"

I tire of the familiar sermon of brimstone and hellfire he has given before. Trying not to twist my head and receive another reproach from Mother, I turn my eyes to the window. Most Sundays, I stare at the mountains in the far distance. Make-believe what lies beyond their peaks. More wilderness, I suppose, and certainly laden with savages, yet to venture there must be an adventure liken to those I have only read about.

Today is different from any other Sunday.

This morn, I see a pair of mounted figures on the horizon line.

I estimate they ride fast toward church. For a moment, I fear them natives come to raid us at last. But there are only two. Hardly a raiding party of any note to strike fear in our hearts when there be so many men at church to defend us.

I vaguely hear Reverend Corwin continue. "But still the Lord goes on. He gives us further hope of freedom from these abominations."

I am not alone in having seen the pair of riders. More pews creak. And there be whispers now that do not go unnoticed by Reverend Corwin.

"In the same book and chapter"—his voice rises to a near shout—"He says, 'I will raise them up a Prophet from among their brethren, like unto thee, And will put My words in his mouth; and he shall speak unto them all that I command him.'"

The two riders halt near the circle of wagons. Both remain mounted. The windows blur their visages. They do not appear to be Indians, or at least not how I picture savages to look. Both wear clothing for one, and neither has styled their hair in Mohawk fashion like George claims all savages do.

Why do they not come in?

Reverend Corwin clears his throat. "Understand then, brethren," he says. "We have but to *listen* when the Lord speaks to us."

A sense of nervousness, urgency even, for him to finish his sermon storms over the congregation. Despite it all, he does not end his sermon any earlier than his usual hour and a half of speaking.

And all the while, the two strangers wait outside.

The moment after Reverend Corwin gives the closing prayer, Father stands. He turns down the aisle to lead the Winford men outside. On any other Sunday, I know they would take their leisure in vacating the premises. Talk with one another. Shake hands. Now, they resemble a gang of boys come across a pair of wild dogs they mean to chase off.

I watch through the window as Father and the others surround the two riders. Though I cannot ascertain whether the strangers be friendly or hostile, I gather from the raising of arms the men of Winford are not welcoming.

Mother ushers me out of the pew after a seeming eternity. I do my best to act dignified, but all I truly desire is to inspect these new strangers to our community at a closer distance.

The other women seek the same. None gossip per their usual Sunday routine, nor pay any mind to us as we make our way down the aisle. They crane their necks over and around one another like a flock of geese searching for crumbs to fetch up.

I exit the church. Edging through the crowd, I find it easy to spot Father. He is near a head taller than the other men. His grim face makes me worry for the strangers to run afoul of him.

I feel Mother's hand clamp upon my collarbone as she guides me away from the gathering. She cannot shut my ears, however. I hear a man speak loudly to the crowd. His voice is foreign—rhythmical, and not one of malice.

The wall of men will not permit me to see his face though, nor can I rightly hear what the stranger speaks of. Their argument drowns both the words the stranger speaks as well as their own.

The second stranger I see well, however.

Mounted bareback atop a red stallion, his tanned skin and long black hair might easily trick one to believe him a native in the wrong light. There is an inherent wildness about him that equally intrigues and frightens me. His disengaged demeanor is unsettling; either he cares naught of the commotion his friend stirs amongst the Winford men, or he is unafraid of the consequences. His dark eyes, hollow at first, flicker when locked with mine.

I cast my eyes to the ground. Hurry to join Mother and the other women nearby. Silly. I know he caught me staring.

Mother's eyes shift to the seedy stranger atop his mount. She must think him an Indian too, or at least that he has a bit of their savage blood running in his veins. "Sarah," she says, her voice quivering. "Find your sister and bring her. I like it not she be gone with these strangers so nearby."

"Aye, Mother."

All about the area, older women cluster together. A group of boys hide under wagons near the gathering of men. Ruth's brother, Andrew Martin, and George are among them. I gather all attempt to listen in on the conversation of men and learn the strangers' intentions.

Shielding my eyes, I find the young stranger again.

He sits so still he almost looks a bronzed statue dressed in black rags. Only when he nods at me is the ruse broken.

"Sarah!"

I turn to see Emma skipping toward me.

"You look for Wesley Greene, do you not?" she asks.

"I—"

She playfully slaps my shoulder. "Do not deny it! I know you fancy him!"

"But I—"

She looks at the crowd of men and blushes. "He is handsome."

I had not noticed before Wesley stood with them. Nearly eighteen, his presence there speaks to our community viewing him as a man.

Emma grins. "I know it is wrong to gossip, but I would like to share a secret with you. Promise not to tell?"

"Aye, I prom—"

"I think he fancies you too!" Emma says. "I hear he will soon be looking to take a wife. Isn't that grand? You will be so blessed if he chooses you! Every girl in Winford hopes to earn his favor."

My thoughts go then to Mother and the other women waiting on the men to finish their business with the strangers. My gaze turns back upon the younger newcomer without my meaning to.

He watches me still. Unlike Wesley, however, the stranger is not so keen to break his gaze from mine.

"Or..." Emma's voice wavers as she follows my stare. "Or do you not fancy him because you desire another?"

"I don't—"

"It is Benjamin King you want, isn't it?" Her voice breaks as she looks at the young man beside Wesley. "Tell me true... you desire him."

"Emma..."

"You desire him, and you shall win him because you are beautiful and I am plain." Her head hung low, she walks away from me brooding.

I go to her. Take her hands in mine. "Hear me, Emma," I say in earnest. "I do not fancy Benjamin King."

"Truly?" She sniffs.

I shake my head.

She casts a fearful look at Benjamin. "Well...but why not? Is there something wrong with him?"

"No, the—"

"*Psst*! Sarah," a scratchy voice interrupts me.

Emma gasps.

A seeming corpse, risen from beyond the grave, stands behind the church, removed from the sight of all but Emma and me. Her once fine dress is tattered. Dark circles make her eyes appear shrunken, their whites lined with pink. Her left shoulder twitches unnaturally, liken to a horse's haunch will do. She seems not pained by it. In fact, I gather she is not to have noticed it at all.

"*Ruth?*" I make my way over to her. Pull Emma to join me.

"Aye," Ruth answers in a voice not her own.

"What happened to you?" I ask.

Ruth winces at the sunlight, and raises a hand to shield her face from its light. "I experienced the night! You both shall come to dance this eve, won't you, sisters?"

Emma shifts uneasily beside me. "I shall not...no." She shakes her head. "Ne'er again will I attend a gathering."

Ruth scoffs. Her fingers reach for me. "But you..." She suddenly pulls her hand back like it is on fire. "You will join, won't you, Sarah?"

"I think no. My father suspects—"

"You must!"

I look around the area to see if others heard Ruth's outburst. All are engrossed in their own affairs...all save for the stranger astride his horse. He has urged his mount aside to keep me in his sights. Yet now I reckon his stony stare is no longer meant for me. It is firmly poised upon Ruth.

"You must come," Ruth says. She scratches at her face, and not for the first time either. I see faint lines where she has continually done so, picking at her skin like one with the pox.

"Ruth, I cannot."

She clutches at me. "*Please,* Sarah..." her voice deepens. "You must come!"

I back away. "But why must it be me?"

Ruth's face begins a new series of ticks. Her eyes dart around, never focusing. "I…I…I need a witness." She nods several times. "They will not let me join if I have no one to witness."

"But what of Charlotte?" I suggest. "Where is she? Can she not—"

Ruth kneels to the ground. She reaches for the back of her head, pulls at her hair, and rocks on her heels as one attacked by invisible harpies. "No…no…*no*!" Ruth paws at the hem of my dress. "Charlotte joins also. W-we both need you to witness. You are the only one who can…"

I glance away, nervous Mother or Father might come around the church side at any moment and see Ruth in such a state. My fears are unwarranted. I see all still engrossed by the arguments between the Winford men and the newcomers.

"*Please, Sarah.*" Ruth calls my attention.

"Don't…" Emma whispers.

Ruth ignores her. "Please…" she begs. "Say you will witness."

I stare into this poor girl's eyes. This one I formerly called friend. I pity her. "Aye. I will come. I will witness for you both."

Ruth releases me. Howls with what I can only assume is happiness. She stops to scratch at her shoulder.

My gut warns she did not mean to.

Ruth takes my clammy hand in hers that feels aflame. "You are a true sister. I shall tell Charlotte."

Ruth scrambles away from us, bound for the woods. It is not lost on me she is careful to stay clear of any parishioners and the church itself. She runs at a dead sprint, never once turning to glance back at us.

"What devilry happened to them last eve?" Emma asks.

I watch Ruth vanish inside the tree line.

"I wish I knew," I say. "Perhaps I shall discover it when I witness for them."

"*Sarah!* You cannot mean to!"

"I promised her I would, Em—"

A shrill whistle pierces the air.

I turn.

Father has already boarded Mother and Rebecca into our wagon. He whistles again.

I must hurry back. A patient man he may be with many aspects of his life. Disobedience from his children is not one of them.

I run for my family with Emma trailing close behind. No doubt she fears to remain so near the woods alone. I bid her farewell as I reach the wagon and jump in the back. It once made Father laugh that I, a girl, could do it so easily. It tempts not even the smallest of smiles from him now.

I nearly tumble into the belly of our wagon when Father yanks on the reins. He climbs out and hands the reins over to George. "Take your mother and sisters home. I want the horses fed, watered, and stabled ere I return."

"But, husband," Mother calls. "Why do you not come with us?"

"I would hear more of what these men have to say without inquiring ears." Father answers brusquely. Then, he makes the walk back to church alone.

Our wagon lurches forward as George heeds Father's command quicker than I expected. He sits proudly at the driver's seat. Almost like Father bestowed some rite of passage upon him.

With so few men left to block my view, I notice the stranger I could not see before. He is old, ancient even, and walks with a limp. I do not for a moment think him frail, however. He moves and speaks with a conviction Reverend Corwin could only begin to pray God for. I wish I could hear his words. By the tone of it, I gather his speech would be far more interesting than any sermon I have yet heard.

Most of the Winford men do not share my view. Many ride away, shaking their heads. I see not a few wives catch their husband's ear once out of range. No doubt they hope to learn what news the stranger brought. Soon their gossip will spread amidst Winford. It will then be nigh impossible to discern what were truly said and that dreamed up for the sake of telling.

And throughout it all, I notice the younger stranger remains a statue. His gaze fixed on the point where Ruth entered the woods.

-four-

I LIE AWAKE WITH THOUGHTS OF RUTH RUNNING IN MY MIND. IF I do not go to the gathering, I am both liar and oath-breaker. That it is written God damns all liars is not lost on me. My conscience reminds me of Reverend Corwin's sermon, and that God damns witches also.

But I am no witch. Not truly. The love of night and dancing beneath the moon is all I ever wanted. I cannot recall any punishment in the Good Book for those. I shut my mind of hellfire torment, and turn my thoughts to the question I have asked myself a hundred times already.

Why did Father send us home without his protection?

My brother had no such questions. I lost count of the times George mentioned his want to bravely take on any who might bear us ill will, whether savages or some other foul creature. Upon our arrival, he even went so far as to carry Father's best rifle with him to and from the barn.

One mention from me that Father oft checked the barn of an evening with no weapons to safeguard him unseated my brother. I further shamed his claims with the reminder if Father truly thought him a man, he would have been asked to stay behind, like Wesley Greene and Benjamin King.

George had little to say after. Less still once Mother shooed him to bed.

She allowed me to stay up but a while longer. I think she wished to not wait alone for Father.

Later, I found Rebecca snoring when I entered our room. She lay there still, sound in her deep, peaceful sleep. And why should she not? There be no further chore she can press me into now Father gave me the worst of hers.

I reach for a small candle and flint near me then strike a flame to the wick. I scoot to the wall to sit with my back against the chimney stones, warmed by the hearth directly below, and then reach for my apron. I drape it over a chair to keep it from wrinkling. Then I retrieve Thomas Putnam's journal. My fingers linger on the leather. Dare I read more? Is that a damnable punishment too?

I open the journal to my placeholder, look upon the page, and take up my reading again.

18TH DAY OF JANUARY, 1692

Our plot begins this eve.

I met with Dr. Campbell earlier today with my wife away. Once I welcomed him inside, he produced from his satchel a flask of sherry, several vials, and a package containing a blackish substance I first believed gunpowder.

My hand claps over my mouth to stifle my gasp. I reread the entry to ensure I did not imagine it. Only a description, but nearly identical to what I saw last eve.

A silly notion. I remind myself on the second reading. *He mentioned a blackish powder. Not one with purple flecks.*

Still, the thought disconcerts me, albeit not enough to bar me from further reading.

He poured the powder and sherry inside the vials, and then shook the mixture to resemble a watered down, blackberry jam. Dr. Campbell mentioned the concoction would conjure spirits and lend credence to our cause.

I asked him then how he came by such knowledge. Were he a witch? A wizard?

Neither, sir, came his reply. A man of science only.

Then, he took his leave to visit Reverend Parris and Dr. Griggs. I write this letter now even as I wrestle with my decision. Aye, and my soul.

Do I give the doctor's potion to my child when I know naught what the results may be? I confess, no small portion of me desires to taste it and see for my own self what spirits the lad claims it will conjure. After all, he did not claim the spirits would be evil. What must it be like to peer into the invisible world?

Yet would doing so cast the spoils owed me aside?

I must think more on it.

24TH DAY OF JANUARY, 1692

God, what have I done?

This morn I awoke to Ann's cries of pain. I ran to her side, but my daughter seemed not to recognize me. She convulsed in grievous fits and shrieked of bewitchment. I sent my wife to fetch Dr. Campbell. Upon her return, she mentioned others said he left for Philadelphia yesterday afternoon with Dr. Griggs. 'Tis rumored they shall not return until next month.

Curse both of them. Neither mentioned such travels to me. My good wife also heard tell Betty Parris and Abigail Williams suffer in the same manner. Even now their cries of pain echo throughout Salem, casting fear upon those who hear. She said nothing of Elizabeth Hubbard though. Mayhap Griggs did not give her the potion.

I should have listened to my conscience and not given it to Ann.

For now, we attempt to quiet her until I learn how others in the village react to the other girls' afflictions.

My wife mentioned also she heard it said the girls danced in the wood at night.

The rumors and gossip have begun, as Dr. Campbell predicted. How did he foresee as much? I must discover the answer.

Another question plagues me more: what else has Dr. Campbell foreseen and not mentioned?

A horse whinnies outside my home.

I blow out the candle, ere it gallops past, and creep to the window.

A figure emerges from our barn, but bears no lantern to light its way.

It must be Father to walk in darkness so confidently.

I shrink back into my room so he will not see me. Beneath

the floor, I hear the wooden latch from our front door lift open, followed by the scraping of Father's heavy boots. My conscience warns I should return to bed. Curiosity encourages me not to.

I sneak out of my room to eavesdrop.

Both Mother's and Father's shadows are made giants upon our vaulted ceiling. I keep watch of them in case they grow smaller, a signal they move from the fire where I could be seen if they glance up.

I hunch low to the floor. Crawl for George's hammock bed, strung near the upstairs railing. I have little fear of him waking. He has ever been a hard sleeper and it is not to save space alone that he sleeps in a hammock. Father oft turns to dumping George out of a morning for it seems the only way to waken him.

I slide beneath the hammock to provide some little cover, and keep close watch of the greater shadow on the far wall—Father walking toward the dinner table.

"Do the children sleep?" he asks.

"Aye," Mother answers. "I believe so. Did you catch anything of note in your wares?"

There is a small, carved hole in the wood. I grin in my recalling the memory when I once dropped breadcrumbs upon Rebecca's head. I later convinced her it must have been God providing her manna from Heaven. If I crane my neck, I can peek through the hole with one eye.

I see Father idly spoon the stew Mother placed before him. With no one but she around to see, he slouches in his chair; something he would never permit us to do.

"I did not check them," Father says. "Only wished to be alone with my thoughts awhile. The children...did they overhear what others said outside church?"

Mother joins him with bread. "I do not believe so. George was the only one near. You might speak with him on the morrow. I believe he were saddened you did not ask him to stay behind with the men."

"Did he come to realize it on his own? Or was Sarah's hand in it?"

Mother brushes the creases from her dress.

"I thought as much." Father sighs before spooning his stew. "I suppose I were curious, too, at such an age. Would that I had not been."

Mother sits and touches his forearm. "Who were those men, husband? A pair of drifters?"

"Highwaymen, more like," Father replies haughtily. "They did not give their names. *Refused* to, in truth. Such a thing speaks to their character and purpose. The younger ne'er said a single word."

"And the elder?"

Father snorts. "He spoke enough for the pair of them."

He eats slowly, like each bite brings with it a new line of thought. I cannot help but wonder what these men might have said to make Father so ponderous. Ne'er have I seen him so before. He near finishes his bowl ere Mother speaks again.

"Of what?" she asks finally.

"Witchcraft in Winford."

"Oh..."

"Aye," Father drops his spoon to lightly clatter in the empty bowl. "No sooner do the rumors and ghosts of Salem grow quiet, than these men seek to resurrect them."

"But what cause have they to speak such?"

Father pushes his empty bowl away. "I do not know. And

they would not say. The elder soured himself with our friends. He asked more question than gave answers. I assure you the others liked it not at all."

"And did you believe him?" Mother lets the question hang.

Father rises from the table. Adds a log to the fire. He stays to watch it catch flame. "Aye," he says so quietly I scarcely hear him. "I believe they have seen things."

My nose wrinkles. *What kind of things could they have seen that Father has also?*

My back aches. I shift to stretch it.

A board creaks under my weight.

I silently curse myself when I see Father glance to the ceiling.

"Are you certain the children sleep?" he asks.

"Aye." Mother impatiently dismisses the question. "But what cause have you to believe the elder's claims? Has he seen that which you did whilst in Salem?"

I nearly choke at her words. *Father visited Salem? When? In what time?*

Those and a hundred other questions arise to torment me. Torments furthered by the lengthy passage of time with no reply from Father.

An ember pops and fizzles inside the hearth.

"Perhaps we should not speak of such evil at this late hour," Mother says.

"Perhaps not." Father returns to his seat, resumes his gaze on the hearth fire.

Mother clears the table. Not a word, touch, nor glance passes between them until she is finished. "Husband..."

Father seems lost to her voice, his gaze lingering on the flames.

She calls for him several more times ere giving up and going to him. I watch her drape her long, pale arms about his chest in a show of tenderness I have not often seen from either of my parents.

"Do not dwell on your time there," she says. "'Tis not your burden to bear for that which overtook them. Evil existed in this world long before you. It will be here long after you and I are gone."

I see tears trickle down Father's cheeks as Mother strokes his hair. Despite her best efforts, she cannot tempt him to look away from the fire.

His stare reminds me of how I must have looked whilst watching Hecate; yet where intrigue birthed mine, regret fatigues Father's.

They remain together, Father locked in Mother's embrace, whilst I marvel such a secret has been kept from me. *What right did he have to not speak of such things? What other secrets do they yet keep from us?*

Mother seems to understand Father has said all he means to. "You are a good and just man, Paul Kelly."

I watch her kiss the top of his head ere leaving his side. But Mother cannot see what I do. She does not witness the cascade of tears now freely flowing down Father's face.

Not those of sadness, nor pride, but heart-wrenching shame.

-five-

I AWAKE BENEATH GEORGE'S HAMMOCK. THE HEARTH EMBERS burn low, the reddish gold amongst the ash hinting they wish stoked anew.

Father fell asleep in his chair; he lay there still.

I slide out from my hiding place. My limbs popping with the movement after having been left so long in the cramped position I foolishly remained in.

I reenter my room. Rebecca still sleeps. I dodge the creaky boards and go to the window. It is nearly midnight by the moon's placement. I must leave soon if I am to keep my promise to Ruth.

A sidelong glance at Rebecca promises it would be far easier, and safer no doubt, to climb under the quilt next to her and fall asleep. I think of Ruth and the insistence in her voice. The way she clawed at her own body. What terrible things may happen to her if I do not witness? Ruth has always been a good and loyal friend. It would stain my honor to not show her similar courtesy.

I swing my legs over the ledge. Drop out the window. Like last eve, I wait for sounds of Mother and Father. Hearing nothing, I run across the yard, not stopping until I reach the cornfields. With Father's threat fresh in my mind, I enter slowly. Far more careful than needs be not to bend or break, the stalks.

The cornfield is different tonight. Long shadows envelope me. Without Ruth to tease Emma, I now think any manner of creature with ill intent might lie beyond the next row. I try to banish such thoughts away, but fear is a stubborn foe that rushes them back to the forefront of my mind.

An icy October wind howls down the row. Warns I should turn back. It follows me until I exit the field where it promptly dies, its power lost at an invisible boundary line.

I hear the familiar beating of drums and playing of flutes. With no fire in view tonight, they sound much further away, deeper inside the woods. I follow their tune, humming hymns to keep evil spirits at bay.

Odd, I think. *That I should seek God's protection in these same woods where I sought witchery last eve.*

Perhaps that is why the hymns bring little comfort.

Each step I take brings me nearer to music that stirs my soul in a different way—a wilder, sensual one. I walk through the woods for near half a mile, all the while feeling I am no closer to the source.

An owl hoots above me. A twig snaps to my left.

I wheel about, silly with fright. I see nothing. Nor do I have any intention of veering from my course to learn what made the sound. I turn back.

A shadow stands before me.

I open my mouth to scream. A leather glove clamps over it. Fingers tighten on my jaw in warning. A sinewy arm wraps around my chest. Yanks me closer until my back is flush against my assailant. I struggle to no avail.

Hecate's guards! It must be them. How could I have trusted Ruth? No. Not Ruth. A specter of my once beautiful friend cornered me at church.

Emma realized the queerness of the request. She warned me to not heed Ruth.

Oh, but why did I not listen?

There is a crunch of dried leaves as someone walks over them. A shrub moves. Then, speaks. "Now, what's a pretty lass doin' out on a night like this?"

I try to scream again. My assailant keeps it muffled. I open my eyes and see no shrub. I see a man, an older one of a grizzled nature. His stringy, unwashed hair is black and grey as a wolf's pelt. The dark forest green tunic he wears is mud stained. So, too, are his leather breeches. An axe dangles from his worn belt. He leans heavily on a long rifle.

"Goin' to a gatherin', mayhap?" he asks. His accent is unfamiliar to me. There be no man in Winford who speaks in such a sing-song manner.

I shake my head no.

He beams at me. "Well, that's good to hear, isn't it? Cause if ye *were* headin' to a gatherin', I'd find meself owin' the strappin' lad behind ye a pint. And the poor bastard ne'er shuts up as it is, so I'd be hearin' about it for quite some time."

I notice a scar over his left eye and extending up to his forehead. Another wraps around his neck. Still, I find he is not nearly so frightening as I first reckoned him to be. He struts about gaily, despite a slight limp, and he makes no attempt to hide his paunch. He plops down on a fallen tree. Squints at me with his unscarred right eye I suspect is his good one.

"Do yer mother and father know ye be out in the woods this eve?"

I shake my head again.

He *tsks* and rubs his coarse beard with an equally dirtied hand. "Bein' a father once meself, I can't let ye go on now, can I? Not with such dark things afoot." He looks around the woods.

Gives me the impression he fears the trees hearken to his words. "Darker things than ye can imagine, lass, I'm quite sure of it."

I hear my assailant snort.

The old man glares past me. "Ah, shut it! I promised ye a pint, and it's a pint ye'll get. Have ye ever known me to go back on me word?"

My assailant grunts in answer.

"Don't ye be mindin' him, lass." The old man shakes his head. He looks past me again. "What's say ye let her go, lad? Methinks we've nuthin' to fear from the likes a her."

I quickly step away upon my release, and turn to see who held me. The mere sight of the roguish young man forces me to take another step back. "You..."

The stranger from church!

Now I see him close, he looks of a median age between Father and myself—or perhaps the scars make him appear older. Four diagonal lines stretch over his face as if a mountain lion raked him with its claws. He is dressed all in black. Even now, he blends with the woods. Like the old man, he carries weapons on his belt—a tomahawk, and several daggers—yet he bears no rifle. With his raven hair strewn about his face, I would almost think him feral if not for the stillness in his coal-like eyes.

"A sorry lot, isn't he?" the old man says behind me. "Shoulda left him where I found him. But that's another matter." I feel a light touch upon my arm. "What did ye say yer name was, lass?"

"Sar—Sarah Kelly."

"Ah...course it is." The old man winks at me before turning to his companion. "Ye know where this one lives, lad?"

I glance over my shoulder, see the younger man finishing his nod.

How does he claim to know where I live? The thought terrifies me. But should it? There is no one here with us, so deep in the woods. If either of these men wished me harm, surely they would have done it by now.

"Good," says the old man. "Why don't ye escort Miss Kelly home so we can get down to business then. This night won't linger forever, ye know."

I turn again. The younger stranger is gone. I do not know whether to be impressed or frightened he slipped away so silently. He must be out there somewhere, hiding. Watching me. I search the trees, but cannot spot him amongst the other shadows of the night.

"'Twas a pleasure meetin' ye, lass," the old man draws my attention. He takes me by the hand. Pats it. "Ye stay put at home from now on, ye hear me?"

I feel the wet kiss of a horse's nose upon my neck. I turn, and see the young stranger sits astride his red stallion. How did the horse come so quietly too? Are they both ghosts?

He extends his hand in offering to help me mount.

I hesitate. There is something dangerous about him I cannot place; it excites me more than flutes and drums ever could.

"Go on, lass," the old man urges. "He'll talk yer ears off, but he'll get ye home safe. On that I swear by the blessed Muther Mary herself."

The young stranger's face is unyielding. His hand remains inviting.

I take it.

With a quick jerk, he slings me up behind him. The force of it nearly throws me across the horse. I unintentionally wrap my arms about him to prevent a fall. His chest feels carved from wood. I let go, but only a little.

The older man steps closer. Pats the stallion's haunch. "Now ye take her straight home, lad. Don't have too much fun. We've nasty work to do yet, and I don't plan to start till ye get back. It's nigh the only thing ye be any good for."

I hear the slapping of skin upon skin. The old man's laughter rings in my ears as the stallion jolts forward into a run. Wind whips the stranger's hair around me. It reeks of smoke and a life lived outdoors. I cling closer to him as he guides and weaves our mount through the trees, never slowing until we burst clear of the woods. I immediately loosen my grip.

We ride in painful silence as I await him to speak. He never does. Nor does he even bother turning his head to ensure I am still with him.

"Who are you?" I finally ask.

He gives no reply.

"I saw you at church," I say. "My Father said your friend angered the other men from town. He said you did not speak at all."

The thought occurs to me my guardian may be mute. George once told stories of Indians who took the tongues of their prisoners as trophies. Mayhap they took my guardian as such a prisoner. I try to content myself by listening to the soft clops of his stallion's footfalls upon the grass, but my impatience will not stand.

"Father says he believes you and your friend have seen things. Pray, do you know of what he speaks?"

If only I could see his face. Perhaps it would give the answers I seek. The back of his head tells me naught.

"Father saw things once," I say. "In Salem."

His muscles twitch.

"Did...you come from Salem?" I ask. "Have you ever been?"

The stallion halts suddenly, and my guardian dismounts.

I feel ashamed at my prying rudeness. "My—my apologies. I meant noth—"

He casts his gaze westward.

We are but a hundred yards from Father's barn.

How did we arrive so soon and I had not noticed? I look back at the stranger.

He offers to help me down.

I slide into his arms.

He catches me before my feet can hit the ground. Lightly settles them to earth and holds me till I release him.

"Thank you," I say quietly.

He only nods in reply. Before I can say more, he swings astride his mount and kicks his heels. The stallion races off into the night. Gone like a dream I suddenly waked from.

I am left wanting. Waiting for him to turn his head. Give me a parting look. Anything to speak he too felt something akin to that which pulses through me even now.

He never does.

-six-

Rebecca tips the milking stool she sits upon back and forth. I wish she joined me to aid in the chore once hers. The truth of it is far simpler. "He spoke not at all?" she asks.

I squeeze Lila's teats with all the strength I have. "Not a word," I say.

"Boys are queer indeed."

I would agree if she spoke of anyone else, but he was a man. More of one than the likes Winford has to offer.

"And you say he were handsome too..." Rebecca prods.

I try Lila again for milk. A few drops ting the bottom of the pail. "Aye. Handsome, but...scarred." I shrug. "I could not rightly see all in the darkness."

My answers are not enough to sate my sister's curiosity. "What was it like to ride with him?"

I chuckle. "Windy. His hair in my face for most of it."

I pause to think back on it. In truth, I have never felt anything like I did last eve. Not even when I danced beneath the moonlight did I feel such stirrings in my soul.

Warm liquid wets my face.

Rebecca laughs. She has sprayed me with milk fresh from a younger cow's teat. She jumps up from her stool, startling Lila anew.

I am nearly knocked over by the old cow before I can give Rebecca chase throughout our barn. We scatter the chickens, and I follow her up the ladder into the very top of our hayloft. I chase her through the stacks of hay Father has taken up to dry for the coming winter. The smell is sweet and fresh, a welcome reprieve. I tackle her into the loose straw.

Laughing, Rebecca shrugs free of me. I watch as she spreads her arms and legs back and forth as one would when making a snow angel. "Sarah, what was his name?"

The question takes me aback. Odd I gave both strangers mine, but do not remember theirs. "I...I cannot recall."

"Do you think they will return?"

I sit up. Brush the straw from my dress. "I cannot speak to that either. The elder mentioned they had business to attend."

"What manner of business?"

For a moment, I wish Rebecca had been with me last night. She would have asked all these questions I thought not of. "Trappers, I should suppose. The only work requiring them out so late at night."

"But you are no trapper and were in the woods."

My sister's words strike further doubt in my heart. What were two strangers to our community doing out so late? Now I think back on it, the older rid me of their company quick enough. Faster still once he learned my name.

"Mr. Kelly! Mr. Kelly!"

Rebecca sits up suddenly, a marked concern spreading over her face. "That is Andrew Martin's voice," she says.

Together, we run toward the hayloft door. I have to use all my strength to push open the heavy double doors. Once free, the weight of them makes a booming clatter off the roof eaves.

Far across the yard, I see Andrew riding a withered mare up our dirt drive. The mare collapses ere it reaches our home, pitching him off. Even still, Andrew rises, yelling hoarsely. "Mr. Kelly!"

Rebecca points to the fields. "Look!"

From our high vantage point, I see Father hurrying through the rows. He runs for home with his scythe cutting the wind like an extension of his arm. George trails far behind him, burdened by the weight of his own scythe.

"Come," I say to Rebecca.

We hurry down the ladder, and then to home. By the time we arrive, Andrew is slumped in Father's arms. He weeps openly, not bothering to wipe his face clean, even upon seeing us girls. His face is flushed, clothes soaked as though he climbed out of the river.

"Speak to me, Andrew," Father says.

"It is...my...sis—sister." Andrew sputters.

"Ruth?" I say.

Andrew nods. "Father says a—d-demon—lives inside her."

A demon...I cover my mouth to keep back my guilty moan. *Did they wreak some ill spirit upon her because she had no one to witness?*

Mother hurries to take Rebecca inside so her dreams will not be filled with the terrors shrouding Andrew's face.

"She moans and flails about," Andrew says. "Tortured by some evil spirit."

George's face turns to ash when he arrives.

Father holds strong to keep Andrew from wilting further.

Andrew chokes on his tears. "Father sent me to fetch you. He would have come. But sh-she is so strong now, Mr. Kelly. Between us, Mother and I could not restrain her. Fa-father said you could aid her." Andrew gropes at Father's shoulders. "Please, sir! She is so strong! How can it be so?"

"Rest now," Father calms him. "I shall fetch my things and go at once to your family."

Father leaves Andrew's side and runs into our home.

Mother returns, sans Rebecca. She pushes George aside and helps Andrew to his feet. "Come, dear," she says, ushering him closer to our door. "Inside with you and rest awhile. My good husband will care for your sister."

"She is not my sister!" Andrew cries before entering. "Not anymore. A demon lives in her...poisons her spirit and wracks her body."

Father pushes past them. He carries a black satchel with him I have never seen and slings it over his shoulder as he strides to the barn.

"George," he calls. "Fetch some water for the Martins' mare. See her to the stables when she can walk again. Then help your Mother calm your friend. He can do no more good this day."

Father's sternness brings life back to my brother. "Aye, Father."

"Sarah..."

I step forward. "Aye, Father?"

"Once I ready the wagon, you will come with me," he says. "I may have need of you."

Father leaves me beside the parched mare. I kneel to stroke her sweat-soaked skin. The mare jerks at my touch, as if she too saw what Andrew spoke of and is affrighted. Father has never asked me to accompany him before. What cause has he to do so now? And what aid could I possibly provide he could not do himself?

I do not have long to ponder. I hear the creaking of our wagon ere George can return from the well. Our draft horses, Moses and Hickory, barrel out of the barn, near tipping the wagon over as Father drives them.

The Martins' mare screams at the thunderous beating of their hoofs. She tries to find her footing. I throw my body over her side to keep her from rising until George can arrive.

Father will not permit me to stay. "Come, Sarah," he commands. "Now."

I climb into the wagon, and sit beside him in place of Mother. Father cracks the reins across their backs so hard I think he will draw blood. Unused to such rough treatment at Father's hands, Moses and Hickory tug hard at their straps. They drag us along faster than ever I have seen the wagon go. More than a few times, I fear a wheel will break for Father scarcely bothers to steer us from striking rocks.

On and on he drives us. To the point I think our horses will collapse.

It takes near an hour for us to reach the Martins' homestead—a smaller one than our own, but still respectable in the community. Ahead, I can see the two youngest Martins standing in the yard with no one to keep watch over them.

Six-year-old Henry's arms wrap about his wailing younger sister, despite he too cries. I hear Ruth's screams even before we turn down their dirt lane.

"I need it! Give it to me!"

Keeping the reins in hand, Father leaps from the wagon ere it stops. He loosely ties the horses off to the Martin's wooden stable post. "Sarah! Look to the children. *Do not* bring them inside!"

"Aye, Father," I say, though I know he does not hear me.

He bid me come to keep watch over children?

The Martins instantly recognize me. Both children run to join me. I pick Mary up, and clutch her close. Henry wraps his arms about my waist.

"Help me, Father!" Ruth screams from inside their home. "I need it!"

I feel a jerk on my apron. "Sarah..."

"Yes, Henry?"

"Is Ruth going to die?"

I lead both children further from the house. "No. Ruth will be well again," I say. "My father will aid her."

"Give it to me!"

"Why don't we play a game?" I suggest.

"But what shall we play?" Henry asks.

"Do you know hide-and-seek?"

Mary wipes away her tears with the hem of her dress. Flashes her white legs for me to see. Like her brother, she too grins at the prospect of a game.

I smile back. "You two hide. I shall count."

"Help meee!"

I ignore the shouting as I walk to the nearest tree and cover my face. I count loudly in an attempt to drown out Ruth's screams. "One..."

"No! No! *Nooo!*"

"Two!" I peek between my fingers to ensure the children are hiding. I see Henry take his sister by the hand and run for their small barn.

"I need it! My soul...they can keep it!"

I leave the tree the moment I see both children disappear into the barn. The Martins' home is only a single-story, unlike mine. Lucy, Ruth's mother, sobs at their dining table near the open door. I swing toward the back window wherein I know Ruth shares a room with her siblings.

Her father, Timothy Martin, stands in the window. His arms straight and face red, he struggles against a thrashing figure dressed in white.

"Damn you, Father!"

A thick headboard slides to block my view. The sound of wood screeching makes me cover my ears. Ruth writhes so mightily she moves the bed with even her father's weight atop it.

Father appears in the window next to Timothy with a leather belt in hand.

"Nooo!" Ruth howls.

Father swivels, dodging her kick at his face. He does not shrink away. Father bends, disappearing from my sight. The belt is gone when he rises. I watch him leave the window; return a moment later opening his satchel.

"Nooo!"

Father removes something from within it. What it is I cannot see for the bed shakes more mightily still, further blocking my view of Father and Mr. Martin.

"Damn you to Hell, Paul Kelly!"

Father sneers as he descends upon the bed.

My cheeks sting with hot tears. I shut my eyes, and cover my ears with my hands. Even that cannot deafen Ruth.

"Get away from meee!"

The screaming stops suddenly.

I open my eyes.

Mr. Martin's face is white as the painted siding of our home. He breathes like one short of breath.

Father pats him on the back. Looks up and sees me.

I duck to the side of the house, and shrink beneath the windows. I know he spotted me. He will scold me later for not doing as he bid. Perhaps even strap me.

"Is it gone, sir?" Mrs. Martin asks.

"For now," Father replies.

"Oh, bless you!"

"Pray," Mr. Martin says, "what stone did you give our Ruth?"

"Not a stone," Father says. "Medicine to help her to sleep. I confess, however, I know not how long it shall last. My stores were old. Time might well have lessened the potency."

"Do you fear it witchery such as Reverend Corwin mentioned?" Mrs. Martin asks, her voice trembling.

"It be hard to say. I know naught the face of witchery." Father sighs. "I warrant something has afflicted her—"

I hear Mrs. Martin moan.

She is afflicted! Could it be the powder to give her such fits?

I hear laughter not far away, the children running in my direction.

"Sarah!" Henry stops and calls from afar. "You could not find us!"

"I could not," I say brightly. "You both hid very well!"

"Come." Henry waves. "Play a new game with us!"

"I—"

"Did the Lord strike you deaf, daughter?"

I look up to the window. See Father glaring down at me, his face red with anger.

"I told you to keep the children away, did I not?"

I cast my gaze to the ground. "Aye."

"Then go. I would speak with the Martins in private."

"A-aye, Father."

Trembling, I leave to join the children. Still, I cannot help but glance back at Ruth's window and question whether I heard those same pains Thomas Putnam wrote of witnessing.

And if Ruth is afflicted, as those in Salem were, what dark days lie ahead for the Winford community?

-seven-

THE MORNING HAS WORN INTO AFTERNOON ERE I SEE FATHER leave the Martin household. The children laze upon the grass around me, long since weary of the tasks I set their hands to hours ago.

I rise upon watching Father and Mr. Martin shake hands in the doorway and run to join them.

"I fear your son nigh killed your mare in reaching me," says Father.

"I care not for a mare in this grave hour," Mr. Martin says. "Is there naught we can do further, sir? Nothing to drive this evil spirit from her?"

"Pray God take it from her," Father says. "My family and I shall do the same."

"Thank you, sir," says Lucy. "For all that you have done for us."

"Fear not, madam," Father says kindly. "God is on our side."

Father leaves their house. He frowns upon seeing me so close to their home and turns back to Ruth's parents. "Madam, would you allow us to care for the children? Sarah could stay if you like..."

"No," Mr. Martin says. "Our thanks for your offer. Ruth will want to see them when she..."

It is a hard thing to see a man cry. Harder still for him to do it publicly, or so Father has said in times past. I look away to not shame Mr. Martin further.

"Once she is well again," Mr. Martin finishes.

Father nods. He briskly walks toward our wagon.

I cannot say why, but I find myself drawing near to Ruth's family. I take Mrs. Martin's hands in mine. "Please, tell her I visited. Ruth has a spirit like none other. I know she will be well again."

My words seem to comfort her. She grips my hands strongly. Even Mr. Martin forces a smile.

"Sarah..." Father calls.

I rejoin him at the wagon. If I judge his demeanor rightly, the ride home will not go pleasant for me. I bid farewell to the Martins ere climbing into our wagon.

Father clicks his tongue. Moses and Hickory heave their massive bodies at his familiar signal. The wagon rolls steadily forward.

The Martins wave to us.

I give them a likewise reply, my gaze again drawn to the window wherein Ruth lies. Ne'er have I heard such wretched cries as she screamed earlier. I wonder how long it will be until I can forget them.

I scoot closer to Father, wrapping the coarse blanket about my shoulders tight. "Father..."

"Aye?"

"Will Ruth ever be well again?"

"You are not certain she will?" he asks.

"In truth, I am not."

He clears his throat. "Then you should not have said otherwise to the Martins. A lie remains a lie. No matter your goodly intent."

"Aye," I say quietly.

I listen to the bustling leather straps tighten to their limits as we roll along. I have heard some families place bells upon the harnesses. Father says to do so is both folly and prideful. Folly because the bells sing to any nearby Indian a rich man drives by who could not, most like, defend himself. Prideful to show your horses bear more riches upon their backs than the indentured servants working in the fields.

I turn my thoughts to the changing of seasons. Most of the leaves are already turned. The reds, yellows, and oranges blend together in a collage of beauty I much prefer to the greens of summer. It occurs to me then God must love color; He changes His palette so often. Soon, all will be replaced by wintery nothingness.

"Father, is it true what Andrew said? Does Ruth indeed have a demon inside her?"

I watch his face tighten. "Something lived within her, aye," he says. "Whether it be a demon or no I am uncertain, but her brother spoke true of her strength."

"Have you ever seen such things before?"

The horses whinny at the sudden choke of their reins. Our wagon rolls forward, striking both Moses and Hickory in their hind legs.

Father looks at me warily. "And where am I to have witnessed such evil before?"

He knows. I cast my gaze to the ground. "I—I...overheard you speaking with Mother. She said you were...in Salem at one time."

The leather reins creaks in Father's grip. "Damn that town," he mutters. "And its people with it. Will I never be rid of its curse?"

Ne'er have I heard Father swear before this day. I try to conceal my alarm.

Father takes my hand in his. I look into his face and see no trace of anger there.

"Hear me, Sarah," he says softly. "But speak naught of this to others. I was there for a time, aye. I rid my conscience of the evils done there and locked any memories of that wretched place away long ago. I mean to keep them buried."

I debate whether to tell him of the journal. Surely if Father were in Salem, he would have crossed paths with Thomas Putnam. Perhaps he could tell me more then, being safe in the knowledge I took him into my confidence also.

My conscience is quick to remind Father will ask how I came by such a journal. It would not take him long to tease a confession out of me.

I gather Father senses I struggle with my dilemma, yet he does not ask me of it. Whether he does not care, or fears to hear the truth, I cannot tell.

He releases my hands to take up the reins again. "We will speak no more of this. Nor of *Salem*," he spits the word.

"Aye, Father."

He does not speak the remainder of our journey.

The silence and long ride gives me much time to ponder what memories plague him. It must be sore memories indeed for Father to shy away from speaking them.

It is late afternoon ere we arrive home. Outside our cabin, a dappled grey mare waits. Alongside it, the young stranger sits upon his stallion's back. He puts two fingers to his mouth at seeing our wagon and whistles.

Father cracks the reins so hard it sounds like a quick clap of thunder. He drives us straight at the stranger.

The younger man does not flinch. Not even when Father pulls at the choke. Our wagon halts within an inch of him.

"What brings you to my land unbidden?" Father growls.

The stranger yawns and looks away.

Father throws the reins into my lap. "I said—"

"I think the lad heard ye..."

I glance toward our cabin. The old man I met in the woods stands in our doorway. He holds one of Mother's tulip-painted cups in his right hand and lifts it as if to toast Father's good health. "And how are ye today, Mr. Kelly?"

"What business have the pair of you here?" Father asks.

"Thought we might have a wee chat," the old man says. "It were awfully loud yesterday with the other men shoutin'. I feared ye might not a heard me warnin'." He takes a drink. Licks his lips. "My that's good and proper hot. Would ye like to come inside, Mr. Kelly? Yer wife's cookin' up a fine stew. I dare say 'twill be the best I tasted since me own wife's, nigh on thirty years ago."

Mother appears in the doorway. She is physically unharmed, or as best I can tell, but her arms shield Rebecca from leaving the house. She casts a fearful look at the older man, and then to Father.

From the front window, I see the barrel of Father's flintlock slowly extend outward. The top of George's head breaches the sill. He aims at the young stranger.

Before I can shout a word of warning, the young stranger's hand flies to his waist. I see a flash of silver as he flicks his wrist.

George's rifle barks.

"George!" Mother screams at the sound.

Smoke blankets the area and fills my nostrils. The horses whinny.

I clutch back on the reins to keep them from running off.

The smoke clears.

A dagger, only a single hair's breadth away from George's face, twitches in the windowsill. It takes me a moment to realize the labored breathing I hear is my own.

The young stranger's left hand drifts to hide beneath his tunic. He does not seem nearly so tired, or passive, now. His eyes dance in wait for Father to move.

"Oi, lad!" the old man shouts. "Do ye want the Kellys to run us off ere we've had a wee bit a supper?"

The intensity from the young stranger vanishes. He dismounts and strides toward our home where he dislodges his dagger from the windowsill.

"Colonial bastard," the older man mutters ere taking another drink. "Now...what's say we put all this aside?"

Father watches the young stranger swing back astride his stallion. Then he turns his dangerous gaze on the old man. "You swear to not harm my family?"

"Us?" the older man's voice cracks. "I do believe yer lot fired upon this sorry lad that follows me everywhere I go. But, aye." He nods. "Ye have me word. Neither of us are here to harm yer family. Came to warn ye, in truth."

"Warn me?" Father says. "Pray, about what?"

The old man waves a stubby finger. "Ah, Mr. Kelly, ye squirrely devil. Why, if I told ye, here and now, I'd ne'er taste yer wife's stew! And I've a fearsome hunger to match yer curious mind."

The corners of Father's lips turn down. He looks toward the window where my brother and Andrew yet hide. "Boys," he calls. "Get you to the barn, and Rebecca with you."

Andrew Martin does as he is told. Even takes my sister gently by the hand once outside. My brother lingers. A dark cloud over his face speaks to one who knows he is yet considered a boy in his Father's eyes. Even I can tell it will not be long ere the cloud thunders.

Father must sense it too. He reaches for his belt.

To prove some little defiance, George climbs out the window rather than use the door. He does not look at Father on his slow march to the wagon, yet I notice he is careful to give the young stranger a wide berth. George climbs into the wagon next to the other two. Taking up the reins, he quenches his anger on horseflesh, driving them faster than Father would approve of.

"Sarah..." Father calls me back to the situation at hand. "Help your Mother."

"Aye, Father."

I walk past the old man. He pays me no heed. I am thankful he does not give away we have met before. Still, it strikes me as odd neither of the strangers has once looked at me since we arrived.

Upon entering our home, I see the table already placed for seven. By my count, we will have eight to share the meal with us. I go to Mother's favorite cabinet; the one Father had specially shipped from England to gift her for Christmas five year ago. I remove the extra bowl and cup carefully.

A dragging footstep scoots over our floor. I turn round to see the old man take his seat upon the wooden bench typically reserved for us children. He has tracked dirt into the house.

It does not escape Mother's notice. If any of us did so, we would be clapped round the ears and forced to clean. Instead, I watch Mother busy herself about the hearth. No doubt she nibbles her tongue to a near nubbin to keep her silence.

I go to her that she may ladle stew into the bowls I give over.

She thrusts them back so fast she nearly spills them.

I take the bowls to the table, and lightly set one before the old man.

"Thank ye kindly, lass," the old man says jovially. He dips his head low toward the venison stew and closes his eyes. At first, I believe he means to pray. He inhales the scent so deeply it almost seems as though he is snoring. "This truly does smell the right side a Heaven, Mrs. Kelly."

Mother mutters a reply. I do not for a moment believe them words of gratitude as I hand her the eighth and final bowl to ladle.

"No need for it, lass," the old man interrupts. "Ye've enough here already."

I count them again. Father, Mother, Rebecca, George, Andrew, myself, and the two strange—I cease my count. The young stranger has not graced the inside of our home.

Father takes his seat at the head of the table. "Your friend will not join us?"

The old man motions over his shoulder. "*Him?*" He snorts. Shakes his head. "He don't like houses."

Something in his tone suggests it is no mere dislike. I gaze out the window to see he watches us even now. *Does he stay to keep watch? Or some other reason his companion neglects to mention?*

The old man licks his dry lips as Mother pours the small beer.

He drains the draught with a single swig, picks up his spoon, and eats without waiting for Father to say grace. He eats voraciously, stopping only to pour himself more beer.

Mother looks at him with disdain ere she places a freshly baked loaf of bread upon the table.

"Ah!" The old man quickly tears a hunk off. He dabs the bread into his stew, stuffs it into his mouth. "Wouldn't go so far as to call us friends neither," he says between bites. "He just follows me around is all. Aye, and the term friends carries with it a sort of, er, attachment, ye might say."

The old man pauses to guzzle his beer, then places the now empty cup back upon the table with a satisfying sigh. "I don't do attachments. Least not anymore."

I cannot imagine why. The mere sound of him slurping the last bits of broth from his bowl makes me not want to eat of my own. When he takes the bowl away, I see a bit of the dark, greasy liquid lingering in his beard. He quickly cleans it away with the back of his mottled hand.

"I'll take another, if ye've more of it," he says.

Mother shudders when the old man takes up his fork to pick his teeth.

It is Father who takes up the stranger's bowl and carries it to the hearth. Taking the poker in hand, he pulls the blazing iron rod the black kettle hangs upon away from the fire. "You are welcome to it, Mr.—"

"Oh," the old man winces. I suspect he pricked his gums with the fine point of his fork. He takes it from his mouth. "I don't hold with names either."

"Odd you have no name," Father says as he ladles the stew.

"Augh," the old man says. "Of course I have a name, sir.

Me muther, God rest her blessed soul, granted me with a right fine one. I just don't use it's all."

Father lightly sets the bowl before the stranger. "And what cause would a man have to not use his name? Be you ashamed of it?"

The old man picks up his spoon. "I'm ashamed a nuthin'. Names carry attachment." He brandishes the spoon as if a wand to conjure stew. "And I don't do attachments, I remind ye. 'Askin' for names nearly always leads to trouble,' me pappy oft said to me. 'So steer clear of 'em, lad.' Sounder advice I've ne'er been given."

He pauses then to scratch his head. "Then again, he also told me don't go round pissin' on leprechauns' heads. The wee bastards are an unforgivin' lot, or so he claimed. I've ne'er had the pleasure a meetin' one meself. But who's to say I won't still find one to grant me three wishes, eh, Kelly?"

The old man laughs himself into a coughing fit, as a man in his cups is wont to do. In truth, I wish to join him in laughter. Never have I crossed paths with a man who could sit before Father so comfortably and make sport. This stranger must be mad indeed.

"A man's name," Father says, "his character, and words are all he truly has in this world."

The old man settles himself, nodding at the last. "Aye, therein lies the issue as I see it. A man's name, why, it follows him, it does. Now, while I've no shame, I can imagine lotsa reasons why a man wouldn't use his own name." His grey eyes twinkle. "Or mayhap take another."

For a moment, I think Father's face darkens.

The old man stabs a bit of potato and holds it aloft. "However, bein' of sound mind, I can appreciate how havin' a name makes a person more familiar and easier to trust. Ye be church goin' folk, are ye not?"

"We are," Father says. "As any goodly soul ought be."

The old man takes a bite of his potato. "Right, then. Why don't ye call me...Bishop." He points his spoon at the window. "And the lad outside, the one who ne'er shuts his mouth long enough for anyone to get a wee word in, ye might call him Priest."

"Pardon, sir. But we are not Catholic here," Mother says staunchly. "Nor do we hold with those who are."

Bishop seems to weigh her words thoughtfully before swallowing his last bite. "Well, none of us are perfect, Mrs. Kelly."

Oddly, he laughs himself into another coughing fit.

The boys and Rebecca enter the house together, their expressions not hiding the intrigue of laughter in our home. Mother takes Rebecca as far away from Bishop as possible. The boys sit on the bench with me. Bishop's laugh is soon infectious, and the two boys begin to chuckle, though they have no common cause to.

Father and Mother do not share their sentiment.

I watch Bishop's face turns a light shade of purple from laughter. He takes another swig of small beer and nearly chokes as he dabs at his forehead with the torn sleeve of his shirt. "Ye have to understand, Mrs. Kelly, attachment's no good for anyone in me and the lad's line of work. In truth, it proves fatal."

George picks up his spoon. "What manner of work are you in, sir?"

Bishop leans across the table like he means to share a gravitas secret with my brother and Andrew. "I hunt witches, lads."

George grins. "Witches?"

"George!" Father says.

Andrew shifts beside me. "My sister is a witch," he says meekly.

Bishop sits back. He takes another bite of stew, chewing it slowly this time. "Is she now?"

"George," Father speaks. "Andrew. Take your bowls outside, and Rebecca with you. Stay there until I bid you come otherwise."

"But why not Sarah too?" Rebecca asks.

"Your sister is almost a woman. She must needs learn how we treat guests," Father says. "Even unwelcome ones."

Rebecca does naught to hide her disappointment.

I think it must be hard for her to look upon Father sweetly and not receive her way. I cannot recall if ere it has happened before.

I watch Bishop eat. His gaze never leaves Andrew Martin. Only when the door closes behind them does he push his bowl away. "We heard a girl named Ruth Martin afflicted by witchery. That lad's her brother, isn't he?"

"We do not hold with gossip, nor rumors, in this household," Father says. "Pray, where did you hear such talk?"

Bishop shrugs. "Rumors come, and rumors go, but is it seeds of truth or fear they sow?" he asks, his gay demeanor in full swing again. "It don't matter where I heard it, does it, Kelly? What matters is I *heard* it."

Father folds his arms.

"Did the girl convulse? Seize uncontrollably?" Bishop savors each question more so than even the bowls of stew I watched him put down. He looks at me queerly. "Were her eyes the color a blood? Aye, and did a feverish fire burn through her?"

Father stirs. "Mr.—"

Bishop turns back Father. "And did ye find her...*stronger* than any woman, nay, any person ought be? Tell me. Did it take several of ye to hold her down?"

"Aye," Father says as one realizing it will be less painful to rip a scab off rather than peel it back. "It did."

Bishop scratches his neck. "Well, then. I'd say there indeed be witches in Winford."

"Witches..." Mother says in disbelief.

"Aye," Bishop says. "There still be witches in the world causin' mischief about. The hailed Reverend Cotton Mather can preach all he likes about the invisible world, but they're in the here and now as plain as day. I ought to know. Killed a fair lot of 'em. The wee bitches keep comin' though."

Father stands. "You will mind your tongue in my house, sir."

"Beggin' ye ladies' pardon," Bishop says to Mother and me. "But what would ye have me call 'em, Kelly? These aren't the same lot ye've heard tale of from Salem. They're not wee lasses what point the finger and accuse they been witched. This lot's happy enough to do the killin' themselves." He points to the scar over his eye. "Aye...ones that would flay yer family before yer very eyes and cackle whilst all ye can do is scream."

Mother gasps.

"Mark this, Kelly," Bishop says grimly. "Ye and all yer house. Bitches from the depths of hell is what they are. I've tracked their lot 'cross an ocean. Up and down yer colonies and stood toe-to-toe with 'em. Until ye've done the same and can tell me different...bitches is what I call 'em."

"I would rather you not speak of such to frighten my family," Father says. "Even if you truly believe witchery exists."

Bishop shakes his head. "We both know it does. And I'm tellin' ye they're already here."

Mother shudders. "The last witch hanged in Salem when I was but newly a woman."

"*Salem,*" Bishop scoffs. "To tell it true, there weren't ne'er a witch in Salem, only greed and spite. But yer noble husband coulda told ye that, couldn't he?"

Father's hand is dangerously close to the knife by his right hand.

"Father..." I say.

Bishop grins at me, then Father. "Ye haven't told her, have ye?"

"Father?"

I watch him move his hand away from the knife.

Father seems calmer now and clears his throat before he speaks. "Mr. Bishop, you strike me as a man on a quest for vengeance."

"Aye," Bishop's eyes gleam. "And ne'er will ye meet a man more bent on it than I. Save for the lad outside."

Father nods and leaves the table. A moment later, he returns with his Bible. Pursing his lips, he turns through its pages. "Do you know what the Lord says of vengeance, sir?"

"Why, I can't rightly recall the last time I had a proper lecture from the Good Book," Bishop says. "But do preach on."

Father stops, placing his finger upon an earmarked page. "Romans, chapter twelve, verse nineteen; Dearly beloved, avenge not yourselves, but rather give place unto wrath: for it is written. Vengeance is mine; I will repay, saith the Lord." Father turns the open Bible toward Bishop. He motions for him to read the verse himself. "You understand its meaning, I trust?"

"A good verse that, but I've another for ye." Bishop absent-mindedly flips through Father's Bible. He stops, places his finger upon the page. "To me belongeth vengeance, and recompence. Their foot shall slide in due time for the day of their calamity is at hand," Bishop's voice rises. "And the things that shall come upon them make haste."

Bishop thumps Father's Bible closed and pushes it back to him. "Deuteronomy thirty-two; verse thirty-five."

"Father!" George's voice comes from the yard. "Come quick!"

I see the young stranger, Priest, ride his horse away from our home.

Bishop's limp does not hinder him from beating Father out the door. I am the last outside. I see Rebecca. She cries in the yard with only Andrew to comfort her ere Mother reaches her.

Priest has George by the wrist and examines what is in my brother's hand. I cannot see what it might be from so far away, but it shines in the sun's rays. I watch him release my brother, shield his brow with his hand and look to our cornfield. Suddenly, he leaps atop his mount and with a swift kick, drives the beast toward the field.

Now close, I see my brother holds a crude, bone-hilted dagger in his hand. The base of it is carved into a skull with two strings—one black, the other red—tied from either eye socket. They run down its cheeks as if the skull weeps colors.

Bishop wrenches it away. He turns the blade over in the palms of his hands. "Where did ye find this, lad?" he asks.

"Pray, what is it?" Mother asks.

"I-I..."

Bishop grabs George by the shoulders. "*Where?*"

"S-stuck in the barn...in a milking stool."

I wait for Father to place his hands upon Bishop. Shake him to the ground for seizing George so roughly.

Father does not. His face is pale, and the whole of his body trembles.

The dagger holds his gaze.

I see Priest gallop back to us. His long hair trails behind him in a wave of black. I wait for him to look upon me.

He never does.

Bishop releases my brother. "Did ye see the ribbons?" he growls at his companion.

Priest nods.

"The lad says he found it in the barn..."

Priest wheels his stallion. Spurs it away in the direction of our barn.

Mother pulls Rebecca close. "Pray, sir, what is this meaning of this dagger? Why does it upset you so?"

Bishop ignores her. He scans the tree line, murmurs to himself words I cannot understand. Then he turns to me. He takes the dagger from George. Points it at me. "Lass! Have ye ever seen this before? Ever seen its equal?"

I shrink beneath his stare.

"Did ye take the Devil's powder?" he asks. "Is that why ye went in the woods? Goin' to meet 'em?"

I shake my head no.

"Sir!" Mother shouts. "I will not have you speak to my daughter so! If you do so again, my husband shall—"

Bishop turns the dagger's point to Father. "He'll do nuthin' but run, Mrs. Kelly, if he be who I think he is."

Even at the taunt, Father does not stir. Indeed, he blocks out all sense of what occurs around him after having seen the dagger.

"Please, sir," I say, near on the verge of crying. "What is the meaning of this? Why do you torment my Father so?"

"What? Yer goodly father ne'er told ye about the witches in Salem carryin' these?"

"Of course not!"

"Oh?" Bishop's face contorts into a man gone insane. "That's because *there weren't any witches in Salem!* All those sent to the gallows and prisons...the men, and women, and the child—" Bishop ceases his rant. His fists quake. "The wee children locked away!"

"Sir, you have the wrong man," I argue. "My Father could not have been—"

"Mark me words," Bishop sneers. "If ye and yer kin weren't here, I'd send yer father to Hell right now." His gaze falls on the ribbons and he grows quiet. "But I reckon the debt he owes will be repaid soon enough."

With a quick flick of his wrist, Bishop throws the dagger into the dirt at Father's feet.

Only then does Father come back to life. He blinks, looks around at us as one amongst strangers. He touches the dagger's hilt, and pulls it from the dirt. A scornful mask passes over him. Father rises, turning his hateful glare to the corn. Then he runs for our home.

"The dagger's how they mark the houses," Bishop says to Mother and I. "The arrogant little bitches tell ye which ones they mean to take. And I'd bet me life any a yer neighbors with daughters have a bone-hilted dagger in their barns right now."

"Daughters..." Mother clutches Rebecca closer. "Why?"

Bishop looks between Mother and I. He looks at the ribbons dangling from the dagger. "Red for the innocence stolen from 'em. Black for the histories that'll forever darken their names." Bishop looks at Mother. "It's Salem's vengeance, Mrs. Kelly. Come for its due and proper!"

A piercing whistle cuts the air.

I look to the barn to see Priest shake his head. He points to the fading sun. To my family, it may look as though he only points at the corn. I know he means far beyond it; his true aim is to the clearing. The deep woods where the gatherings occur.

Bishop hurries to his dapple grey. I watch him swing astride his mount with surprising dexterity for a man as old as he.

"Bishop!" Father calls. His voice is strong again. The voice of Father I have always known, not the weakling I witnessed but a moment ago. I turn to see him exit our home with a flintlock in hand. "I go with you."

"Oh?" Bishop asks. "And who will protect yer family while ye be away?"

Father looks at us each in turn. He passes over me, but lingers on Rebecca.

"Stay with 'em," Bishop says. "After all, this isn't Salem. This lot won't be idly clapped in irons and led to the gallows."

"Mother," Rebecca says. "Does he speak true? There are witches in Winford?"

Bishop winks at my sister. "Aye, lass. And I go to hunt 'em!"

He laughs himself into another mad coughing fit, and spurs his horse away toward the corn. I watch him follow the path Priest left, riding just beyond the reach of corn, yet never venturing inside. He becomes a tiny thing ere much time passes and soon vanishes, along with my family's hope for more answers.

-eight-

Night has fallen with no sign of Bishop, nor Priest. A strange fear took over my household when they left. I like it not at all.

Father has been sullen ever since and disappeared to the barn with the bone-hilted dagger. Mother took Rebecca several times to cheer him. I gather she intended to learn if Father abandoned us to follow the strangers into the woods.

Each time they return, Rebecca tells me they find Father upon the milking stool; his gaze lost in the sockets of the skulled dagger. What spell is cast upon it not even Rebecca can break him from its transfix?

With Father out of his wits and Mother beside herself with worry, George lords about our home. He and Andrew brought down gunpowder and shot from our stores to place near the windows. Why he does this I do not pretend to know, but his enthusiasm for it keeps them busy.

I am forbidden to leave the house, even to gather firewood. All because Mother fears witches may truly come for her daughters. I notice, too, she will not allow Rebecca five feet from her since Bishop's warning. I banish myself upstairs rather than be consumed by the fear gripping them. On my way up, I see Rebecca rise to follow me. She takes but two steps ere Mother wrangles her close.

Even my own room has been taken over. A rifle leans against

my window. I wonder if George expects me to use it, or if he plans on manning all the positions he has laid out. With naught else to do but wait, I light a candle, lie upon our pallet, and resume my reading of Thomas Putnam's journal.

2ND DAY OF FEBRUARY, 1692

Would that I could have murdered Captain Alden today. To my deep regret, the savage-lover has already departed for Quebec. An honest man told me Alden offered to seek out a Wabanaki medicine man to rid my Ann and the other girls of their affliction.

As if I would allow he or one of his red men near my home, let alone touch my daughter.

I cannot fathom why Alden be allowed to come and go as he pleases. The man is a traitor to his people.

12TH DAY OF FEBRUARY, 1692

Doctors Campbell and Griggs returned to panic in our town this afternoon. Good doctors both, but they are far better actors. I nearly believed their distress at the woeful affairs they returned to in Salem. Griggs insisted upon examining each of the afflicted girls at once, with Dr. Campbell to aid him. A crowd followed them to Reverend Parris's home, tittering of evil spirits and the Devil come to bear.

The pair of doctors tarried in the home not an hour ere returning to an even larger gathering outside, all eager to spread their words throughout the countryside. Griggs refused to speak until he had examined my Ann.

I gather this is Dr. Campbell's ploy. The delayed response only sowed the seeds of fear deeper amongst the crowd.

I would not permit any, not even Parris inside my home. Indeed, I barred my wife from witnessing also. Once alone, Dr. Campbell apologized for his lack of communication, but insisted it necessary for panic to truly take hold. I again am left to wonder what sort of mind devises a plot such as this; to bend a town so easily to his will? I admit, I am envious of such power, yet feel blessed I am partnered with it rather than pitted against him.

With only I to watch, the doctors ceased their examination pretense. In truth, Griggs stood beside me trembling whilst Dr. Campbell removed his satchel. From it, he took what I first believed a small rock. He first required Griggs and myself to restrain Ann, a feat which took near all our strength. She continued to moan, and lash at me, a sure sign of the Devil if ever I saw one.

Dr. Campbell insisted she were not witched. He closed her nostrils and forced the rock inside her mouth, then placed his hand over it to prevent her from spewing it out.

She nigh choked upon swallowing, yet I felt her body go lax beneath me after. She slept soundly then.

Dr. Campbell assured me she would awaken by nightfall. He then preached we must proceed as agreed upon in the woods, and asked Griggs to address the crowd.

✤

Newfound strength, the moaning, and lashing; each word I read only serves to transport me back to Ruth's home. Could what afflicted the girls in Salem truly have come to Winford?

I am torn by the thought. My friends snorted of a powder, not drank it as Thomas Putnam claims his daughter and the other Salem girls did. Mayhap the powder and drink are different substances.

I wonder what is this remedy Dr. Campbell gave to calm her? Could it be similar to that which Father gave Ruth? Perhaps someone discovered a cure and made available for others to remedy afflictions of witchery on their own after Salem ended.

I think on Father's satchel. Given his current state, mayhap I could sneak the satchel away to better learn what else may be hidden inside.

No. If he discovered the theft...

I return to my reading.

⁂

Later, I overheard Griggs relay to the village the girls acted in accordance to how the children did when bewitched by Goody Glover. I heard gasps from the women and more rumored whispers than I care to recount.

Dr. Toothaker, spoke then, he who had come at our request to examine the girls before doctors Griggs and Campbell returned. He went amongst the crowd claiming he and his daughter have killed witches in the past, and could do so again if necessary. The superstitious man has always been a nuisance, but now the crowds hearkened to his every word. Several asked how could he tell a witch from an afflicted?

I did not stay to hear his ridiculous answers. Instead, I returned home to find Ann awakened. She told me spirits beckoned her to dance after she had drunk of the potion. Aye, and felt lifted to heaven as if she could fly. She next asked of me for more of it.

I admitted I had none.

She grew unruly, begging me to obtain more whilst claiming an unquenchable thirst. Her body twitched as if possessed anew, and she would have torn her face off, I fear, had I not halted her from doing so. When I restrained her, she kicked at me and flailed about until her release. Again, she demanded I retrieve her more. Again, I refused, and she beat upon me with a furious strength no mere child should possess.

'Twas shock bid me strike her, I realize now, yet she seemed not to feel the blow that should bring an average man to his knees. I do not recall the knock upon my door, nor can I remember when Dr. Campbell entered the room, but he was suddenly there. I watched in wonder as he approached my Ann, unafraid, with a vial of sherry in his hand. He gave her but a spoonful of the drink, and that she drank down greedily.

I scarcely heard what Dr. Campbell said next to me, my attention being solely for my daughter. She turned calm not a few minutes after she drank of what he gave. Falling back into bed, she smiled and moaned lecherously.

Dr. Campbell asked if I preferred her in such a state, or would I have him return her affliction. Before I could speak, he held the remainder of the vial before my eyes. The evil shall retake her without this, he told me softly. He then set the potion on my table and reiterated my family's role to play in the dastardly plan. Then he took his leave.

My precious Ann turned feral again but two hours later.

I gave her the remaining lot, and, as if magicked, she grew calm again. Yet now the potion is gone, and I fear it will not be long ere she has need of it again.

25TH DAY OF FEBRUARY, 1692

There are multiple girls in Salem now afflicted, my own servant, Mercy Lewis, chief among them. I fear all have drunk of Dr. Campbell's potion. Could it be he spread it amongst the girls in fear I shall betray him? If so, I must relay his threat well-received. I shall play my role to the fullest, as my partners continue to act their own, so long as my Ann is given what she needs.

To the public, Griggs claims he can find no remedy for the girls' affliction but they be witched, and so the villagers have turned to superstitious remedies.

I heard tell the slave, John Indian, was ordered to bake what he named a witch cake—a foul concoction made from the urine of Betty Parris and Abigail Williams—and fed the cake to a beastly dog, it being said the animal is a familiar of the Devil. I am told the mongrel ate the lot, yet both girls remain afflicted.

Fulfilling his obligations to the plan, Reverend Parris preaches of the Devil in all his forms and how even the most faithful in heart may be corrupted.

Dr. Campbell visited me later under the pretense of examining Ann once more, though I knew he came to assuage my concerns. He made mention I would soon witness a sign he is a good and honest partner to me. The time is ripe to earn my reward, he said. And I shall understand his meaning soon.

27TH DAY OF FEBRUARY, 1692

Betty Parris mentioned this morn their savage, Tituba, caused her torment. Accusing a slave of such witchery seems of little offense to me, but she and Abigail later accused Sarah Good also.

Dr. Campbell saw both women clapped in irons and led away. He then asked if there be anyone I reckoned a witch.

Then, I fully understood the doctor's meaning two days past. My partners be the truest allies I could ever have hoped for. called my Ann into the room where first Dr. Campbell gave unto her a potion that caused her to convulse. I planted the name in her mind, and she went with me to seek a legal warrant for the arrest of Goody Osborne.

I cannot imagine a test more suited to our plot. A slave, a beggar, and a thief; with these three souls, we lay the foundation for that to come.

I hear footsteps walking up the stairwell. I close the journal, and shove it in my apron. Rebecca appears in the doorway.

"Mother says it is time for supper," she says.

"Aye, I shall be down in a moment."

Rebecca remains. Her fingers play about the handle.

"What keeps you?"

"I-I have not told Mother, nor Father, of your leave for the gathering," she says tenderly. "Can you not tell them you that put the dagger in the barn?"

She cannot mean it. "But I did not do so."

"No?"

I swing my legs out of bed. "Where am I to have acquired such a dagger? And the mastery of carving such intricacies upon its hilt?"

My sister puzzles over my words.

"Do you truly think me a witch?" I ask.

I am surprised to hear not a little of Mother's voice in my own. A queer feeling near strikes me down as I watch Rebecca run away in answer. How could it be my own sister believes me capable of such evil? I have told her we do naught but dance at the gatherings. Does she truly think I would sport as such to put fear in both the hearts of her and Mother?

I hear our main cabin door open below and close as quickly. I hurry to the window. Mother carries a plate of corn, carrots, and a slab of venison toward the barn.

Father must be there still, and she off to serve him.

With both out of the house, I slip downstairs. In truth, I am happy Father does not join us. He believes children should be silent in the presence of adults and so our meals together have ever been a bleak affair. At least Mother's absence will allow me the chance to eat quickly and leave the table.

I reach the bottom of the steps. George and Andrew have positioned themselves off to the sides of our front windows as lookouts. Each holds one of Father's long rifles across their laps. They barely acknowledge me as they eat in watchful silence. I wonder if the pair of them gave any real thought to what Father will do should he find his best rifles taken without consent.

Rebecca sits at the table with her poppets strewn about to keep her company. She is deep in conversation with them as I make my plate. I take my place down the table from her. With Mother gone, I sit comfortably with a leg tucked up beneath me as I read on to discover more of Thomas Putnam's scheme.

1ST DAY OF MARCH, 1692

The witches have turned on one another. Parris's slave Tituba named Osborne and Sarah Good as conspiring with her and the Devil.

I sense Dr. Campbell's hand in this; perhaps he whispered a subtle word she may free herself by admitting guilt and condemning the others.

Later, Sarah Good admitted conspiring with the Devil. She turned on Osborne not long after.

However, an earlier fear of mine has come to pass. Martha Corey called the afflicted girls liars, and spoke of her disbelief in witchery also.

Dr. Campbell cared naught of it when I told him the news. He would only say Corey will be dealt with in due time.

I pray he is right.

He did praise my choice in condemning Osborne. Prideful and stubborn, she will not confess, nor name other supposed witches as Good and Tituba have done. Dr. Campbell mentioned her refusals only serve to strengthen the resolve of all in the village now seeking answers. It will not be long ere they find some.

I shall see personally to that. I admit to a sense of joy in seeing Osborne suffer so. The woman has tormented me these many years in her withholdings of the lands that by rights belong to me. Let her rot in jail and think on the wrongs she showed me. Many will join her if I have my way. My list is long, and the good Dr. Campbell gave unto me the keys to fortune and vengeance. I should be a fool not to use them.

12TH DAY OF MARCH, 1692

Our cause grows stronger.

Dr. Campbell has further swelled the ranks of afflicted girls, including my servant, Mercy. All do as they are bid or risk facing the terrible agony my daughter spoke comes from the absence of potion.

Would that I knew the contents of it. I have asked Dr. Campbell, but the man has smartly refused. At least my partner is no fool to give up his secrets so easily.

Martha Corey also now stands accused of witchery. It will be a mighty blow for our cause if she be condemned; she being so highly regarded for her faith.

Parris means for her to face the rope, but I could not fathom a means to blacken her name. Would that I had more faith in our reverend. He aims to spread talk Martha is both whore and mother to the bastard slave boy, Benoni, who lives with her and her equally wretched husband, Giles.

24th day of March, 1692

A sadder sight I ne'er saw than that I did today. Dorothy Good, the daughter of Sarah Good, was arrested for witchery and she being only four years old.

I choke on a bit of venison. *Bishop spoke true...there were child prisoners in Salem!*

I look down the table at Rebecca. She is double the age of Dorothy Good. Even the thought of her in chains shudders me.

How could one so young be thought a witch and, worse, imprisoned in a dank cell?

The notion robs me of my appetite. I rise from the table, and clear the scraps into a bucket for George to give the hogs later. There is a small basin to wash the dishes in. I do so hurriedly, ere Mother returns with more for me to clean. Rebecca comes to help me dry the plate, one of her favorite tasks. I carefully place it back inside Mother's cabinet so as to not chip it.

Our watchful guards drowse at their posts. I collect the rifles and return them to their rightful home beside Father's bed ere he discovers the boys' misstep. It would not be proper for Andrew to receive a strapping for obeying my brother's commands whilst he is a guest in our home.

Rebecca, too, seems tired. With a yawn, she lays on the floor in front of the hearth amongst her dolls. I think to scold her for keeping them so close to the fire. If a spark popped just right, it could singe her dolls, or catch fire. I think better of it.

"Rebecca," I say. "Won't you come to bed?"

"I wait for Father."

I know better than to argue. Nothing will give her cause to move once her mind is made. As I climb the steps, I think on how long Mother and Father have been gone. The thought frightens me some, but not enough to journey outside and be scolded for leaving the safety of home.

Once in the confines of my room, I thumb through the few remaining pages of Thomas Putnam's journal. Sleep is calling my name, and, while I do not wish for night terrors of children clapped in irons, I must know the fate of those condemned.

I had not thought it should ever come to this. I sought only vengeance against those who trespassed against me, not children.

Dr. Campbell made mention that the villagers allowed the

child led away further proves our hold over them. No one dares speak against the accusers now lest they be clapped for doing so.

Indeed, even I have not raised objections though I fear the afflicted girls go too far in this. I wish I could coerce them and my Ann into reversing their claims against Dorothy Good, but to do so would weaken our position. Still, the thought of such a young girl shivering in the cold cells next to her mother haunts me.

19th Day of April, 1692

I grow fearful our position weakens.

Dr. Campbell refuses to meet with me any longer, instead communicating through Reverend Parris. Blast him! Has Campbell not come to me on several occasions for information on my neighbors? Did I not warn John Proctor should be dealt with sooner? Proctor has ever been dismissive of the afflicted girls' claims, and more vocal still once the girls accused his wife.

It matters little with Proctor now also accused, but I have heard others say it was only because he protested his wife's arrest. It takes but a small crack in the rock for water to split it; I fear Proctor may have begun what will be our undoing.

Furthermore, we are now forced to deal with the Proctors' servant, Mary Warren. My daughter mentioned to me some time ago Warren eagerly wished to join the afflicted girls', but Proctor would not allow her to leave his home. Warren claimed Proctor beat her for claiming she, too, is afflicted and warned of further torments if she continued her claim. Two weeks past, she admitted before the magistrates she were a liar and neither afflicted, nor a witch.

Dr. Campbell warned such would happen. He said it necessary for one of the girls to break from the fold that the others bear witness to Warren's pains when his potion is withheld. In this way he keeps them loyal.

I have seen Warren scratching at her body already; a sure sign the lack of potion affects her.

On the matter of potion, I have asked Dr. Campbell to wean my daughter of its evil power since first I learned of its power. The damnable man obliged me, but only when I pay him handsomely to do so.

Parris mentioned he requested the same but quickly grew short of income, and so sent his Betty away to live with the Sewalls. He hopes time might draw the poison from her. However, he did not send Abigail Williams away, in keeping his end of the bargain to supply an afflicted girl.

Indeed, despite my own misgivings, I, too, have seen my share in this plot upheld. I had Ann allege the spirit of a man rumored murdered by Giles Corey many years ago now torments her. The specter requested Giles not be shown the rope, but rather, be pressed to death to extend his suffering.

I shall do all in my power to see the so-named specter be pleased. Aye, and see Corey's body crushed in equal to the fortune he stole from me.

7TH DAY OF MAY, 1692

It appears Dr. Campbell's reach has no bounds.

I had Ann accuse our former reverend George Burroughs of witchery less than a week ago, but ne'er expected to see him returned to Salem. Today, I witnessed him drove in, clapped in irons.

More of my earlier written fears have also been assuaged, for now.

Mary Warren recanted her position but a few days after my

last entry. The lack of potion must be a wicked sort. Now she is deemed a hypocrite, and defies the Proctors who employed her.

Indeed, the accusations are daily routine here and now.

I find myself again marveling at Dr. Campbell's plan; because the crime of witchery occurs in Reverend Cotton Mather's invisible world, there be no evidence but what the girls allow. Yet even I, who well know their claims false, am amazed at how convincing their portrayals of affliction be. The girls act a marvelous show before the accused, none more so than Abigail Williams. Where she rocks and condemns, the others are quick to join, aping her every whim.

10TH DAY OF MAY, 1692

I am again repaid for my part in this plot.

Goody Osborne died in prison today. Her lands now belong to me until her sons come of age. I mean to profit much from them until then. And who is to say, in time the boys may also be condemned for witchery...

18TH DAY OF MAY, 1692

I must needs remind Griggs to thank me for the part my daughter played today, she being chief among the accusers against his competitor, Dr. Toothaker. It helped our cause Toothaker performed medicine these many years with no proper education. "How is it one could acquire such knowledge without being schooled," others have asked. "And how is it a man and daughter who have killed a witch came to know what a witch was, but they be witches also?"

"How indeed?" I whispered in their ears.

Reverend Parris is also repaid for his loyalty. His ill will struck again at Rebecca Nurse and her goodly family of high esteem by way of my servant, Mercy.

Upon the declaration and freeing of Nurse's sister, Mary Easty, this afternoon, I had Mercy accuse her anew. Easty now rots in chains again, not a few hours after her release.

I am told she wishes her accusers judged in court.

We deemed it a fool's defense for a woman to so boldly speak to such learned men.

Her challenge went unheeded.

Is this the truth Hecate bid me find? I wonder as I turn the page. *That the Salem trials occurred only because corrupt men warranted it for vengeance sake?*

31ST DAY OF MAY, 1692

I swear Dr. Campbell has aged ten years since I saw him last. Tonight, whilst giving Ann her treatment of potion, he looked over his shoulder so often I feared he had drunk of his own stores. He attempted to take his leave quickly, but I bid him stay a moment.

I mentioned a point I have recently thought much on...many of the afflicted girls are orphans. Aye, and made orphans by the Indian war. I admitted I had thought little of this earlier, but the plan is genius. If the girls are found frauds, their lives mean little to anyone with no family to speak of. Likewise, they cannot betray us lest they face the torments Mary Warren experienced.

I had always deemed Dr. Campbell's choices wise, but of late I am less sure.

The girls seem now vindictive. Indeed, Abigail Williams revels in her newfound power, tossing accusations against some with no guidance from any of us.

Dr. Campbell did nothing to assuage my doubts. He said only he would think on what I had told him.

I have been most discomforted ever since he took his leave. There has been a reason for all he set in motion thus far. I would be a fool to not think he has further plots. But what plans are they, and where do I place among them?

I wish to end this eve's entry on a note of happy circumstance. I saw Captain John Alden, Jr. recently seized and arrested for witchery. I had seen him accused, but not yet heard he returned from ransoming prisoners. I wonder how a traitorous dog will fare when locked away in the dark? I mean to visit him there. Aye, and ask if he yet feels his Wabanaki medicine man could strike witchery from the countryside.

3RD DAY OF JUNE, 1692

I woke this morning to Griggs beating upon my door. I answered believing he meant to relay news about a Court of Oyer and Terminer recently issued, with Lieutenant Governor William Stoughton appointed to rule over it. Stoughton's close friendship with Reverend Cotton Mather makes his judgment nigh invincible, and it is said he will allow spectral evidence into the courts. I could not see how any of the accused may hope to clear their names with these good tidings.

Griggs bore ill news. He claimed Dr. Campbell never came to him with potion for his niece. Indeed, he feared the founder of our plan disappeared in the night. A visit to Ingersoll's inn proved it so.

God, but where can he be? How could he abandon us now?

Parris has ventured off to find him, claiming business abroad. He asked of me to keep watch over Abigail Williams, which I agreed to readily.

We have since agreed to proceed as planned until Campbell be found. If he is, mayhap the young doctor will learn what the accused experience. He is still a stranger to these parts, after all, and it would be easy for me to convince the others such a man does not tarry here with good intent.

Clink!

"Sarah!" The familiar voice comes from outside. It sounds like a girl's, but croaky and deeper. I close the journal, and go to the window.

"Sarah!"

"Ruth?" I ask.

"No. Come down..."

I look to the rifle beside me. Father once taught me to shoot when we heard the Tuscaroras raided nearby. He claimed me not a bad shot for a girl with no experience. It angered me so that I practiced until I could shoot an apple off a scarecrow from fifty yards away. But that were four year ago. I have not felt the coldness of a trigger since.

"Who are you?" I ask. "What do you want of me?"

The bushes rustle. A living, twitching nightmare steps from behind it. I would think she shivered from the cold had I not seen Ruth's body do the same.

"Charlotte!" I say. "Oh, Charlotte. Where have you been?"

She seems not to have heard me. Her head snaps nervously

in the direction of every sound in the night as if she is privy to whispers I am not. "Come with me, Sarah," Charlotte says. "You must come with me to the gathering!"

"I cannot. My father will—"

"Come with me!" Charlotte insists. "You must. I-I have need of a witness."

"But I do not think I should."

Charlotte falls to her knees and weeps. "They will not give me more without you. I-I have need of it. Please come with me—" Her head jerks up. "*You!* You could take of the powder also! Then we can truly be sisters, Sarah. Aye! Moon sisters forever and ever!"

"Charlotte..."

"I need it, Sarah! I nee—"

A shadow leaps from the corner of my home. It spears Charlotte to the ground. Her wails of torment die, replaced by furious hissing as the shadow attempts to subdue her. It climbs atop her belly and sits with its knees upon her shoulders. Charlotte scarcely seems to feel its weight. Swinging her arms about, screaming like a wounded pig, she claws wildly at the shadow.

"Where are they, Charlotte Bailey?"

Father...How is it he came there?

"Tell me, child!"

I leap from my window.

"Why do they come for me now?" Father demands of her.

Charlotte chuckles, the sound of it laced with scorn. "You know why..."

Father slaps her. "Tell me!"

"Nooo!" she screams.

I pull at Father's shoulder for striking her. He roughly pushes me away, sprawling my body to the ground.

Charlotte continues to flail. "Release me!"

Mother restrains me ere I can speak sense to Charlotte. "No, Sarah," she says. "Leave her be!"

Mother means to drag me to the house.

"Charlotte," I say, fighting through tears. "Charlotte, it is I, Sarah."

I see her writhe and buck with the ferocity of an unbroken stallion.

"I need it..." She snarls. "I need it..."

Father struggles to stay on top of her. "I will help you, child. But first tell—"

"They will kill you!"

Father succeeds in grabbing Charlotte's wrists. He strains to push her arms to the ground.

Charlotte is too strong. "I need it!"

She shirks her arms straight out like she be crucified. The sudden move pitches Father forward, crashing him headlong into the grass. Charlotte rises and makes for the corn like a startled fawn bolts for the thicket.

I hear twin rifles bark.

George and Andrew awoke with the commotion. The smoke clears. I look to the window. Both reload powder and shot.

There is no reason to do so.

I thank God for their poor aim as Charlotte disappears into the field.

Mother releases me that she may help Father.

He pushes her away. Then he glares at me. "Where is she going?"

"I-I do not—"

Father crosses the few feet between us and slaps me. "Do not lie to me!"

"*Paul!*" Mother yells.

I rub the sting in my cheek. When I draw the courage to look up, I see Father is gone, replaced by a mad man with murderous rage pulsing through him.

"She mentioned a gathering," he says. "Do you know of what she speaks? Where it occurs?"

I nod.

He grabs my arm. Pulls me back to my feet. "And the Devil's powder—did you take of it?"

"No..." I say quietly.

Father studies me. By the look of his face, he wrestles with the truth of it. He releases me, but the force of his grasp leaves a mark soon to bruise upon my wrist. "What did he look like?"

"He?"

"Aye. *He*," Father sneers. "The man who offered the powder to you. What did he look like?"

I cannot understand this. Why should a man have been at the moon dance? "But no man offered me anything, Father."

Father raises his hand. "I will not warn you again, Sarah. Describe him to me."

Mother steps between us. "You will not strike her again."

"You do not command me, woman," Father says. "I will stop the moment she speaks truth."

I flinch, but do not shy away. "I tell you true. There was no man. A woman offered me the powder. I swear it on my soul. The others...they named her Hecate. The Devil's daughter."

"*Daughter?*" Father lowers his hand. My answer has thrown

him. He looks up at the moon, puzzled. I see him grimace. "So that be his plan...Very well. Then I must away to meet this...*daughter*... of his. Sarah, fetch my rifle from your brother."

Father leaves Mother and me. Her tears wet my arm.

"I'm sorry, Mother," I say. "I never meant—"

She tries to pull me close. I will not allow it, lest she keep me in her embrace until Father arrives and strikes me again for not doing as bidden. I leave her there, and away to fetch Father's rifle.

For a moment, I fear George will not part with it peacefully. For a moment, I hope he does not. Anger I did not know existed swelled in my heart the moment Father struck my cheek. It must be plain upon my face.

George gives the rifle over willingly.

I hear the barn doors kicked open.

Father rides our painted mare, the one Rebecca named Callie, the fastest we own. He barely stops to allow me up behind him before kicking Callie's ribs so savagely it sounds like the booming of a drum. Tearing across the yard, bound for the distant woods, she carries us toward a gathering beneath the moon.

-nine-

Like Priest and Bishop, Father keeps us within sight of the corn yet he will not approach the rows. He gives our mount no rest until we reach the field of dandelions. All their whimsical florets are gone now. Killed by a frost.

A pillar of smoke rises deep within the woods. Already the dark melody plays from somewhere deep inside. Tonight the tune is different; the once gleeful pipes replaced by ominous drumming.

Father slides off Callie. He pulls me down and gives me the reins so he might load his rifle.

Callie quivers with cold sweat. I wish I had an apple to give her. I tie her off inside the woods so her silhouette will not stand out against the field. I turn back to find Father waiting on me.

"Lead on," he says.

I do so slowly, listening for any sign we are not alone. I hear not even the rustling of underbrush behind me from Father. With him silent, the darkness sports with my mind. It makes me recall when I once shared these woods with my friends. The happy memories I have are changed, however, replaced by those with friends tearing at their faces in scratching fits of agony.

A twig snaps beneath my foot.

"-arah," Father halts me with a stern whisper. He intentionally leaves off the S in my name rather than let anyone who may lie in wait hear the hard sound it makes. He points to his feet, then to my chest.

I am to follow where he steps. I nod.

He shakes his head then takes the lead.

The ill thoughts of my friends return. I push them away by concentrating on Father's feet. I pretend we are Indians sneaking upon our victims as George and his friends used to play.

My pretense does not work. It only serves to remind me there may truly be painted braves waiting to scalp me ere I knew the deed had been done. I tell myself Father would not let anything happen to me.

The dull sting in my cheek cautions to doubt even that once certainty.

The gathering is much further than I estimated. On and on we walk, deeper into the wild than ever I dared venture alone or with my friends. The wood spirits whisper to one another high in the trees. They creak the branches in mockery of my fears.

All prayers I offer they be silenced go unanswered. I sense a black magic in the leafy canopy that prevents them from rising to Heaven for God to hear.

A pack of wolves howls in the distance.

I halt. "Father, I can go no further."

In answer, he roughly grabs the shoulder of my dress to pull me along. I shut my eyes, and allow myself to be led.

The music grows louder with every step I take. I try and give over to its rhythm again, but the power it once held over me is now lost. It must know I turned away from Hecate's flock and has excommunicated me for my betrayal.

I run into Father's back. We have stopped behind a sprawling oak. Beyond its woody borders I see firelight.

Father squats and peeks around it.

I follow his example, and gasp at the sight of nigh a hundred followers dancing in the circle of oneness.

The dancers are different than those I met in the woods before. White, black, red—every color of skin God ever painted upon His children dances there.

I see white men dressed in animal pelts and not a few Indian braves also. Most look of an age near my own, but some as old as Father. A few wear leather jerkins, others bits of raggedy cloth. All are dirty. A breeze carries their musky, sweat-ridden stench into my nostrils.

The moon dance is different, more ritualistic and primitive. The followers twitch and scratch. I cannot discern whether that be part of the dance or from the lack of potion Thomas Putnam wrote of.

A two-tiered earthen mound the size of our cabin sits behind the bonfire. Stone-carved steps make a path up its steep incline. A gaping, black cauldron sits at the first landing with its own smaller fire beneath it. Its flames have a bluish tint to them that greedily race up the sides whenever the liquid contents boils over the edges.

A pair of hooded figures dressed in flowing violet garb stand beside the cauldron. One stirs the vat with a wooden spoon so large it seems an oar. The other unties a tethered black ram and leads the beast up to the second landing.

And there, at the top of the earthen mound, an obsidian table gleams in the firelight. Behind it stands Hecate...the Devil's daughter.

With the hooded figure ascending to her, Hecate takes a dagger from a hidden sheath in her violet robe. With her other hand, she lifts a golden chalice from the table.

The ram bays loudly.

Hecate quickly bends. In a single, swift motion, she slits the ram's throat.

Bile rises in my own as she holds the chalice before this sacrificial fountain of blood.

Hecate steps away. Lifting both the chalice and dagger skywards, she offers them first to the moon. Then, pours it into the flames.

A raucous cheer rises from the crowd.

"Father..." I whisper.

His gaze will not leave the ritual, nor will he answer me.

I turn back to see Hecate's honor guard lift the ram's carcass onto the table. The guard moves his arm back and forth in a sawing motion. A moment later, the ram's head rolls away from the body.

Hecate takes it by the spiraled horns. This too she offers skyward before thrusting it down upon a pike inserted near the head of the table. With a hammer given to her by the guard, she taps the animal's nose, forcing the severed head to stare upon the table. She tosses the hammer aside without care and bows low before the sacrifice.

The drumbeats taper until only one is heard; the gathering's living pulse.

"Sisters." Hecate's voice rings out above the rest, quieting them. "Brothers! Family all! Tonight another heeds our Father's call. Let her step forth!"

All sit in the circle of oneness, save for a single girl.

"*Charlotte...*" I whisper.

Father places a steady hand on my shoulder to keep me from moving.

Hecate beckons Charlotte come closer.

I cannot rightly see her face, but Charlotte's gait is stilted as she climbs the mound. Reaching the top, the guards guide her to lie across the table with her head directly beneath the ram's gaze.

A hooded guard kneels beside Charlotte's feet and rises with chained iron fetters in hand. The guard pulls the first chain taut. Closes the shackle around Charlotte's left ankle. I watch the guard perform the same action at all four corners of the table, binding each of her limbs to form her body into a human X.

I see movement at the lower mound. The pot stirrer lifts the spoon from the cauldron to rest upon the lip. With her free hand, she reaches into her cloak and removes an empty vial. She brings it under the spoon and pours the cauldron's concoction inside.

Hecate lifts her arms in praise. "We welcome this girl into our fold. With a willing heart, her soul she hath sold!"

Another drum begins, opposite its brother; the two slow beats resembling the thunder of draft horse footsteps over cobbled stone.

The circle of oneness begins anew. The followers clasp forearms, each pulling at their neighbors, chanting. "*Todi-ras-ela-nahana. Hama be-la de-za sustana!*" the choir of voices rise and falls. "*Todi-ras-ela-nahana. Hama be-la de-za sustana!*"

The vial carrier reaches Hecate. Kneeling humbly, she offers it up.

Hecate takes the vial in hand. She empties its contents into Charlotte's mouth then claps her free hand over my friend's face to prevent her from spewing it out.

Charlotte arches wildly. Her hands yank at the bindings. She cannot break free of them.

Father stifles my scream. He pulls me behind the tree so

I cannot see further. I hear the drums crescendo then go immediately silent alongside cries of approval from Hecate's minions.

I struggle for Father to release me.

He does without much fight.

I poke my head around the tree, and gaze up at the mound.

The whole of Charlotte's body convulses. I see the chains are meant not only to restrain her whilst she lay there. They prevent her from seizing off the table. She shrivels and straightens like a green sprig thrown upon a flame.

Hecate casts a pouch into the fire. Its flames transform to an emerald hue to match her eyes. She places her hands about the ram's jaws. Kisses its nose. Then cranes her neck back and howls joyously.

Those in the circle cheer louder.

I cannot look upon Charlotte anymore. I put my face to the ground for the earth to soak up my tears. I feel my body lifted as Father bears me away from the madness.

He strides knowingly back the way we first came, almost as if he laid a trail of crumbs to follow. Not until we are a hundred yards from the gathering does he set me down. He grips my face with his calloused hands. "Go," he whispers. "Ride for home."

I shake my head.

"Do it, child," he insists. "And quiet—"

A witch's war cry cuts him off. Father pitches me aside.

I land in a patch of brambles. Hear scuffling not a few feet from me.

"They're here!" a craggy voice yells. "Mistress, I've found—"

I hear a grunt and then the voice is silenced.

A hand reaches for me. I scream ere recognizing Father. His face is bloodied. So too is the dagger in his hand.

He pulls me free of the brambles and leads me, running, through the trees.

The thrashing of brushwood follows us.

I glance over my shoulder, and instantly wish I had could unsee the fast-moving torchbearers giving us chase.

"Come back!" Voices maliciously cackle. "Come back to play!"

Father stops. He drops to earth and pulls me down with him. "Wait here," he whispers.

He is on his feet and vanishes ere I can speak against it.

I place my cheek against the cold ground like a scolded pup. With darkness and little foliage about me I feel naked and vulnerable to any who might pass. I spot a fallen tree but ten yards away. The long scar up the side tells me lightning felled the tree. I crawl toward it.

A cackle is cut short, replaced with cries of pain.

"They're here! Fetch the mistress—" Another voice is silenced.

The tree is five yards away.

"Nooo!" A third voice is cut down.

Two yards.

A cloaked figure appears where I previously lay. It halts to sniff the air.

I crawl into the hollow of the tree to shield me. The dead bark chips easily away. Insects making their homes in it slither over my body. I bite my lip to not scream as I bat them away. It does little good. I feel them crawling down my collar and over my arms.

"-Arah?"

Father...he came back for me! I squirm free of the wood to run for him. Then I hear the laughter echoing throughout the woods, quickly joined by the mirthful hooting and crows of others. I cower back inside the hollow.

"Torches," Hecate says somewhere in the dark.

Near twenty are lit in a halo of light, and I barely outside their perimeter. Indeed, it seems a miracle no one discovered me. A torchbearer, an Indian brave with blood painted all over his body, stands but fifteen yards away from me. In the broken moon rays, he looks a demon cast out of Hell. His body twitches subtly for wont of Devil's powder. I see him grin at the prey they have surrounded.

Father...

He stands in the middle of the circle. His rifle aim trained on Hecate. "Who are you?" he demands.

Hecate steps toward him. "Do you not know a witch when you see one, good doctor? I thought surely one such as you would recognize the Devil's daughter when she stands before you."

The ring of followers laughs with their mistress.

"The Devil has no daughter," Father says.

"Oh, but He does," she coos. "And you helped birth her... Dr. Campbell."

*Dr. Campbell...*My mind reels with the accusation. *She confuses him. Mistakes him for an evil man. A poor resemblance mayhap—*

"That man died in Salem," Father replies quickly, confirming my belief. "Along with all the other evils there."

"Not all of them," Hecate says. "And you *are* Dr. Campbell. It may have taken nineteen years to find you, but I will never forget the face of the man responsible for my fate in Salem."

"Seek you out Thomas Putnam then," Father says. "It be little secret—"

"I have," Hecate cuts him off, stepping closer still. "My Salem sisters and I visited him in due course. So, too, did we find his wife, his brothers, and his brother-in-law. In time, we will find the others who played their parts. But you..." She shivers, but I gather it is not due to the cold. "I have desired you most of all."

Even from where I lay, I can see the delight dancing in her eyes.

"Young, handsome, *Dr. Campbell.*" Hecate relishes his name. "Tell me, sir. Did you feel an evil presence near the night you fled, hunting you for a betrayer? It found me instead. Took me under its wing and taught me the dark arts of your science."

"Step no further," Father warns, his aim poised at her heart.

"Your drugs made me as I am." Hecate spits. "Aye, and blackened my good name for all time with it."

Father sneers. "And what be your cursed name?"

"Why, I am Hecate!" She turns and plays to her crowd. "The Devil's daughter, sir."

I cringe at their mockery of Father.

Hecate grins spitefully at him. "Do you not recognize me yet, Dr. Campbell?"

The ring of witches takes up her claim. "*Dr. Campbell...*" they whisper. "*Dr. Campbell...*"

"He died in Salem!" Father insists.

"As did the innocent girl I once was," Hecate shrieks back. "Hecate rose from her putrid corpse with a vengeful claim for the nineteen souls you bid my Salem sisters and I condemn to the gallows!"

I see movement high in the trees. A noose dangles over Father's head where he cannot see, flung over one of the highest branches. I try to call out. Warn him.

My voice will not work.

"Then back to Hell with you," Father shouts. "And see its fires stoked for me!"

Hecate's minions let the noose fall round Father's neck. I witness it tighten as they lift his entire body into the air with a great heave.

Father's aim is thrown. His rifle barks. The light of the shot is blinding, made worse with the smoke it produces.

My cry goes unheeded amidst the shouting, scuffling, and war cries that follow.

Hecate yet stands when the smoke clears. Blood trickles from the open wound in her shoulder. She seems not pained by it, unconscious of it even.

Father has been uprooted. His toes dangle within an inch of the ground. His arms wave freely in torture.

But there is the minions' misstep.

Father raises his hands over his head. Grasping the taut rope, he pulls himself up enough to breathe. I see his muscles straining to keep the weight of his body from pulling him down.

Hecate snatches a torch from one of her followers. She removes her hood and tears off her mask of raven feathers. Tangled, rat-colored hair spills over her shoulders. She stops shy of Father, holding the torch before her wild face. "Do you recognize me now, Dr. Campbell?"

Father's face is purple, his strength waning.

Hecate tiptoes around him. "Do you think on your family? I laugh at your calamity, sir, and will mock the fear I bring upon them! Their destruction comes like a whirlwind for the anguish you caused me!"

Hecate throws away her torch. She jumps and grabs hold

of the rope. Her added weight yanks Father higher. His mouth soundlessly opens and closes like a barn door caught by an unrelenting wind.

The voices in the circle begin to chant. "*Ersna tela pox-igada! Kruca mera tashee-dada!*"

"Call upon me to stop!" Hecate taunts. "I will not answer!"

"*Ersna tela pox-igada! Kruca mera tashee-dada!*"

She releases her hold on the rope.

Father falls a few feet. His body bounces beneath his own weight. A low gurgle escapes his lips.

Hecate's followers hold strong.

Father's feet again dangle and kick an inch from the ground, desperate to find any small hold to leverage upon.

"Curse them!" Hecate addresses her audience. "Hang them! We damned without care." She points at Father in a demonic rage. "Tomorrow, his daughter's scalp I shall wear!"

She reaches into her robe and from it produces her dagger. Holding it in both hands, she sneers at Father. "But now, Dr. Campbell...it's your turn to die."

"To die," the crowd chants. "To die."

"I offer you to Satan, sir, and so—"

Hecate strides quickly to Father...and plunges the dagger deep into his chest.

"Goodbye!"

-ten-

My screams go on long after Hecate's crowd finishes their own joyous cry.

Rough hands grab me ere I can run.

I punch and kick to no effect.

Hecate's worshippers drag me before her. They restrain me near the pendulum of death that is my Father's body, the rope creaking with his weight at every tock. I see Hecate's blade buried to its hilt inside him. A river of blood pulses from it, feeding the growing pool beneath his feet.

"*Sarah...*" Hecate sings my name.

My captors force me to look at her.

Her angelic face and creamy skin bear no trace of the pockmarks, or scabs littering the picked faces of those around her. She lightly traces one of her fingers over the bruise on my cheek where Father struck me. "Did you find truth in the gift I gave you?"

"I...I..."

"*Yes.* I see it in your eyes! You learned truth, as I did, and were so grateful you brought me a gift in return." Hecate laughs and shoves my father's body.

I shut my eyes of the sight, but cannot block out the creaking of wood and rope.

"And now you wish to dance with your moon sisters in celebration. Come." She bids me rise with a touch of her hand. "Let

us dance with your friend, Ruth. We shall fetch her tonight and remedy what your father afflicted her with."

I hear the pendulum tick.

"Please..." I beg of her. "Please let me go."

"But I made a promise to your father," Hecate says. "I cannot recant unless you would join us."

"You mistook him...H-he is...his name is P-Paul Kelly."

"Poor, innocent girl. He spoke many lies to me also." Hecate strokes my cheek. "Look at me..."

I open my eyes. Stare into her green orbs that sparkle in the firelight.

"*No*. This can't be. You've learned nothing, have you?" Hecate frowns. "Spineless as your father, you'd flee this instant if I allowed it."

"I-I—"

Hecate turns to her followers. "What say you all? Should Dr. Campbell's daughter join us...or him?"

Someone touches my hair and sniffs it.

"Such a pretty thing..." a deep male voice says lustfully.

I mean to slap him, but there are several strangers hovering about me.

They laugh in my face.

Backing away, I trip over my dress.

The strangers surround me. A crone with crazed eyes and black-stained teeth pokes at me. "You will join us, won't you, dear?"

"Join us!" a man calls.

"Aye!" another girl appears, scratching at her pockmarked and bleeding cheeks. "Welcome, sister!"

I cover my face with my arms. "Help me! Someone, please!"

Hecate's followers cackle. "Help me! Help me!" the collection of voices shouts over one another. "She cries. She cries!"

"Pray, not to her father..."

"He dies! He dies!"

"Leave me alone!" I shout.

"She does not wish to join us?"

"The poor little dear—"

"Look on Hecate"—the crone grabs my chin—"and you will learn fear!"

Hecate pushed the crazed woman aside. With a raised hand, she silences the group. "Sarah Campbell," she says quietly. "It is now your turn..."

"*Her turn,*" the crowd whispers. "*Her turn...*"

"Which will it be, girl?" Hecate steps aside to allow me a glimpse of my fate: several of her manservants stacking a pyre of logs. "Join us, or burn?"

I shake my head and moan.

The witches cackle at my tears.

Something whizzes past my ear.

The witch nearest me falls at my feet.

Another drops beside her, and then a man.

All have arrows shot through their hearts.

The circle of followers erupts with screams at the murder of their companions. Some search for the source. Most scatter into the woods. The few building my execution pyre leave it to protect Hecate, their mistress.

Another witch seeking escape falls in front of me with a long arrow embedded through her throat.

I look to the woods. See the torchlights extinguished one

by one; swallowed by the woods, or some unseen presence that makes their bearers cry out ere they are silenced.

A shriek near Hecate wills me back. One of her guards falls with an arrow through his temple.

The others tighten their circle around her.

Another whooshes past me and a second guard falls, this one with an arrow through the neck. He seizes on the ground, trying to remove the arrow even as his lifeblood slips away.

The remaining three form a triangle with their backs shielding Hecate. They speak to one another in a guttural tongue. I gather they try to discern where the assassin is. One of them points to the woods.

A shadow emerges from the wilderness. His face colored with a bloodied handprint overtop it; a seeming Indian painted for war.

Priest...

Slinging a longbow about his back, Priest takes a tomahawk from his belt. He kneels by a still writhing witch. Finishing her with a single strike, he rises with her blood staining his blade.

Hecate laughs scornfully. "You! Oh, *you*." She closes her eyes and moans. "I have missed you so. Did you come longing for my sweet embrace again?"

Priest takes a dagger from his belt. He motions both it and his tomahawk's blade toward his person, ushering her to come closer.

Hecate makes a pouty face. "No? Then I have little use for you." She pushes her guards toward him. "Kill him."

Each takes a knife from their belt before rushing him. Priest throws his own dagger at the first and buries it through the assailant's eye.

The other two are undeterred. They spread out, one to garner Priest's attention, the other to flank him.

Priest moves with serpent-like speed. He blocks and parries their blows while making deep slashes of his own. Catching the heel of one with his tomahawk, he trips the man. Almost faster than my eye can follow, he rises, swings his dagger upward into the next man's throat.

It knocks the man off balance, near cleaving his head off.

In a final, sweeping motion of merciless efficiency, Priest brings his tomahawk crashing down upon the tripped guard's skull. I watch him pluck his weapons free, step over the twitching corpses, and make for Hecate.

She seems to find the deaths of her guards a small matter, for she grins even as he comes on. Kneeling, she takes a fallen torch in one hand and unsheathes her dagger from Father's chest with the other.

It makes a deep, sucking sound as it emerges; one I know will remain with me all the rest of my days.

"There is little need for this," she says to Priest.

His face is stone.

"Come..." She slinks toward him, the rubies in her dagger winking in the torchlight. "Throw down your weapons. Serve me as you once did. Mayhap I shall serve you also." She licks the length of her dagger's blade.

Priest strikes at her.

Hecate whirls, matching his precision and strength with anticipation and speed. She dodges his blow, slices his cheek.

Priest kicks her in retaliation.

Hecate's pretenses melt away. She charges at him in a blood lust, raining fire and steel upon him.

Priest will not retreat. He steps forward, snarling at her fury, as he makes new strikes of his own.

I watch their deadly dance. Listening to their blades sing against one another.

I feel a tap on the shoulder. "Come, lass."

Bishop stands behind me, his face equal parts blood and sweat. With a strong hand, he aids me to stand and leads me from the fray.

"You cannot escape, Sarah Campbell!" Hecate shrieks as Bishop and I run away. "I will find you!"

I glance back a final time. Four torches hurry from deeper within the wood toward Priest.

"Priest..." I say.

Bishop leads me faster. "The lad can take care a hisself. If not, he'll owe me a pint for havin' to save his arse."

We run as one, the sounds of cackling in our ears. I am again surprised Bishop's limp does not hamper him. I hear the pawing of hoofs nearby and soft whinny of horses. Bishop leads me to his dapple grey, tied beside Priest's red stallion. Both move with skittish urgency.

Bishop reaches beneath my arms. He heaves me atop the stallion. "Can ye ride, lass?"

I clench my legs over the stallion's back. "Aye, I believe so."

"Good." Bishop unties the horses. "We've a long way to go yet, and we must needs leave quickly ere the witches find us."

"But there were...men." I recall the terrible faces amongst the circle. "I saw men also."

"Aye, highwaymen and fur traders." Bishop spits. "The Devil granted that succubus some unholy power betwixt her legs. I'll warrant she's swayed a man or fifty with it." He looks back the way we came. "Blast it." He sighs. "Where are ye, ye wee bastard?"

"My father—"

"He's dead, lass," Bishop says, not unkindly. "Can't change that now."

The thought of Father's body, swaying in wait, returns to unnerve me. Bile rises in my throat ere I can fight it down. I vomit to the side.

I hear Bishop curse.

The stallion moves beneath me.

I dizzily sway to the side. Then fall into blackness.

I stand alone at the base of the earthen mound. Gaze to its peak where the polished table lay before the blaze. I am alone here, all the torches and followers gone with Hecate.

The fire still blazes.

Atop the earthen peak, I witness the ram's head slowly turn upon the pike, of its own accord. It lingers on me. Watching.

My feet step forward, called by an unheard voice that bids me walk up the stony steps. The vat at the first landing gurgles and slops dark liquid over its edges. The Devil's drink smells both sweet and decaying at once. I turn away from it, fearing what ingredients may bubble to the surface.

I am willed to the next landing where Charlotte yet lies upon the table. Now close, I see elliptical runes engraved upon it. Stone-carved, hooded serpents snake around the legs, their hoods and mouths open, fangs ready to strike.

Charlotte looks peaceful in death. Her limbs no longer twitch, nor does she mar her face by picking at it. She lies unbound, save for a black ribbon keeping back her hair. A necklace with a wooden crucifix is draped upside down upon her chest.

I reach forward to right it in the proper holy position. A frigid trap grabs my wrist. Yanks me to the table.

Charlotte's eyes flutter open. "They have me, Sarah," she says. "Yet I fear for you most of all."

I struggle to free myself.

"*He* has marked you." Charlotte tightens her grip. She laughs cruelly at hearing my bones snap. "Desires you"—her voice becomes deeper, craggier—"needs you!"

"Who?" I can barely ask the question.

Charlotte cackles. Her free hand palms the top of my head, forces me to look directly above her. "The Devil..." she whispers in my ear. "He sends His daughter to fetch you."

I pull away as far as Charlotte will allow. A wet, slippery sound draws my attention. I look up.

The ram's head oozes down the pike.

Transfixed by some evil magic, I am bound to remain until its bloodied nose touches mine. Fiery warmth spreads instantly through me, like its nose were flint and mine the striker. It holds me there, bids me stare into its dead eyes and watch its horns spiral out into the night.

"Awaken," it bays.

Soft candlelight hovers above me from the timber rafters in my room. "Wh...wh—"

"Sarah..."

Mother? I try to rise. Pain shoots up my left wrist. I scream.

"No, child," Mother says. I turn and see her worn, tired face. Her cheeks flushed with sorrow. "It is sprained. Lie back now."

I obey. "How did I come here?"

She strokes my hair. "Mr. Bishop brought you. He carried you in..." her voice breaks. "Sarah...y-your Father—"

"I-I saw it Mother."

Sobbing, she leans in to kiss my forehead. "Oh, my Sarah... Praise God you are still here."

"I am, Mother." I comfort her, though I too am weeping. Her back trembles at my touch. "I am still here."

-eleven-

THE UNTOUCHED GRITS BEFORE ME HAVE LONG SINCE GROWN cold.

Like Father in the woods, the dark of my conscience speaks.

I have no tears left to weep. No strength to fight the voice away. I lent all to Mother last eve, and, for that, she will not scold me to finish my breakfast now.

She rolls dough beside me on the table, the commonness of daily routine taking hold of her. The lump in her apron is Father's Bible. A talisman to ward off the accursed witches who killed Father.

I wish I heard all Bishop said to her. She would speak naught of it this morning, and I cannot bring myself to ask. Not that I wish to relive what I saw to her.

Rebecca plays with poppets in the corner. I gather she, too, uses them to shield her from a horror no young mind should ever face.

Our cabin door opens with a loud creak. Mother automatically reaches for her apron. From it, she draws a knife.

I once heard it said some women oft keep blades secreted away, for one never knows when Indians will attack. A hidden blade would not be enough to fight off the savages entirely. It would serve to open one's own veins and keep the Indians from their prize. Seeing only George at the door, she tucks it away and resumes her rolling of dough.

I watch George carry the milk pails, sloshing a bit on the floorboards as he walks too fast. "Move, Rebecca," he says in a commanding tone reminiscent of Father. His voice has not yet made the change, however, and it breaks with a higher pitch.

Rebecca will not budge.

George makes sport he will kick her. "Move!"

"I am waiting for Father," she replies.

"Father is dead."

I wait for Mother to clap George for speaking so.

She feigns the same deafness to his claim Rebecca does.

With no reproach, George looks at my sister squarely. "The witches killed him. He's never coming back. Now, move!"

Rebecca shrugs his comments away. "I am waiting for Father," she reiterates, stroking her poppet's horsehair.

"George," I say. "Leave her be, or I'll knock you down with my good hand."

George sets his pail upon the table.

I see in his face he means to test me. But there is a growing seed of doubt also. I water it by rising, standing between he and Rebecca.

His gaze flickers to my left arm, slung from a strip of cloth and wrapped in a poultice. "She needs to hear the truth, and face it. That is what Father would say."

"Father would tell you to leave her be."

His face reddens at my retort, but he has no reply. He knows my argument is sound. His hand quivers like wishes to strike me, an inferior female, for speaking back to him. The largest part of him is still a boy struggling with his own fears though.

I leave him to it.

Surprisingly, George walks round the table and sits opposite me. Only then do I realize he is alone. "Where is Andrew?" I ask.

"Mr. Bishop took him, after he carried you into the house near daybreak and set your arm. He bade Andrew lead him to his homestead that they might gather up his family. I-I wanted to go," George stutters as if he fears I would mock him for a coward. "Mr. Bishop bid me stay. He said I was a man now"—I notice his stance and shoulders straighten.—"and a man's duty is to protect his family. He bid me shoot anyone dead who approached our home, save for he or his companion. 'If God himself rides on your home, you shoot Him, lad.' That is what he told me."

On any other day, I might chuckle. I can hear the old man's voice as clear as Rebecca speaking soft words to her poppets.

"They have not yet returned." George quiets his tone. "I fear they never will. And why should they when Father rebuked them?"

"They will," I reply. My thoughts drift back to the ferocity with which Priest fought against Hecate and her minions. A nervous fear courses through me. George said nothing of Priest... only that Bishop returned. "Was the younger man, Priest...was he with Mr. Bishop?"

George shakes his head.

I think back on the torches running toward him. *There were too many.*

It seems I have a few tears left within me after all.

"Sarah," George says, more quietly still. "Is Father truly dead?"

He senses the weaning time has ended yet is still wanton of the teat.

My answer is not to come. The sounds of fast-running hooves

echoes through the door George left open. I run to the window to see who comes.

Two riders approach the end of our drive, one of them leading a riderless horse alongside their own.

A rifle cocks beside me.

George opens the window with its barrel. He balances the end upon the ledge as he takes the first rider in his sights.

For a moment, I think to take it from him. I have seen him miss twice now. It may well be I have the truer aim between us. My thoughts vanish when I see the barrel slowly turn as George follows the first rider's movement. I see his finger massage the trigger. I cover my ears to shield them from the deafening blast to come.

George removes the barrel from the window. He grins. "It's them."

My heart races at Priest's safe return. I think on what I might say. How to properly thank him. I freeze upon seeing Mother.

She has moved from the table to sit behind Rebecca. Her right hand tucked into her apron, her fingers knead beneath at that which I cannot rightly see. I think it no coincidence she sits so near her youngest and Father's beloved.

She means to do it. My conscience warns. *To keep those who stole her husband from taking any more of her family.*

"Rebecca," I say. "Come to me."

"I am waiting for Father."

I go to her, lift her with my good arm. She screams and kicks as one possessed, but I will not give up. I carry her outside and away from Mother. We sit upon the frost-covered grass where I promise to hold her in my lap until she tires of fighting or her body gives out.

Rebecca stops only when the horses draw near.

I think she believes it may be Father.

We are both disappointed; it is only Andrew Martin atop Callie, and Bishop upon his mare. The third, our largest draft horse, Hickory, bears no rider. Two wooden kegs hang off either side of Hickory's back, slung together by a bit of rope.

"Lower yer aim," Bishop growls. He swings off the mare and removes his rounded hat. The dome of his head is like a halo of bare skin, surrounded by untamed wildness. Wiping his sweaty brow, he dons the hat again. Then he goes to Andrew and pats his leg. "Come down, lad. We've work to do, and yer not doin' any sittin' on yer arse."

Andrew dismounts slowly. His face is grimy, blackened with soot, save for two light colored streams down his cheeks that his tears washed clean.

I watch Bishop place his gloved hand beneath Andrew's chin. "Oi. Ye keep this up now, ye hear me? Ye'll make yer family right proud tonight."

Andrew nods and wipes his nose with stained sleeves.

Bishop turns to see me watching. With the slightest of nods, he acknowledges my grief. A second later, he lifts his hat in welcome. "Top a the mornin' to ye, Mrs. Kelly," he says brightly. "Have ye any more food in the house?"

Mother stands in the doorway. Her right hand still in her apron. "A-aye," she says.

"Right, then," Bishop says. "Lads, get yer bellies full. We've a long day's work ahead and an even longer night, I'll warrant. Best to work both on a full stomach."

A strange kinship has formed between George and Andrew. Before, my brother would have begged to hear stories from his friend; ask on the ride with Bishop, learn what they discovered there. Now, he waits for Andrew to make the first move. When Andrew does not, I see George's face tighten like Father's oft did when trying to solve a problem.

"Mr. Bishop speaks true," George says.

He turns back to our home, seemingly without care if Andrew joins him or no. At first, I think him rude. When Andrew trudges after him, I wonder what unspoken message passed between them.

Rebecca is right, I think. *Boys are queer.*

No sooner do both enter the house, than Bishop looks to Mother and me. "The Martins are dead," he says. "Their home burnt to a shell. The lands and them with it."

"Ruth..." I say.

Bishop's eyes flash. "Don't ye cry for her, lass. Yer friend's not dead."

"But how can you be sure?"

"'Cause I haven't killed her yet. And before ye get the weepy eyes on me, know this. That girl, Ruth, and any others ye might know who took the Devil's powder...they're not yer friends anymore. They'll do anything to have more of it. Includin' killin' ye if that's what the Devil's daughter bids 'em do. They're slaves to her will now."

Mother shakes her head in disbelief. "This is madness."

"Aye, madam," Bishop says. "And ye'll witness it firsthand tonight."

"I don't understand. Why would they wish to harm us? Why did they kill my husband?"

Bishop strokes his beard. "I don't like to speak ill a the dead, but yer husband weren't the pious man he claimed to be."

Mother's lip curls. "My husband was every bit the man he said—"

"Did he tell ye his true name...Simon Campbell?" Bishop asks gently. "And that he lived in Salem for a time?"

Mother looks at her feet. "A-aye. I knew him for a Campbell."

She knew? I cannot contain my rage at all the secrets withheld from me. "Mother! How could you and Father lie to us?"

Mother rubs her temples. "He sought a fresh start, Sarah," she says weakly. "We both did. I was indentured when first we met. Kidnapped and ransomed by savages. Your father...he paid the debt off. Took me for a wife when I had naught to offer him in dowry but forgiveness."

She takes me by the shoulders and stares into my eyes that I might believe her words.

"You *are* a Kelly, Sarah," she says. "Your father gladly took my maiden name for his own and buried the sins of the man named Campbell. He passed it to you children rather than you be stained by the man he once was. It is why he took the name Paul also; Paul who saw the light of God upon the road to Damascus and changed his ways."

"Beggin' yer pardon," Bishop says. "But a man can't change who he is, Mrs. Kelly."

"Look you to your Bible then, sir." Mother straightens her chin. "And you will understand it is possible. My good husband struggled every day with the sins he committed in that cursed place—"

"Salem," Bishop says.

"A foul place with even fouler citizens." Mother throws back. "They had their grievances long before my good husband arrived. Let them reap the blame upon themselves."

She steps toward Bishop, her hand tucked into her apron. I see the dagger hilt pull from her apron. "Simon Campbell may well have partook in those malicious dealings. I married Paul Kelly. A good and just man who rescued me from my torments, gave me a life I never deserved, and helped raise Winford to a community of high esteem."

Bishop nods. "And now his demons come to burn it all away."

He leaves Mother speechless. Hickory paws with his hoof at the approach of one whose scent he does not recognize. Bishop whistles a strange tune to calm the beast.

I watch him slowly loosen the knots binding the barrels together.

Mother storms to his side. Her movement gives Hickory pause to jerk in Bishop's grasp. "I thank you, sir, for bringing me my daughter. Now I think it best you move on."

Bishop produces an apple from his saddlebag and gives it over whole. Hickory chomps at it, snorting, and allows Bishop to continue about his business. If only he could placate Mother so easily.

"Sir!" she says. "I think—"

"I heard ye, Mrs. Kelly, and I care more about this horse's arse than what ye might be thinkin' on."

Mother's jaw opens like one slapped.

"Ye'll be singin' a different tune tonight. The Devil's daughter will be comin' soon. Aye, and she'll bring witches and highwaymen with her no doubt. A few savages too, mayhap."

"Savages..." Mother whispers. "But wh-why would they want my daughter?"

"I ne'er said *they* wanted yer daughter," Bishop says. "*He* wants her. The one they call the Warlock. One a the bastards yer husband betrayed. The Devil's daughter comes to claim ye for her master."

One of the men Father betrayed? Thomas Putnam, mayhap?

I fall to my knees. Dry heave.

Bishop kneels beside me, bids me look at him. "I don't mean to scare ye, lass, but it's better ye learn the hard truth now. Know this, too. I don't mean to let her have ye. I swear it on me own soul."

"Why?" I ask. "Why would you protect us if my father was the man you say?"

I see the old man's shoulders sag.

"Aye. How is it you to know all these things, sir?" Mother asks. "Of my husband's secret past, and this...Devil's daughter? Why do you come to help us, if it indeed be help you offer?"

Bishop's cheeks quiver at her questions. He says nothing for a moment. His gaze distant in reliving a memory I am not privy to.

"Yer daughters aren't the first marked for the Warlock," he says.

I hear a whistle from the drive. Mother helps me to my feet, and I turn to see a new pair of riders. Priest leads the way atop his red stallion, followed close by Wesley Greene on a chestnut quarter horse. My hand flies to my breast seeing Priest alive and well. What I cannot fathom is why Wesley rides beside him.

"Bah," Bishop mutters as they halt near us. "This lad all ye could rally?"

Priest nods.

Bishop takes his hat off and smacks his leg with it. "Ye couldn't talk sense to any more of 'em?"

Priest looks away to the corn.

Bishop kicks the dirt. "Why don't they ever listen? Makin' it easier for 'em is all they're doin'."

Priest says nothing; only watches Bishop until the older man tires of the charade.

With a shake of his head, Bishop picks up his hat and dusts it off. "I know, I know." He sighs. "They don't know better. Well, they damn sure don't listen neither...*colonial bastards!*"

I feel Priest's eyes upon me. I cannot tell if he wishes me to speak and mayhap give him thanks for his heroism last eve. His gaze lasts but a brief moment and is gone. Then, I see Bishop looks at me with the same bit of eager study.

"Aye, yer right, lad." Bishop says to Priest.

Right? About what? Priest never spoke a word!

Bishop spits when Priest nods at him. "Well, ye don't have to brag about it, damn ye. Off to it with ye." He turns his head to my house. "*Lads!* Bellies full or no, out with ye. It's time to work!"

George appears in the doorway with Andrew. "Wesley? What brings you here?"

Wesley turns his attention to Priest. "This stranger came to church and brought word we face our doom this eve. He bid any who wished to live and see the morrow come with him."

"Wesley," Mother says. "Are you saying there are others at the church?"

"Aye, Mrs. Kelly. Reverend Corwin called near the whole town there in light of the burning of both the Martin and Bailey homesteads. He said God wreaks vengeance upon our town for this new witchery and we beckoned it come hither by our sins. He claims we must go to God and pray for Him to take this cup from our lips."

"Pray," Bishop scoffs. "Does yer Reverend remember how that worked for the last one to request such from the Almighty? At least ye had the sense in yer head to leave 'em, lad."

"I did not leave because my faith wanes, sir," Wesley replies harshly. He looks upon me. "I came to protect Sarah and her family."

He dismounts and strides toward me. "I near wept when this man brought news of your father's death," he says, taking my hand in his. "I pray God grant mercy on his soul."

"I-I thank you," I say, reeling for such kindness from one who has scarcely spoke ten words to me before this day. "But what of your family? Do your parents not object to your leaving?"

"Aye, they did. But I am a man grown," Wesley says with willful resolve. "And must needs do what I believe right."

Bishop chuckles. "I like this one already."

Wesley ignores him. His tender gaze focused only on me. "It be little secret I have long wished to take you for a wife. I meant to ask your father come the final harvest, but—"

"Wesley, I—"

"I do not come to ask for your hand now," he says. "Only that you let me serve in his place during this, your time of need."

Bishop claps Wesley on the shoulder. "Right well said, lad!" He drags him away from me. "We'll see what such words be worth tonight. Now—"

"Your pardon, Mr. Bishop, sir," George says. "But if others gather at the church, should we not join them? Father had many friends in the town. It may be we are better shielded there with so few defenders between us here."

Bishop scowls at my brother.

George falters for a moment, yet he will not quit his argument.

"If these witches truly mean us harm, as you have said, is there not safety in numbers?"

"Aye. There can be," Bishop says. "But if those numbers turn fearful, it's not safety ye'll find there."

"I don't take your meaning, sir."

"Why do ye think they went to church?"

"For comfort," Andrew says meekly. "God dwells there."

"The church resides in the people, Andrew," Wesley chides him. "The building is the largest structure to house a town gathering. It is the most defensible outpost we have."

"Aye," George says. "A place to seek fellowship *and* fight together if needs be."

As if signaled, I see Priest gives his stallion a nudge of his heels. He circles the three sons of Winford.

All take notice. They back closer to one another to keep Priest in front of them.

"And what will ye do, lads, when the enemy isn't outside... but *inside*?" Bishop asks. "Did ye ever herd yer father's sheep?"

Priest continues to pace his stallion around them. A smirk teases the corners of his lips when he sees my brother and his friend startled.

"A-aye, many times," George says.

"Right. Then ye know well if ye have one in particular ye want, ye don't rush in after it, do ye?"

"No," George replies, swiveling to keep his gaze on Priest. "You'll fear them and make them spread. It will take longer to catch the one you want. Better to fan out around them. Force them together in the middle so you may weed out the others."

"Aye," Bishop says. "And do ye know what forces 'em to the middle?"

Priest swings off his horse. Andrew and Wesley jump back, leaving Priest a clear path to stride right for George. He stops directly in front of my brother.

"F-fear," George says.

"Aye," Bishop replies. "They move to the middle 'cause it's where they feel safest. Let yer hounds in to nip their heels and they'll move as one, even if it's not where they mean to go."

Bishop clears his voice of the ominous tone. "Now," he says, his tone gay once more. "What's say I could speak to sheep and they'd understand. So I says to 'em, 'I don't need the lot of ye... just that wee lamb right there. Give it over and I'll call me dogs off.' What do ye think they'd do?"

And now I have the understanding of it. "They would give it up," I say.

"Aye. And that's why we can't go. The church is the middle," Bishop looks directly at me. "And we have the one wee lamb they're after."

-twelve-

"Your pardon, *sir,*" I mock Bishop. "But I am no lamb, nor do I have any intention of being sacrificed."

"Well, that's good, lass," he says. "I've no desire to risk me own life if ye were. Right then. I want ye and yer muther to move anything in the house ye'd like to keep over to the barn. When ye've done with it, I'll give ye another job."

I start forward. "But—"

"No buts. The more questions ye ask, the less we get done," Bishop says. "Now, Little Kelly, the Martin lad, and, er—" He scratches his head and points to Wesley.

I watch Wesley raise himself to his full height. "I am—"

Bishop waves him off. "I don't care who ye are. Don't want no names neither. I don't do attachments, ye know. Saves me the time from mournin' ye if'n ye get yerself killed. So"—he claps his hands—"the three lads run along to the barn, fetch the axes, and cut down the nearest trees ye can find to fashion some boards. I don't give a damn what's been said to ye before this day. None of ye are wee boys any longer. It's man's work we do tonight, and I've need for three more standin' alongside me. Now off with ye."

George and Andrew grin at being called men for the first time. Together, they run off to complete their task.

Wesley lingers beside me. "I did not leave my family to chop down trees for a plan you will not speak of, sir," he says. "I came to protect Sarah."

"It's right noble of ye, lad," Bishop says. "But they'll be time for yer chivalry later. She'll be safe so long as the sun is shinin'. Witches only come at night when it's harder to see 'em."

"Then why not track them by day?" Wesley suggests. "Find where they sleep and kill them there?"

Bishop chuckles. He turns his attention to Priest. "Oi! Why didn't we ever think on that?"

Priest takes a small whetstone from his pocket, uses it to sharpen his tomahawk. It makes an awful scratching sound as he drags the blade's edge across it.

"Oh, that's right," Bishop says grandly. "Some of the natives protect and hide 'em. Well,"—he turns back to Wesley—"if ye've an army to raid the tribes with, then by all means, we'll get right to it."

"Why would savages shelter witches amongst them?"

Bishop chuckles. "Ne'er been with a woman, have ye, lad?"

I see the truth of it plain upon Wesley's blushing face.

"There's no shame in it, son," Bishop says. "Safer, truth be told. Course if ye doubt me, ye could ask him over there." He motions his head toward Priest.

I hear the blade's edge sing off the side of the stone. Priest holds it aloft. He glares at Wesley, daring him to ask the question.

Wesley gulps.

"Ah, don't ye worry about him," Bishop says to Wesley. "He'll do naught to ye. Less ye go round stickin' yer nose where it don't belong, that is. Well," he cocks his head to the side. "Off to the woods with ye to join the others. I'll be there soon as I get this lot sorted."

Wesley turns to me. "Sarah, if you should have need of me—"

"I will call," I say, knowing full well I shall have no such need. Not when I see Priest's gaze also lingers on me. I stand quietly by as Wesley walks away. No doubt he wonders what plan Bishop has in store.

"Well," Bishop says to Priest. "Whattaya think, lad?"

Priest leans to the far side of his stallion where I cannot see. I gather he spits from the sound of it.

"Aye, yer right," Bishop says. "A bit green, but they'll do. Now, where's the wee Kelly lass?"

"Rebecca?" I say.

"Aye, unless there be more of ye."

Mother shelters her. "What do you mean to do with my youngest?"

"I've a job for her, naturally." Bishop leans to see Rebecca's golden head peeking from behind Mother. "Did ye think I forgot about ye, lass? Ye've the most important task."

Rebecca eagerly steps clear of Mother, showing the first sign of life I have seen in her since the morning before church. "What is it?"

"I need ye to—are ye listenin' now?"

She takes another step toward him.

"Good. I need ye to make sure every poppet in yer house has a good place to hide in the barn tonight. *Every* poppet, mind ye. Can ye handle that?"

Rebecca bounces on her heels as she gives him a nod.

I wonder what she must be thinking. No man has ever spoken so kindly to her, and especially not of poppets.

"Right then," Bishop continues. "And after ye've done with it, ye make sure everyone else does their jobs. Now, off to yer poppets."

The old man smiles as she runs away. A smile that quickly disappears when seeing Priest also grins. "Don't start with me," Bishop growls at him. "What are ye still doin' here anyway? Ye know what needs done. Off with ye!"

Priest clicks to his stallion and rides away toward the woods.

"Colonial bastard," Bishop mutters as he joins the boys. "Startin' with me on the rules. I *wrote* the rules!"

Mother and I return to our home. For the next two hours, we bundle blankets, clothing, and candles together. I find the work aids in delaying any unpleasant thoughts of Father, Hecate, and my friends, so I do it gladly.

Mother seems invigorated by the work. She does not sing as she oft did before, but every now and then she hums to herself. I leave the books for the boys to carry, and tie the blankets and clothing with twine to take for the barn.

Leaving the cabin, I hear the sounds of axes biting wood afar off. I glance across the open southern field to where the three boys alternate in turns to fell the thin and tall elms all the faster.

Wesley's chest is naked. I see it little wonder why the men amongst Winford have taken him for one of their own.

The change did his body well. Even from a distance, I see it glistens with sweat. I look too long, however, and he catches me watching. He lowers his axe and gives me a grand wave.

Bishop immediately reprimands him for doing so.

I do not return the gesture, not wanting to seem forward. Tucking my chin to chest, I continue to the barn. The cows mooing lend credence to the thought I am performing my daily chores.

I hear Rebecca high in the loft above me, asking of her poppets where they would most like to hide. She comforts the unheard voices, which must be sore affrighted at the notion of being left alone. I sling my tote about my shoulders and climb up the ladder.

Rebecca becomes a mute at the sight of me. I wonder if she believes the poppets' hiding locations must be kept secret even from me, one she knows to have danced in the moonlight. She taps her foot, and I gather I am to hurry so she may finish her first chore and move on to the next.

I hasten to finish and leave her to it. As I descend the ladder, I hear her footsteps running across the floorboards. They send dust and hay fluttering to earth and into my hair. Shaking any remnants free, I leave through the northern door of our barn.

Priest's red stallion comes round the opposite side into my sights, with him leading it. A dead stag is draped over the stallion's back. Its head and neck tied firmly in a way that prevents its rack of horns from stabbing, or poking the mount. The stag's coal black eyes stare at me from beyond the throes of death, reminding me of the dead ram I saw in my night terrors.

The stallion neighs deeply at the sight of me.

Priest dips low under its neck. He quiets it by placing his hand upon the white blaze between its eyes and gently rubbing it.

I cannot discern Priest's demeanor, only that he means me no harm or I would have received it already. "Th-thank you," I say. "For last night."

He seems more interested in calming his beast than in my gratitude. He moves his hand to stroke its jawline, patting it at the last. Only then does he look at me. Though he utters no words, I understand mine did not go unheard. With a dogged grin, he clicks to his stallion and leads it across the yard.

I watch him go, thinking again how he must be a mute to stay so silent. Then I recall Wesley saying he spoke at the church. Why is it Priest would speak to others, but not me? Does he think me plain and ordinary?

He whistles.

I look up, and see him motion for me to follow. I attempt to quell the delight upon my face, for I do not wish him to think I am but a girl on the eve of womanhood. Despite my misgivings at being whistled at, I join him.

Priest waits for me ere he continues on. He looks upon me only once, but that with another dimpled grin.

My heart flutters.

He stops shy of my home where he unties the stag's bindings. With a quick yank, he pulls the corpse off. It lands in a sickening crunch of bone and flesh. Only then do I notice there is no mark upon the beast.

"How did you..."

I scan the body over and back. There be no entry, nor exit, of a shot. No arrow wound. Only the slitting of its belly to allow its guts cleaned out after the kill.

Priest takes a long knife from his belt and kneels at its ribs. He deftly works the blade in with one hand, tugging at its pelt with the other, tearing skin from muscle.

"How did you slay it?" I ask.

Priest wipes his hands clean on the grass. He places an arm around the stag's neck and cups his other hand about its muzzle. He waits to ensure I am watching, and then makes a quick twisting motion.

Even in death, the stag's spine makes a sound akin to a tree branch cracking.

Priest chuckles when I wince. He lets the head fall, its

neck awkwardly craned to take in the sun, and resumes skinning it.

I gather, for now, he is done speaking to me in his own silent way. It is for the best. I hear a rattling cart approach.

George drives it with Bishop seated beside him. Andrew rides atop the fresh cut timber. Wesley walks alongside it, a jealous hurt in his face at my standing so near Priest.

I enter the house before Wesley can voice it.

Priest pays me no mind. I come to realize the man annoys me. *Why can he not speak but one soft word?*

The boys enter not long after me, though Wesley does not join them. George impishly looks at our dining table with an axe weighed over his shoulder. "Ready, Andrew?"

"Aye."

With surprising quickness, both swing their blades upon the benches.

Mother appears from hers and Father's room. The sadness about her gives way to pure ire upon witnessing her benches destroyed by the two newly made lumberjacks. "*George!* What are you doing?"

"Mr. Bishop says we have need of the lumber."

Andrew connects on another swing, cleanly swiping through the wood.

Not one to be outdone, George swings harder and nearly does the same for the opposite bench. He raises it again.

Mother reaches it first and wrenches the axe from his grasp. "I think not!"

"Afraid so, Mrs. Kelly," Bishop enters. His linen shirt, soaked through with sweat, gives off a pungent odor liken to rotten mushrooms. "We need the benches to board up the windows, and the table's weight to bar the door."

"But why?"

Bishop blinks at her question. "They'll try to come through 'em. We need defense lines, wouldn't ye agree?"

"Aye, but—"

Bishop notices Mother's pies left out to cool. Dipping his fingers into one, he takes a hunk of the blackberries to shove in his mouth. "We'll need yer fine dresser as well to bar the hearth when ye've finished emptyin' it."

Mother trembles. I cannot gather whether it be for the marring of her benches or her newly baked pie.

Bishop licks his fingers clean of the fruited stains. "Ye see, Mrs. Kelly. We can't just have 'em come down the chimney like jolly old Saint Nicholas."

"We should light a fire!" George says. "Burn them like they did in Salem!"

Bishop sighs. "There weren't any witches burned in Salem, lad. Their lot didn't have the stomach for it. And we can't light a fire. These girls be afflicted, sure, but there's bound to be one who'd pour water down to douse it. Aye, and smoke us out to boot."

Andrew buries his axe through the other side of the bench. It, too, goes through cleanly. So cleanly his axe blade sticks in the floor. "If they wish to smoke us out, will they not set fire to the house eventually?"

I think he ponders on his family's demise. A cruel thing to witness, your home and loved ones burnt to naught but a pile of ash. But if Bishop spoke true, Ruth may still be alive. Some small comfort if she aided in the burning.

"Aye," Bishop says to Andrew. "That they'll do sure as yer born, but don't ye think on it. The Devil's daughter cried her master wants yer sister. She won't risk fire till her prize is safe and sound. Let others tell ye what they will"—Bishop looks out the window at our barn—"fire has a mind all its own. It's what makes Hell such a fearsome thought. Not even the Devil hisself can wrangle it."

He nods approvingly at the boys' work. "Right, ye lads get these boards nailed 'cross the windows. Leave an openin' small enough to point yer rifle's barrel through. Then we'll move on to the barn."

He leaves before any of us can ask why we should bother with fortifying both our home and the much larger, less defensible barn.

"I'll go to the barn and collect the last of Father's nails," George says.

Mother takes her broom.

I watch her sweep up the chipped remains of wood. Common sense tells me it is all for naught. I notice Andrew staring at me.

"I'm sorry about your family," I say.

He nods. "And I for your father. I wish I could thank him for taking me in. I would be dead if not for his kindness."

I wish Hecate and her minions could hear Andrew's words. Hear that Father was a good man capable of much benevolence. It is the first I have thought of Father since Bishop arrived this morn. Hecate's words yet sting in my heart, as do Mother's.

How could my Father and Dr. Campbell, the crafter of evil in Salem, be the same man?

The weight of Thomas Putnam's journal feels suddenly heavy in my apron. I wish for the time to read more of it. Mayhap there are other answers regarding Father's secret past inside.

"They burnt his home, too." Andrew recalls me from my trance. "Mr. Bishop's."

"The witches?"

"Aye, though a different group in a different time." Andrew clarifies. "Mr. Bishop spoke to me of it on our time along the road. He said crying witchery for personal gain existed across the sea for a long time now. It were only a matter of time ere greedy men of circumstance had need of it here." Andrew gazes at the handiwork he wrought with his axe. "He means for us to make an end of it tonight."

"Did he say anything of..." I step closer to him. Whisper so Mother cannot overhear. *"Of his companion, Mr. Priest?"*

Andrew shakes his head. "He spoke only of himself. Told me a home could be rebuilt. That my family's legacy remains strong so long as I have the courage to fight for my life."

"Then why will you tarry here? Why not go and run away to a far city where you can be safe?"

"My Father taught me a debt not repaid is a sin," Andrew says quietly.

I place my hand on his shoulder. "You owe my family nothing, Andrew."

Unhinging his axe from the floor, he looks at me blankly. "It is not your family I must repay."

-thirteen-

WE BREAK FOR LUNCH AT MIDDAY TO EAT UPON THE LAWN. THE chill has settled in. I reckon it will remain with us for the whole of winter to come. The sun still shines, however. It almost seems as though we are at picnic, save for the grim silence betwixt us.

Rebecca alone remains cheery. She sits nearest Bishop, the lone poppet she has yet to hide away in hand. Occasionally, she murmurs something to it the rest of us are not privy to.

I see George take a knife from his belt, Father's once. Another heirloom George felt the right to confiscate already. With it, he hews another slice of fresh venison onto his plate. "Pray, sir," he says to Bishop. "Why did Mr. Priest leave when we have so much work to do?"

"'Cause he's a lazy bastard." Bishop laughs at his own sport. "He's out rangin'...lookin' for scouts to kill. Pray he finds some, lad, and thins their numbers."

George casts Andrew a skeptical look. My brother has doubts.

I do not. I know Priest could be anywhere. As if seeking confirmation of my belief, I look to Priest's recent kill, the stag roasting on the spit he built. *How does one move so silently as to creep upon a stag and break its neck?* My thoughts turn to Hecate. *I hope he bends her neck like he did the stag's.*

I take a bite of the tender venison. The meat slides off the bone into my mouth. I lean forward for the grease to drip into the grass, rather than stain my dress.

The boys, save for Wesley, are not so well mannered. They wipe at their faces with the back of their arms and smear grease alongside the timber dust from the logs they hewed to a manageable size.

"He'll be back," Rebecca mutters to her doll. "Most like with Father too."

Bishop strokes the doll's hair. "Is yer wee doll hungry, lass?"

"Aye," she answers.

"Augh," He pushes the head of it toward her food. "Then ye must needs feed her that she grows up strong."

The distraction works. Rebecca laughs. "Mr. Sir," she says whilst chewing her meat. "Your voice is odd. Did you come from the old country?"

"A wee bit further, lass. I came from Ireland ere into slavery I went."

"You were a slave?" George asks.

"Aye, for a time," Bishop says. "Sold and shipped to Barbados with me wife. Served there a good long while, but 'twas not to last as nuthin' in this life is."

"Did you purchase your freedom?" George asks. "Or escape?"

"Neither. I let 'em stretch my neck a wee bit," Bishop says. He tilts his head back to show off his scar.

Both George and Andrew crane their own necks to better see his.

Even Rebecca does not shy away. She stands and traces her finger over the scar. Her eyes squint at the touch. "But how did you not die?" she asks.

Bishop barks to frighten her away. He laughs when she takes a step back, but does not scream. "I believe I did," he says. "But the good Lord weren't done with me. Woke me from that dark and quiet sleep, He did."

Bishop folds his arms. "'Oi!' the Almighty said to me. 'Cause ye wouldn't renounce yer faith in Me to them bastards that hung ye, I've a wee job for ye to do. I'm givin' ye back the curse a life. And with it, I mean for ye to kill some right evil bitches.'"

The boys and Rebecca titter at his cursing. I refrain in the event Priest may be watching me, even from afar, and disapprove.

Bishop winks at us before continuing his tale. "'Would that I could, yer Lordship,' says I to Him. 'But I'm a bit too old in the tooth to go huntin' anything now. And me dead body growin' stone cold here, too.'

'Ye'll do as I command,' the Almighty answered in His thunderin' tone. 'I'm sendin' ye to bring some sense to them colonial bastards in the north. And if it's help ye be needin', I'll lead ye to find a lad that ne'er shuts his mouth to keep ye company.'"

I assume he means Priest, though I still do not rightly understand his meaning. Priest never speaks.

I watch Rebecca take the last strip of venison from Bishop's plate with a wry grin. "Where is your wife now?" she asks in an innocent way only children can. "If you were sold together, why is she not here?"

Bishop puts his arm about her shoulder in a half hug. Even he cannot hide the trace of sadness in his normally merry voice. "Augh, right now she's either singin' with the angels, or havin' a pint with St. Peter."

Still, Rebecca's questions and Bishop's mostly good humor gives me courage. "Pray, sir," I ask. "What was she like?"

"A stubborn old wench, she was." The corners of his eyes

crinkle in the retelling. "Right till the end a her days, or so others told me."

Rebecca's lips smack at the food. "You were not with her when she passed?"

Bishop slumps a bit. "I ne'er saw her again after they led me to the scaffold and draped the black hood over me head. I learned she came to yer colonies after me funeral. I journeyed here meself upon me rise from beyond the grave. It weren't long ere I heard tell of an Irish woman who refused to confess as a witch and hanged for it. That's when I knew me poor wife had been murdered."

"They hung her?" George asks.

"Aye," Bishop says gravely. "The Mather bastards saw to it, both father and son. For witchery, they called it, but they had no proof in it. Mark me words, lads. She died for bein' a Catholic, and a woman who wouldn't bend to kiss their heels.

"Ah, she knew the truth when they came for her, most like," he says as one lost in a memory. "What with her havin' witnessed a sham trial when I hanged for the same. Others who saw her die told me she refused to speak in English. Wouldn't give the bastards what they wanted." He smiles.

A silence creeps amongst us at his sad tale. Rebecca is the only one to break it. "Have you been hunting witches ever since, sir?"

Bishop kindly strokes her cheek with the back of his hand. "There's no such thing as witches, lass. Only powder-snortin' bitches and their heathen lovers."

The boys and Rebecca laugh.

I cannot. It be a good thing Bishop keeps their moods light. The faces of those who laughed at my Father's death yet linger in my mind, however. I try to clear my head of such thoughts.

If what Bishop says is true, there will be more than enough fear to go around tonight. Best not linger on it now. I toss the rest of my meat aside for the cats to find.

Bishop seems to take it as a signal. "Right." He grunts as he slowly stands. His ankles and knees pop with old age. "We've rested like a bunch a ninnies far too long. There's work needs doin' yet."

I rise with the others to collect the dirty plates they leave behind. Wesley alone stays behind to help. "Where do you take them to wash?" he asks.

"There be a basin we moved from the house to the barn. We must fill it first."

"Aye," he says. "Is there a stream close?"

Something in the way he asks makes me hesitant. I gaze across the field. "There is, but it lies beyond the corn. I think it wise we not go there now."

He looks at his feet. "You doubt my protection."

Oh, no, I think to say. *Only I do not wish to be alone with you right now.*

I cannot bring myself to tell him.

But what can I speak to him on? This newly made man who has offered my family his protection? I do not have long to ponder. *A lie remains a lie, no matter the goodly intent.* The ghost of Father's voice rings in my head.

"We do not need the stream," I say. "Father dug a well, just beyond the barn wall."

The thought seems to cheer Wesley a bit, but I gather he yet has a lingering doubt. "Here." He takes the plates from me. "You should not be carrying those with your wrist sprained."

"It hurts not so bad." I take them back, and cradle them in

the crook of my good forearm and elbow. "Besides, that is why God gave us two."

Wesley shakes his head. "I have oft heard you bull-headed."

"From whom?" I ask, taking the lead in our walk to the barn.

"Mother told me it is a sin to gossip," he says easily. "God may not strike me down if I shared such secrets, but Mother certainly would."

I laugh without meaning to. The thought of Wesley's mother bending his six-foot frame over her knee and spanking him with a wooden spoon is too much.

"In truth," he says, "I did not wish to seem forward. My father oft preaches to me the virtues spoken of in the Good Book. Of honoring one another and of a wife's submission to her husband—"

I scoff.

"Pray, do not mishear me," he adds quickly. "I like that you are stubborn, Sarah. Most other girls only gossip with one another after church. They ask silly questions and titter at everything I say."

He stops me with a touch of his hand. Then he stands before me that I might better see his plain and realize he speaks from the heart. "You were always different. You, the only one to ever ignore me." He chuckles. "What I mean to say is...I care for you, Sarah."

Surely Charlotte or Ruth would know what to say. Either of them would most like kiss him right here and now. If only Emma—

I gasp.

"It's him, isn't it?" Wesley asks. "That man, Priest. I have seen how you look at him. Hear me, Sarah. He is wild. Savage, mayhap. He will not linger here. A man—"

They will come for her too...Hecate and her witches. Did Wesley not say they burned and killed all the Martins and Baileys? What if they mean to do the same to Emma and her family?

"Oh, Emma," I say.

Wesley's forehead wrinkles. "Have you heard nothing of what I said, Sarah?"

I look up at the sun. It is well past noon. Bishop said the witches only come at night. If I ride for Emma's home, I may yet make it there and back before dusk. I look down at my wrist. If I run afoul of them...

"Sarah?" Wesley asks.

I drop the plates, not caring that they shatter at my feet. "Will you ride with me?"

His grin is quick to appear. "You wish to go riding now? But your wrist is lamed. And where would we go?" He looks around the fields. "Work needs done yet ere night falls."

I hold no doubts Priest would have pulled me onto his stallion before I had asked the question. I wish he took me instead.

"To save Emma and her family," I say. "I have run from here to her home in almost two hours before. If we take the horses—"

"But Emma is not at home," Wesley says. "They are at church with everyone else."

"Was she there this morn when Priest convinced you to come hither?"

Wesley's face hardens. "He could not persuade me to follow him anywhere. I have already said I came to protect you."

"Protect me now, then." I beg of him. "It is a further ride

to church and back. We must go now if we are to return ere night falls."

"Sarah..."

"Please!" I say. "You may doubt Priest and Bishop, but I do not. Believe my words. If they say all at church will die this night, it will be so. We must go there and convince the others to come. Aye, and your parents also."

Wesley scratches the back of his neck. "Bishop said the witches come for *you*. Hecate comes for you. If they find us on the highroad, alone..."

I run for the barn.

"Sarah!"

Fear cautions me against leaving. *Stay here, little girl, and be safe.*

Those at church would not listen to Priest's words of wisdom. Very well. Let them discover what happens when the Devil's daughter comes to call. Let them see with their own eyes what gruesome fate found Paul Kelly in the woods.

Priest is a stranger though, and our community has ever been wary of outsiders. Those at church have known me since I were a babe. They will listen to me. They *must* listen to me.

I reach the stables and fling one of doors open. Hickory and Moses watch me hurry to their stables. I reach my hands to their noses that they might smell them and recognize my scent so they do not startle. I attempt to lift a harness from its placing on the wall with my good hand. The weight of it nearly topples me. Sweat pours off my brow as I try again and fail.

"You are indeed a woman gone mad," Wesley says from the doorway.

"You came to protect me and my family," I say, attempting

a third time. "Why should it be any different that I wish to protect my friend and yours?"

He comes to aid me. The weight of it buckles him a bit, for he is not nearly so strong as Father was, but he is able enough to free it loose.

"Come, Hick," I whistle, and lead Hickory out for Wesley to hitch. Moses is more difficult. He is accustomed to being fed ere he will budge. I give him an apple whole to tease him from the stable.

Wesley is less successful. He cowers as Moses rears, unused to a stranger's touch. I grab the harness roughly to show Moses I have no fear of him. He neighs, but settles. With Wesley's help, we quickly set about hitching them to the wagon.

"Hurry, hurry," I say. "We must leave ere Bishop discovers us."

"Why?"

"He will stop us. Restrain me somehow."

"If you know he will, then why do you go?"

Because I am a stubborn wench. "Please, hurry!"

I leave his side, climb into the wagon, and take up the reins. The leather straps feel sweaty in my hands, or is it my hands that make the reins sweat? I cannot tell.

Wesley joins me. "This is lunacy," he says.

I slap the reins. Hickory and Moses pull away. I jolt back in my seat and catch myself with my good hand. We burst out of the barn, headed for the highroad. I see Bishop notice us at the last. He waves his arms about, calling out for us to halt. Yelling that Hecate comes for the Campbell *family*.

I do not stop.

With us leaving, I wonder what Bishop will do next. Will he

leave to give us chase, or guard my family? I pray he stays. My family will need his comforting lead until I return.

Reaching the end of our drive, I guide Moses and Hickory to turn for the highroad.

There is also Priest to consider. Is he truly ranging like Bishop declared, or did he hide somewhere to keep watch over us? I hope he watched and saw I, too, am a free spirit.

Oddly, I have the audacity to wonder if my newest act will finally loosen Priest's tongue, and if I will live to hear his rebuke.

-fourteen-

WE SET THE HORSES AT A GOOD PACE—FAST ENOUGH TO GUARANtee our quick arrival, but not so slow to trot—when Wesley asks me who the Campbell family is.

"Mr. Bishop yelled they come for Campbell's family," he studies me. "You seemed to recognize of whom he spoke."

His question makes me recall Thomas Putnam's journal. I wonder if it might yet hold some secret to the past I might use to sway those at church, and fumble inside my apron for it.

Wesley looks at me as one gone insane. "You brought a Bible?"

I flip through the pages to find the one I earmarked.

"Sarah..."

"Hush!" I silence him. "Keep us on course."

Then, I begin to read...

5TH DAY OF JUNE, 1692

God help me to finish this letter. The marrow in my bones has only now begun to thaw.

It was after dusk ere I walked for home from visiting Captain Alden in his cell. Halfway there, my horse went lame upon hearing fast beating drums behind me. I glanced o'er my shoulder, and there marked a giant of a man riding hard. He rode a steed as black as the evil we bewitch Salem with.

He halted the stallion ere it trampled me.

The beast screamed terribly at the choke, yet could not throw him.

It being a moonless night, I could not plainly see his face for he kept his hat dipped low over his brow. Even now, safe within the comforts of my home, I admit no portion of me desired to see the full of his face.

He mentioned his search for a young doctor, new to the area. From his pattern of speech, I gathered he hails from across the sea, though claiming he came from Boston.

If this stranger asked me but a few days past I might have lied about my relationship to Dr. Campbell. However, he spoke with an understanding that told me to speak only truth in his presence. I somehow drummed the courage to first inquire as to why he searched for Dr. Campbell.

He gave the stallion free reign, allowing it to stomp around me, snorting wildly. If he intended to frighten me, he succeeded, with great effect. The stranger then related to me the tales of Salem's witchcraft had intrigued him. He next revealed his knowledge to every step of our plot and the true nature of the girls' affliction. Indeed, he spoke so reverently of it I near believed it his own plan.

I saw no sense in lying to him upon hearing this, and asked how he came to acquire such knowledge.

The stranger claimed Dr. Campbell apprenticed under his tutelage. From his tone, I gathered Campbell betrayed him in some manner, and this stranger has searched for him ever since.

Too afeared to ask more of him, I delayed my answers in hopes a kindly neighbor might happen down the road to see this strange man and break his hold over me. I realize now the hope futile. If ever I thought Dr. Campbell had some great foresight, his master had a deeper power reaped from a darker plane.

I related to him all I knew of Dr. Campbell.

⁂

Father served this dark man, then; the Warlock, as Bishop named him. Putnam's musings trouble me for his descriptions paint how I first felt in Hecate's presence. I wish Father still lived to answer my many questions. How could he serve a man like the one Thomas Putnam described? And better yet, betray him?

For a moment, I think to speak aloud the questions I wrestle with about Father, yet to do so would surely bring more inquiries from Wesley.

Hesitantly, I read on.

⁂

The stranger next asked of the girl who made such passionate accusations amidst the court.

I gathered he meant Abigail Williams, for she hath often led the others to do as she bid.

He rightly surmised her an orphan girl, made so by the Indian wars. He said we wasted a girl of such enthusiasms upon condemning the innocent, and questioned if she might consider a grander scheme. Aye, and reap a bit of her own vengeance also. The man claimed a lonely existence since Campbell betrayed him. I gathered he saw in her a pure joy for the malicious work his former apprentice had not the will to carry out.

Then he asked I give Abigail over to him.

I told the stranger she was no slave, nor did I have the power to sell her in any case. She was also a child, only twelve years of age. How could he mean to have her serve him except but through ill deeds best left unsaid.

The stranger insisted he misspoke; he questioned then not whether I would give her over, but rather, would it be Abigail Williams he took with him this night, or my own daughter, Ann?

I heard no pretense in his question.

He bid me make my decision quickly ere he left me to ride for my home.

I gave him my answer. Then, he left me weeping in the dust.

I do so even now for Abigail Williams. God only knows what sinister plot that demon has in store for her, but what choice did I have? For what righteous man would willingly give up his daughter's life in exchange of another?

Abigail Williams is Hecate!

All my thoughts jumble. My hatred of Hecate now mixed with pity for a young girl caught in the schemes of wicked men.

However, Putnam claims the Warlock chose her for the passion she had in condemning others, so should I truly pity her? If what he wrote is true, it is little wonder why Abigail harbors such hatred for Father. The words she spoke of him stealing her life and blackening her name...all of it true.

My mind reels. My body must also, for Wesley reaches over to right me. "Sarah," he says. "What are you reading about?"

"Salem," I say quietly. "Hecate is from Salem. She was one of the afflicted girls."

"How do you know?"

I lift the journal for him to better see. "She wanted me to read this...gave it for me to learn truth."

Wesley squints confusedly at the journal, then me. "Why?"

It is not right to speak ill of the dead. I cannot bring myself to admit Father's shame. "I do not know. I think she mistakes us for some other family."

A lie remains a lie, no matter the goodly intent...

I do it for you, Father. I argue with my conscience. *To protect the goodly man Mother says you became after leaving Salem.*

I decide to put aside any grain of truth Father and Dr. Campbell were the same man. Henceforth, I vow to only think of him in the goodly light he showed me all the days I can remember.

Still, I cannot shut myself to thinking ill of Hecate. Unlike Father, she is alive. I may think all the evils of her I wish.

Did she change like Father? Did Hecate kill any remaining goodness Abigail Williams once possessed? I must learn more of what befell her to better understand the monster she has become. I bend my neck to read more of the few entries left in Putnam's journal.

⁂

10TH DAY OF JUNE, 1692

The absence of Abigail Williams has been noted amongst the court, yet the trials continue. Too consumed are they now by who will go to trial next, and then the rope, to concern themselves with the fate of one afflicted orphan.

I have not spoken of what transpired that night to Reverend Parris, nor do I mean to share the tale with anyone. It matters little. Parris were distraught at first hearing she had disappeared, but he and the others have since reckoned she ran off to Boston to make her own way. He worries more over his Betty, she who yet claims to suffer even from so far away.

I bid my daughter keep up her pretense to safeguard her until the other girls cease their supposed afflictions.

For now, both Dr. Campbell and the stranger I met have vanished entirely. I know not what their fates may be, nor do I care. I am thankful for the vengeance Dr. Campbell helped me claim and the further riches to come, but it is my fervent hope to never see either man again.

In the meantime, Reverend Parris, Dr. Griggs, and I have agreed we must allow this plot burn itself out ere Salem returns to normal.

The executions began today with Bridget Bishop the first to hang on Gallows Hill.

I admit a sense of pride when I heard her neck break, especially when I saw her viperous tongue that spread so many rumors about me loll out of her mouth afterward. A small bit of me desired to take it for a trophy that I might show it to any who think to speak ill of me again.

Alas, I know I cannot and must content myself she be dead. Perhaps it is for good. How else could she beg for Lucifer to quit her torments?

How can a person be so evil to take joy in the murder of another, innocent or no?

Any small bit of sympathy I had for Putnam giving over Abigail Williams rather than his daughter vanishes, replaced with utter disgust.

I think to throw this journal and its history away.

Prudence warns there may yet be some bit of note to save others and learn me more of Father's past. I read on.

16th day of June, 1692

Dr. Griggs came to speak good tidings to me this afternoon, namely that Roger Toothaker died in prison. I am told those who examined him deemed it from natural causes due to his age.

I believe not a scrap of it. Toothaker is dead for no other reason than Griggs desired it.

Griggs also shared with me a bit of gossip heard from Reverend Parris.

Apparently, our head justice, William Stoughton, requested a letter written by Reverend Cotton Mather read to him today. Mather requested the court disallow the use of spectral evidence, meaning to put an end to the afflicted girls' claims evil spirits have been cast to torment them. He also urged the trials be speedy to end this grim time.

I took from that both Cotton and his father, Increase, fear their names blackened from this affair and wish to pawn their actions on Stoughton.

Mather...Bishop spoke the name earlier today whilst mentioning his wife. *They are the ones who hanged her for a witch!*

I find it strange I cannot recall any mention of her in Putnam's journal, however. The only Ann he wrote of is his daughter. Surely a girl so young could not have been Bishop's wife; nor is there any record of her accused in the journal.

There must be a connection, but what?

"We are almost there..." Wesley says.

I glance up from the journal. Indeed, the steeple is not afar off. Lowering my gaze, I read quickly in search of any bit of information that might convince those at church to come with us.

***

Griggs relayed Stoughton is like-minded to our cause, and had Reverend Parris burn the letter after. I am told Stoughton mentioned the trials would indeed be speedy, but neglected the portion of disallowing the spectral evidence to the courts.

After Griggs took his leave, a strange notion came to me. Did only happy chance place Stoughton to head the court, or did Dr. Campbell hold some sway in Boston too?

If so, he placed Stoughton wisely. The man's zealotry for ridding the countryside of witchery is unmatched.

19TH DAY OF AUGUST, 1692

Reverend Cotton Mather visited Salem to witness Martha Carrier hanged. He even named her the Queen of Hell for the entire crowd to hear. I know naught what she hath done to warrant his especial visit, but she surely reaped the vengeance he sought, for his claims to disallow spectral evidence did not save her.

I furthered my own vengeance today; our former reverend, George Burroughs, hanged beside Carrier. Had he only repaid the debt he owed my family in a timely fashion, mayhap he would still live.

I turn the page.

There are shreds where others have been torn out. A single page is all that remains in Putnam's journal.

Wesley nudges me with his elbow. "We are here."

A ring of wagons encircles the church like they are the iris and the building its pupil. A few seated figures come to life. They raise their rifles to aim.

I stow the journal back in my apron.

"Halt!" cries one of the sentries. I recognize his voice for Mr. Bradbury, he who is husband to the missus that drowns my singing at church. "What business have you—"

"Wesley?" another voice interrupts.

"Aye." Wesley pulls back on the reins. He looks at the one who called him by name. "Hello, Father."

Mr. Greene drops his rifle. "For Heaven's sake," he yells at the other men. "Put down your arms. It's my son, come back to his senses. And with Sarah Kelly too! Pray, child," Mr. Greene speaks to me. "Where be Goody Kelly and your brother and sister?"

I cannot find my voice. Though Mr. Greene ordered the others to lower their aim, not all have done so.

"Gone and left them, have you?" Mr. Bradbury asks sharply. "Mayhap she has some of her Father's good sense after all."

"Peace, Goodman Bradbury," Wesley speaks for me. "We have not returned to stay."

"You see, David," Mr. Bradbury elbows Mr. Greene. "It is true what my wife has said. Your son is bewitched by her."

My blood boils at the slight. "Do not name me witch!"

Mr. Bradbury ignores my outburst. He looks to the other sentries. "Mark my words. Wesley rode off with that earlier scoundrel against his father's good advice. Now he returns with this girl to strike discord amongst us. She seeks to divide us."

Wesley stops me from charging Mr. Bradbury. "We do not," he says calmly.

"Then why you have returned, son, if not to stay?" Mr. Greene asks.

"Aye," Mr. Bradbury says. "Our stance has not changed since this morn. Nor will it now."

The sky is already blood red.

We come too late. If we do not leave, and soon, we will be alone on the highroad, unprotected at nightfall. I must do something to save them!

"Please, sirs." I try to quell the anger in my voice. "I have seen that which you have only heard tale of. The witches mur—they murdered my Father before my very eyes. The strangers you met shielded me from a likewise fate."

"You see!" Mr. Bradbury interrupts. "It is a new ploy she speaks of!"

"Quiet, will you!" Mr. Greene says. "Wesley, what say you to this?"

"I doubted it at the first." Wesley weights his words carefully. "But I worked alongside these men today. I believe them,

Father. Even now they seek to fortify the Kelly homestead in preparation for the damnation they claim befalls Winford tonight."

One of the sentries raises his rifle. Another points to the highroad. "Look!"

A lone rider in black approaches fast, the color of his stallion bleeding together with the crimson sunset.

Priest...

I hear footsteps behind me.

"Sarah," Mr. Greene says. "You may stay if you wish. Your father was ever a good friend to those in need. It would not serve for us to send you away now with dusk so near."

Wesley speaks before I can. "We do not wish to tarry, Father. She came for Emma Harney and her family," he takes a deep breath. "And I for you and Mother. Please, I beg you. Come with us."

Mr. Greene puts the butt of his rifle into the ground. His face pains as he glances at the other sentries.

The church doors open with Reverend Corwin among the first out. Mrs. Bradbury, ever one at the forefront of gossip, is not far behind. Families I have known all my life pour out behind them in following two of our community's most verbal leaders.

Yet even Mrs. Bradbury cowers when Priest drives his steed into the heart of their protective wagon circle. He draws both his long dagger and tomahawk ere his feet land to earth. He steps in front of me, stands shoulder to shoulder with Wesley, and raises his blades to the ready.

"Pray," Reverend Corwin speaks. "What trouble is this?"

I watch the women whisper to one another. The men fold their arms and shake their heads with no regard of hiding their disdain. Children I've watched Rebecca play with are ushered behind their mothers' skirts.

Is this what I risk my life for? To hear my name whispered, mocked, and disapproved of?

Mr. Bradbury leans on the butt of his rifle. "This stranger has corrupted Paul Kelly's daughter. Aye, and she Wesley Greene! Careful she don't send her spirit to torment your wife next, David!"

Mr. Greene backs away from Wesley. Almost like he fears it may be possible.

"Father," Wesley says in disbelief. "No one has corrupted me, nor spirits been sent out. We came only—"

"We know what you have come for," Reverend Corwin sneers. "Honest men said Paul Kelly treated Ruth Martin. The next morn, she and all her family lay dead. Aye, and their home and lands burnt to ash!"

I think to refute him, but my voice is lost amongst the many gasps and Mrs. Bradbury's rising voice.

"And my neighbors too," she says, her voice shrill and cold. "The good Bailey family. They had the same evil brought down on them. Their daughter, Charlotte, befriended this girl, this Sarah Kelly!"

Priest draws closer to me. The blade of his tomahawk twitches. I notice his gaze falls on Mr. Bradbury. A moment later, I understand why.

No longer does Mr. Bradbury idly lean on the butt of his rifle. He has brought the barrel to aim.

"I smell witchcraft here!" Mrs. Bradbury continues. "I heard it said Paul Kelly once lived in Salem. Mayhap he brought the evils there back with him!"

Others in the crowd take up her claim. I cannot believe this. It is as I read in Thomas Putnam's journal. A new Salem, come alive with rampant fear run amok.

"My Father were a righteous man," I shout back at her. "Goodman Greene said the same not a moment ago."

They will not hear me, nor will they listen to Wesley's claims. The veins on his neck pulse from yelling to silence them, but his voice is drowned; too consumed are they by the rumors spreading amongst them like wildfire.

"I have oft been heard to say her family did not come to own such fine lands by mere chance," Mrs. Bradbury says above the din.

"Aye, she has," a few of the other parishioners take up her claim.

Their words freeze me. *How do they make such claims with straight faces?*

I see no goodness here. They are naught but dogs gone wild and foaming at the mouth. And there, timidly hiding toward the back, I see Emma.

She looks at me as one helpless to her fortunes.

"Emma!" I say.

She shrinks further at hearing her name called.

"You went with me that night," I say. "You saw of what I speak! Aye, and saw Ruth outside church not two days past. Tell them I speak truth!"

Emma shakes her head. Tears drip down her cheeks. "I-I know not of what she speaks."

My frigidness melts at her betrayal. I quickly fetch a stone up and heave it at her. "You lie!"

My aim is poor though. I miss Emma, but hit Mrs. Bradbury.

She falls as one shot by an arrow. She rolls about the ground, moaning.

Emma is so stunned by my action she stands there still, an easy target to my mind. I kneel to pick another stone.

Priest restrains me.

"Be gone with you!" Reverend Corwin waves us away. "We have no need of your wickedness here!"

I kick and scream. "I came to warn you! Came at the risk of my own life and you dare send me away?"

Priest drags me back to the wagon with Wesley's help. Only when I see Mr. Greene leading his wife from the fray do I pause.

Wesley's mother quivers in her husband's arms, but Mr. Greene will not allow her to rejoin their ranks. He loads her into the wagon with Wesley's help.

"Mother, it is I," he speaks softly, clutching her closer. "It is your Wesley."

Mr. Greene climbs up to sit beside her. "Peace, Goodwife."

I scarcely realize we are moving.

Priest sits beside me in the driver's bench. His gaze fixed on the horizon where the last rays of sunlight wink goodbye. The reins smack harshly as he makes every effort to call more speed from Moses and Hickory. His stallion runs swiftly in front, leading the other two.

I glance over my shoulder at the church my Father helped raise.

Emma is on her hands and knees. Without me to cry witchery against, the crowd has turned on her, the closest associate to a witch they can find.

Benjamin King, the boy she once professed to love, stands over her with a dirt clod in hand. "You all heard what Sarah Kelly said!" he shouts. "This one is a witch too!"

The crowd roars their approval when he throws the clod in her face.

"Turn around," I cry to Priest.

He will not. We are thirty yards from the woods before I understand he is not bound for the highroad. Priest shows no sign of slowing. He drives us toward a gap in the trees. I am not sure we will fit between them. Ten yards away, he shoves me out of the wagon.

My fall is quick, and I have no time to scream. The ground steals my breath away, even as I roll. My groans are met with the snapping of wood, the screaming of horses, and those of Wesley's mother.

I come to a stop, gasping for air. Flat on my back, I stare up at the sky. Then I hear it...

In the distance, steadily growing nearer, the quiet beginnings of a dark symphony orchestrated by flutes and drums.

Night has come.

-fifteen-

I HEAR HOOVES GALLOP TOWARD ME. BEFORE I CAN MOVE, THE sound vanishes as a dark shadow leaps over me. The hooves return to earth a few feet away, bound for the church.

I prop myself up on my good elbow to better see. *Priest.*

The shadow came when his steed leapt over me. He rides hunched low over the stallion's back, a perched vulture with his head dipped between his shoulders.

From a distance, I see torches lit in the wagon circle. I no longer see the parishioners, but I hear them singing hymns. They must have returned inside the church, hoping to sing their fear and doubt away.

My shoulder aches from the hard landing, yet nothing feels broken that were not so before. I hurry to my feet, and then the wagon. One look tells me Priest misjudged the trees in his haste to enter the wood. The horses made it through, but the wagon is stuck between them. The front two wheels are shattered. One in the rear may be fixable, but it will take time.

We have no such luxury.

Mr. Greene climbs out, a pained look about his person as he groans and rubs the back of his neck. His hair is a disheveled mess. I have no idea where his wide-brimmed hat has flown. He smacks the wagon side.

Still in the wagon bed, Mrs. Greene whimpers. She clutches

to the sides as one fearing she may yet be thrown. "Oh, husband. We should never have left," she cries.

Wesley leads both Hickory and Moses around the wagon. He seems puzzled as he lifts the tattered scraps that once yoked them. Even if we could have fixed the wagon, now there is no point.

"Why did you cut their reins?" I ask.

"I did not. Priest must have ere he jumped," Wesley says. "Why would he sabotage us?"

I understand Priest's intentions then. *The wagon would slow us. He would not wish it left in working order for the witches to use.*

"Because he is a madman like the others said!" Mr. Green shouts. I watch him lift his frightened wife out of the back. "Are you well, wife?"

"Aye," she says. "Frightened is all."

I do not believe her. Her lips pursed, she welcomes her husband's embrace too easily for one claiming all is well. Even now, her fingers tremble.

"Wesley," Mr. Greene says. "You are coming with us back to church. We shall be safer there with night upon us."

I know what Wesley's answer will be even before he speaks.

"I stay with Sarah."

"You disobey me—confound it all!" Mr. Green looks to the sky. "What is that accursed racket?"

I venture out beyond the tree line. Across the open field, I see nigh fifty torches. They move inside the woods opposite us. All bound toward church.

"They are coming," I say quietly.

Wesley hurries to my side. "You are sure of it?"

"Who is coming?" Mrs. Green asks.

The music grows louder. My fears swell with each note.

A shadow rides toward us.

I hear a girl's wailing. Without thought, I push Wesley and his family back inside the woods to cover us.

Priest bursts through a moment later, holding Emma upright in front of him. A bruise already forms upon her cheek from the dirt clod thrown by Benjamin King.

"S-Sarah," she says. "W-why did you tell...tell them I went with you. Benjamin, h-he..."

The bleater cannot even finish.

Priest dismounts. He pulls Emma from the stallion and into his arms.

"Were you born daft, sir?" Mr. Greene says to him. "You must have been to wreck the wagon so. If Paul Kelly lived—"

Priest ignores him. He carries Emma toward the wagon and sets her gently inside it. Then, he furiously saws Hickory's harness loose with his long dagger.

"What are you doing?" Mr. Greene demands.

The harness falls beside the monstrous beast with a heavy *thump*. Emma jumps at the sound. Sniffling back more tears, she buries her head in her arms.

Priest wastes no time. He goes to Moses next and makes short work of his harness also.

Mr. Greene strides toward him.

I reach out to stop him. "Please, sir," I say. "We will be faster without the wagon. I know that is why he cut us loose."

Mr. Greene will not listen. He lays his hand upon Priest's shoulder. "Stop—"

Priest wheels and catches Mr. Greene by the neck. In two

steps, he pins him against a tree. His free hand brings the dagger up close for Mr. Greene to see.

"*Don't!*" I say, careful not to raise my voice too loud for anyone nearby to overhear. "He meant no harm. They do not understand what is coming!"

Priest coldly looks upon me. He releases Mr. Greene and points the tip of his long dagger at Wesley. I watch his point motion to Hickory, then Emma.

Wesley gathers what he means faster than I. "No," he says. "You take her. I will protect Sarah."

"What?" I say.

"He wants me to ride with Emma." Wesley explains. "I will not."

Priest again points, more insistent this time.

"I will not!" Wesley says.

Everything happens too quickly for me to react.

Priest covers the distance between them in seconds.

I see Wesley swing at Priest's jaw.

Priest ducks it at the last. With a quick sweep of his foot, and a hard shove, he takes Wesley to the ground. He drops his knee onto Wesley's chest to steal his breath. Faster than anyone can move, Priest twirls his dagger. He buries the blade an inch from Wesley's ear.

I hear Wesley's ragged breathing even above my own. Without realizing it, my fingers clenched the sides of my dress.

Priest grabs the lapels of Wesley's jacket and pulls him to his feet. He shoves my would-be protector toward Emma, ending their one-sided debate.

Wesley looks at me as one shamed, but he will say naught.

He offers Emma his hand. "Come," he says. "We must ride for the Kelly farm."

Emma shakes her head. She looks past all of us toward church. "My mother and father—"

A rifle's shot echoes like a cannon across the field, followed by a cackle. More shots follow in quick succession, not as a single volley, but scattered. Panicked.

I run to the edge of the woods with the others close behind. Mrs. Greene gasps at the sight. She draws closer to her husband. "Oh, David..."

Torches in the wagons light the sentries' faces. Folly. Each torch reveals to the witches where men are positioned.

The sentries fire again, their rifles create brilliant flashes of orange-yellow with smoke following after.

For every shot I hear, the sound of a man screaming follows after. One-by-one, I watch the sentry torches extinguished as easily as blowing out candles.

Mr. Greene starts forward. "We must help them!"

Even I know the six of us together would be hard-pressed to aid but a few of our neighbors. I do not know whether Mr. Greene is brave and I the coward, or if I am wise for desiring to retreat. Mayhap I am heartless for wishing no more than to leave, but I would rather be labeled a live coward than a brave corpse.

I have to say nothing, however.

Priest stops Mr. Greene from leaving.

Strange, but I did not see him there before. How did he move up so quietly behind us?

I gather Mr. Greene means to argue further. He loses the urge upon inspection of his wife; her hand glued to her mouth in horror at what we witness.

The sentries' cries of suffering bring a halt to the parishioners' singing; replaced by the pounding of drums, the cackling of witches, and war cries of men. Horses neigh and move at the strangers flitting amongst them. Dots darken the windows inside the brightly lit church.

I think they must be the faces of those who mocked our claim not twenty minutes prior. I will them to retreat from the windows even as Bishop's earlier words rise to haunt me.

They will all die tonight.

Two of the sentry wagons burst into flame. Horses buck and pull at their yokes.

What fool kept the skittish beasts hitched?

The fire brushes at their flanks, gives them added cause to scream. Spreads fear and discourse amongst those still living.

I see a sentry leap from his wagon. He flees for the church, his torch bobbing with every step. "Let me in!" he shouts. "Open the doors! I beg of you!"

Mr. Bradbury...

For a brief moment, I find a dark joy in the terror pervading his voice. *Now do you know a witch when you see one, old man?*

I push the thought away, lest I be consumed with hate like Hecate and Thomas Putnam.

One of the fired wagons rolls toward the church. The valiant few sentries, who yet held the perimeter, abandon their positions.

I hear them call to one another. Shout they must keep the church from catching flame. I watch the remaining sentries cut down by shadowy blades ere they can ward off the flame's determined progression.

With no one left to stop it, the fired wagon rolls unhalted toward the church doors and Mr. Bradbury.

I warrant he never sees his demise coming.

The wagon pins him, envelopes him in flames. The fire races upwards, wreathing the church's dry wooden doorway, leaving Mr. Bradbury a human torch to writhe in its sweltering heat.

A pair of ladders lifts from the gathering crowd of black-hooded witches and white men dressed in animal skins. More than a few scamper up their wooden steps. Some carry buckets, others torches. All seem to fly across the roof.

"God help them," Mr. Greene utters. "All those innocent souls..."

We watch helplessly as they drain the buckets down the chimney.

The screams inside the church are immediate. Doors that would not open for Mr. Bradbury now burst off their hinges in the parishioner's haste to exit. A heavy smoke pours out alongside those choking on it. It rises in the sky, reminiscent of the pillared whirlwind that carried the prophet Elijah to heaven.

The windows shatter as the many inside abandon their sanctuary, exiting through the double doors.

Their hopes of life and fresh air are short-lived.

I see all met with fast daggers and even crueler taunts.

More screams pervade the night sky. Even from afar, it does not take much imagination to conjure horrific images of their fates.

They are being scalped alive...

Wesley stands beside me, his face drained of color. "Like herding sheep," he says breathlessly.

A horse quietly neighs behind us, yet still I jump.

Priest stands beside all three mounts. He motions his head to go.

No one resists this time.

Mr. and Mrs. Green hurriedly climb atop Moses.

Wesley aids Emma onto Hickory's back.

I swing astride Priest's stallion. He leaps up behind me. His arms rise beneath my own to enshroud and bar me from falling. I lean backward, comforted by the feeling of his hard chest against me.

Even bearing two riders, Priest's stallion is far swifter than Hickory and Moses. He constantly pulls the hairs on its neck to slow its gait that the others might keep up. I do not mind it. Each time the stallion pulls at his touch, Priest's forearm clutches me tighter around my chest.

"Stop, Emma!" Wesley says.

Priest turns us back.

Wesley struggles to keep Emma upright. He slows Hickory to a trot. I see Emma choking for crying so hard. A moment later, she vomits to the side. "My m-mother..." she heaves. "F-father."

My heart goes out to her. By now they are amongst the dead if they are lucky. If not, they will be tortured or scalped with the others who yet live.

"Emma, we must go," Wesley urges.

"N-no," she cries. "We must g-go b-back."

"Emma," I say. She looks up in recognition of my voice. "We must hurry. They will catch us if we linger."

"S-Sarah, I am s-sorry."

"There will be time for those words later," I say. "We must be gone from here. Sit up, no—"

A war cry cuts me off, so close I fear it comes from Priest's own mouth.

Our stallion rears.

The painted brave appeared almost from thin air. His face is pockmarked with scratches. Even now they seem to bleed as he looks upon me with furious intent.

I am the last thing he sees on this earth.

In one fell swoop, Priest cleaves the brave's skull in two with his tomahawk. He wiggles the blade to dislodge it and kicks the body away.

"Heyaah!" he utters to our mount.

We outdistance the other two. The wind whistles in my ears, but it is not enough to drown out more war cries. I glance over Priest's right arm to look behind us.

Several more highwaymen and a pair of witches in tattered dress have emerged from inside the woods. All of them bound for my friends.

Wesley does not halt Hickory. He mows the first of them down under the draft horse's massive weight.

Emma screams at one of the witches who grasped her foot ere being trampled.

Mr. Greene is not so wise. He pulls back on the reins at the sight of a highwayman running straight at them. Moses rears in fright. The sudden movement pitches both husband and wife to the ground.

I feel cold metal pressed into my hands. I look down.

Priest has given me his long dagger. I feel his warm lips upon my ear.

"*Ride,*" he commands me.

The safety net of his arms and body about me falls away. By the time I turn, he is already on foot. With a grim nod, he slaps the stallion's haunch.

"No!" I cry.

I see him run back toward the fray. Then, he is gone to darkness as his stallion bears me away.

-sixteen-

I AM A MILE HENCE FROM THE BATTLE ERE I CAN HALT THE STALLION. Even then, the beast makes as though he means to run again. I look on into the lingering blackness.

Fear cautions me to continue on as Priest bid. Alone now, I pull the tiny hairs of the stallion's mane. "Back! We must go back!"

It only whinnies in response.

I hear hooves approach. I loose the mane, and take up the blade instead. It quivers in my hand. *Do I give what little defense I can, or open my veins and keep Hecate from her prize?* I prick my fingers upon the edge.

Wicked sharp, it calls my blood at the slightest touch.

No. Father did not wilt in the face of death. Nor did Priest when surrounded by Hecate and her followers. I do both an injustice if I falter so easily now.

I remind myself of Bishop's words. *They come for me...Plan to take me before the Warlock. Mayhap I might put an end to him, or even Hecate ere they kill me.*

I hide the dagger inside my dress, and tie the strings of my dirtied apron to bind it close. The coldness of it freezes my naked skin, a reminder I yet live.

I hear echoing shouts of pain in the far distance. Oddly, they give me hope. I cannot imagine Priest to make such noise.

Two mounts approach, each bearing a pair of riders.

"Sarah!"

Emma! She still lives!

I see her clutch Wesley's arm about her. I am instantly equal parts jealous and mad.

Why can she keep her protector when mine abandoned me?

Wesley tries to release her.

Emma refuses to let him.

"Why have you not gone?" Wesley scolds me.

Mr. and Mrs. Greene ride up behind them. Both of them are worse the wear. A long gash streaks up her leg. Blood trickles from his forehead into his right eye.

Only four have returned... "Where is he?" I ask.

My question brings a new whimper from Emma, one that sounds like a dying lamb.

I look to Wesley.

He frowns in answer.

It cannot be. It must not be.

"Dead." Mr. Greene blinks to keep the blood out of his eye. "I saw it at the last. He gave up his life to help me back on the horse. I turned round to help him and saw—"

"What?" I scream. "What did you see?"

Mr. Greene hangs his head. "He felled them like wheat before the scythe. One of the witches...I-I thought surely she was dead... but...she drove a dagger in his back. I—"

"No..."

Mr. Greene draws the courage to look me in the eyes. "I watched him fall. H-he did not rise again."

I hate the sudden wetness of tears upon my cheeks and the cowardice in all who now surround me. "Why did you not return help him?" I ask. "It may be he yet lives."

Wesley urges Hickory closer to me. "Sarah, he is gone. We can do naught for him now...but, we can return to warn the others."

He reaches out to touch me.

I shove his hand away. *Of course he would wish us to return and leave Priest. Did Wesley not point out my affections for Priest earlier?*

"No!" I cry. "I would see his body."

"They are coming, Sarah," Wesley speaks softer still. "Think on Rebecca, your mother, and George. Aye. And Andrew Martin, also. They will need our help if they are to last the night."

I can yet feel Priest's phantom lips upon my ear. Hear his whispering voice...*'Ride.'* Only a word, but in its tone he spoke more than someone else might say with twenty. He would not wish me to stay here and die on the highroad. I know he finally spoke that I might heed him; that his word would push me to go. Push me onward even though it means leaving his body to rot for scavengers to feast upon.

I rub the snot away with my bad forearm. Resting my lamed wrist upon my lap, my elbow brushes the hidden hilt of his dagger. The touch of it bids me think of Thomas Putnam's hatred for those who wronged him. Nervous energy germinates within me.

I will have my own vengeance this night. I brush the hilt again. *With God as my witness, I shall reap a reckoning on* Hecate and her followers for all they have taken from me.

"Let us away from here," I say.

My heart hardened and mind blank, I click to the stallion as Priest once did. It trots me down the highroad toward home. Nothing I do coaxes more speed from it, almost as if it understands the fate of its master and mourns with me. My eyes sweep back and forth in search of any new scouts or traps lying in wait. In truth, I almost wish I found some. My hatred is fresh, my blood hot.

I recall Bishop saying Priest went ranging earlier in the day. It must be he found and killed any of Hecate's scouts close to home. We find no more to bar our path.

Even before turning down the dirt drive, I see tiny sprinklings of orange light inside my home. The lights are broken up from the planks Bishop and the boys nailed to the windows.

Spurring Priest's stallion ahead, I leave the others behind.

I see smoke escape from our chimney.

Are they so foolish to cook inside even now? I chide myself for thinking so poorly of Bishop. I suppose it does not matter if they are. We know Hecate and her army comes for us. Why should my family not enjoy a final meal?

I hear nothing upon my approach, however.

Odd...surely they heard me upon horseback. God forbid George or Andrew have their aims trained on me and mistake me for a witch.

"It is I, Sarah!" I call upon my approach.

They must hear me for there is no shot. I tug on the stallion's mane to bring him to a halt. Sliding off, I wonder why Bishop and the others have not yet opened the door to welcome my return?

I run to the cabin and pound upon the door. "Mr. Bishop! George! We have returned!"

There is no reply.

Why will they not let me in?

A cold wind blows. It shrieks in my ears and freezes my soul.

What if they cannot hear me? I back away from the door slowly. My mind tortures me, recalling images of Father swinging by the neck, and the screams of those at church. *What if Hecate or a scouting party came here first? What if all that remains of my family lies dead inside?*

I look to the road.

Wesley and his father have turned up our alley.

My conscience speaks they will be here in a moment. *I should wait for them ere I check inside. That is what a sane person would do.*

Father gifted his patience to Rebecca and George, though. I step close to the cabin. The tough wooden siding against my back reminds me of Priest. I reach into my gown, pull the dagger free, and remind myself to breathe.

It does little good.

I raise the dagger to strike any attacker, and peek my head around the window.

There is a slight crack the plank defenses do not cover. I am outside the kitchen.

Inside, I see the hearth aglow. Three figures of similar size lay prostrate around it, each covered with quilts. A larger, unmoving fourth slumps against the far window.

Only four...

I hurriedly count how many we left behind. *Bishop, Mother, George, Andrew, and—Where is Rebecca? She would be far smaller than all laying inside.*

Hecate's threat rings in my ears. *Tomorrow his daughter's scalp I shall wear.*

No. I cannot believe it. Not Rebecca. Perhaps she sleeps upstairs in our bed. Aye. She must be upstairs. I run around the corner, careful to keep in the shadows. I look up to where the window of our room is. The shutters are closed, barred by wooden planks.

"Rebecca!" I call out in a hushed voice. "Rebecca!"

"She's not there, lass." Bishop emerges from the dogwood Emma and Ruth once hid behind. His jovial expression disappears when he sees me holding Priest's dagger.

"He's dead," his voice wavers. "Isn't he?"

The tears I hated so much to cry return. I nod. "A witch upon the road," I say. "How did you know?"

He snorts and clears his throat. "That's his father's blade. The lad would ne'er part with it if he yet lived." He kicks the cabin wall. "Stubborn bastard! Told him not to go. Now he's dead and for what?"

He looks past at me at hearing the others approach. "Augh," he scoffs. "An old man and a couple cryin' wenches, eh? Yer pardon, lass, but I'd rather have me lad back."

I know not what to say. He is rightfully angry, yet I see three souls saved for his one sacrifice. *Some small comfort if we are all to join Priest in death tonight.* I think grimly.

"Where is Rebecca?" I ask.

Bishop jerks a thumb over his shoulder. "In the barn with the others."

"But inside—I saw bodies lying on the floor—"

"Ye saw what I wanted ye to see," Bishop replies, a bit of humor coming back into this voice. "And what I mean for the bitches to ere I send 'em to Hell. Now, come." He motions me to follow. "We'd best hide away in case their lot watch us even now."

The others wait patiently in front of my home.

Foolishness. I shake my head. Witches could have taken me on the other side and kept me hostage, for all they know. Instead, they sit patiently upon the back of tired mounts. What if a raiding party befell us now, out in the open? I doubt Hickory and Moses have the strength to bear them away a second time.

Wesley sits straighter upon seeing us. "Mr. Bishop, sir. These are my parents—"

"I don't give a wet fart who they are. Get inside the barn, and quick. Or stay out here if ye like, but make yer decision and make it now."

Wesley shifts uneasily and opens his mouth to speak.

His father does before he can. "We are indebted to your companion, sir," Mr. Greene speaks solemnly. "My family and I will do whatever you bid us that we might repay his sacrifice."

Bishop nods. "Get in the barn, then. Up in the hayloft ye'll find the lads. Give 'em a break from their watch. If'n they're still awake, that is," he adds under his breath. He watches them ride away. With a shake of his head, he turns to me. "The rest of 'em die at the church?"

I nod. "Th-they burned it," I say as we begin our march for the barn. "And the ones who made it out..."

"Scalped 'em, I'll warrant." Bishop says. "Aye, made to look like the work were done by the natives. Ye know they learned it from white folk?"

He must gather I did not. He chuckles darkly as he continues limping along. "A few years before the Salem trials, folks offered bounties for every native scalp brought in. Three pounds a head, I believe."

"That cannot be," I say. "It is a savage custom. Everyone knows—"

"All people know is what they been told, lass. And usually what they're told *first*. Before last night, ye know yer father for Paul Kelly. A good-hearted man who cared for his family, not the Dr. Simon Campbell what sparked the Salem trials."

I stop walking. My thoughts dwell on Thomas Putnam's journal and all he had written. "And how did you come to know my father for Dr. Campbell?"

Bishop hangs his head. "I was there, lass," he says heavily. "Like I said to yer father. Now would ye like to hear this tale again and be scalped yerself? Or may we continue to the barn so we're not out in the open when they arrive?"

I understand his urgency, but I want answers Thomas Putnam's journal did not give. In my anger, I outdistance him to limp behind me. I catch Wesley embracing Emma just outside the barn.

He lets her go upon seeing me.

Emma is crying again.

How does her body produce so many tears?

Wesley sighs at my questioning look. "She is afeared there might be..."

"Snipes," Emma says. "They will drag me inside—"

I laugh. With everything that has occurred to her these past few days, she is afeared of an imaginary creature? I wish I could tell Ruth and Charlotte.

The thought of them kills my laughter.

Nothing will ever be the same again, I realize. *They are gone forever now.*

As I look upon Emma, I note our friendship, too, is ended. I pity her, as I always have, yet her betrayal drove a wedge between us I cannot pluck.

Both Wesley and Emma look at me like they do not know what to make of me. Indeed, I must seem mad to both laugh and grow dour in such a short span of time.

"Better the snipes take you than Hecate and her followers," I say.

Fresh tears form in the corners of Emma's eyes.

I enter the barn, leaving Wesley to mend the broken spirit she will always be. I hear the cows shuffling about in their pen toward the back. Their moos bid me think it is any other night. I would happily milk them now to make it true.

Mr. Greene stabled both Hickory and Moses. They neigh at my scent and bump the wooden sides with their huge haunches. I find my way past and to the hayloft ladder. My eyes adjust to the darkness as I climb, and I see dim shapes by the time I reach the top.

Two figures guard either side of the great loft opening. George and Andrew.

I fondly recall watching Father raise hay bales from the rope and pulley hung from the rafter outside it. He would fearlessly reach out into the empty air to pull them inside and then stack them in preparation for the winter months. Sometimes, he would even let us build forts of hay bales to play inside of.

The doors are only cracked open now though. Not enough to make our presence inside known, but enough to allow us some bird's eye view of anything outside. A bit of pale light from the hunter's moon shines through it.

The rustling of hay in the far end of our barn unnerves me. Never have I been up here at night. Perhaps I should not have been so cruel to Emma.

"Sarah?"

Rebecca's voice...She is safe!

"Where are you?" I ask.

I hear the patter of her small feet run across the boards. A moment later, a shadow leaps at me. I catch my little sister in my arms. Even when she releases her hold on me, I refuse to let go of her.

"Saar-ah," she says, and tries to wriggle free.

I force myself to let her down.

"You made it back!" she says happily. "And you brought Emma too!"

It is hard for me to not be caught up in her enthusiasm. "Aye," I say. "Wesley's parents also."

Rebecca leans close to me. "I heard Mrs. Greene speak to Mother," she whispers so low I scarcely hear her. "She said you met misfortune on the road, but Mr. Priest delivered you. She said savages killed him! I know the truth of it though. He will return with Father!"

There is plenty of somberness amongst us already, I tell myself. *Let Rebecca be the one to keep our spirits alive.* "Where is Mother now?"

Rebecca takes my hand. "Come."

She escorts me to the furthest corner of the barn. I hear crying from the opposite side, then Mr. Greene's soft *ssh-ssh-ssh* as he hushes his wife.

"Mother..." Rebecca says. "Mother...Sarah has returned."

"Sarah?"

She says my name like one who knows but has since forgot.

I follow her voice as she continues to repeat my name. I find her lying in an unbound pallet of straw. I kneel beside her. Taking her hands, I place them upon my cheeks. "I have returned, Mother. I am safe."

"Did you bring your father with you?" she asks. "I fear he went to the taverns again. You did right to fetch him."

I do not know of what she speaks. Never did I see Father drink like other men. In fact, he oft preached the use as a tool of Satan to corrupt otherwise goodly men.

"Y-you did find him," her voice sounds pained at my lack of answer. "Did you not, Sarah?"

"A-aye, Mother," I say.

A lie remains a lie, no matter the goodly intent. I hear Father's voice in my head.

"He will return home soon."

Mother takes my hand and pats it. "Good. That is for good. I hope he comes not too late. There have been rumors of savages raiding the countryside."

With one hand, she pulls Rebecca close to her side. The other reaches inside her apron. "I hope they do not come here." She strokes Rebecca's thin hair. "The red-man does...terrible things to white women."

My wits tell me I must needs go on now without Mother as well. Hecate has stolen almost all from me. I will not let fear of her take my sister as well.

"I-I believe the raids put down, Mother," I say. "Come, Rebecca. Let us look after your poppets."

Rebecca will not move. "I already hid them."

"Ah," I say. "But we must check on them. You would not want them afeared, would you?"

My sister's teeth gleam as she smiles. "No. I will go at once."

"Do not go far," Mother calls at our leave.

We are but five feet away when Rebecca squirms her hand from mine. "I wish to tell them alone. Elsewise, it would not be a secret."

"Aye, I understand, but come back to me when you are done. We must let Mother rest."

I watch her disappear into the further reaches of the loft.

The ladder creaks behind me. Two figures climb its rungs. Emma comes first, her eyes warily searching out snipes. If anyone but Wesley followed her, I would laugh she fell for a boy's scheme to look up her dress. He is too gentlemanly for such a trick, however.

I hide behind a hay bale so they do not see me. There I watch from the shadows as he leads her from the opening in the floor and on to where his parents sit.

From my position, I hear George and Andrew speaking in hushed whispers. They talk on what Bishop said to them of being men. How he mentioned they should envision shooting wolves tonight to shield their minds from the truth.

Both seem nervous, to my mind.

I suppose I am as well. I take a seat on the wooden floor and place my back to the hay. A sharp tinge in my thigh reminds me of the journal I carry.

The journal!

It seems ages since I read its contents. Can it be I read not a few short hours ago? Opening it, I near rip its pages to where I left off. A lone entry remains. I squint my eyes to better see in the dim moon rays. Then, I read the last words of Thomas Putnam.

24th day of May 1699

It seems my gift of foresight is proven a final time; my sins are come to bear this eve.

Even now I hear the skittering of feet outside my home. Aye, and their accursed cackling.

Why must they torment me so? Is it not enough I suffer in the knowledge they come for my life?

I shot at the first sign of blackened teeth through the slats of lumber barring my windows. I know I missed, for the witches laughed wickedly at my aim.

They plague me still with their infernal chants.

Thank God I sent my wife and children away upon learning of Dr. Griggs's death. I only pray they stay gone and escape this retribution for my trespasses.

I heard it said others discovered Griggs with a dagger in his chest. Aye, with both red and black ribbons tied to its bone-hilt. Did he sheath it within himself because he could not withstand this same mockery I experience now?

A similar dagger sits before me. Indeed, the longer their chanting persists, the more I find myself staring upon its blade, desiring to silence their voices.

A dark melody has begun outside my home.

I gather they come for me soon.

I write this, my final entry, now to beg forgiveness of any who find it. Heaven help me, I lusted for power and had it granted for a moment. What cruel joke is it God plays upon us that all men must falter? Perhaps I shall discover its truth in Hell, for I am not like to discover th

There is nothing further, almost as if someone plucked the quill from his hand.

"What are ye readin', lass?"

Frustrated, I toss the book into the straw. "A dead man's journal."

Bishop picks it up and thumbs through it. "And why would a lass be readin' that?"

"Hecate gave it to me. I think she meant for me to read it and turn against my Father when I learned the truth."

He turns a page and holds the book afar in front of him to read. I gather his vision must not be well for he blinks several times. "Would ye if he were alive?"

"No," I say. My own answer surprises me. "He was my father. Ne'er did I see the man she claimed him to be. Nor Thomas Putnam neither."

"Putnam, eh?" Bishop shakes his head. "There were an evil man if ere I met one."

I sit up. "You knew him?"

"I *met* him," Bishop clarifies. "I gathered he weren't the grand schemer, but he did little to hide his hand in helpin' breathe life to it. His daughter accused most folk hanged, ye know. I suppose he's payin' for it now. Greedy bastard."

I sense the chance to have answers to my questions. "You said you were in Salem."

Bishop settles his back against a hay bale and continues to read. "For a time..."

"And," I pause. "Did you sense my father had anything to do with the accusations?"

Bishop turns another page. "No. He was smarter than the others. Didn't guess his part in it until long after when I wrestled the truth from Putnam. There were other plotters too." He studies the page. "But I reckon ye already know that."

"So you met both Dr. Griggs and Reverend Parris?"

"Aye."

"And did you..."

"Did I murder 'em?" Bishop chuckles. "No, lass. Vengeance is best served by those betrayed. If ye want the hard truth, it's why I stayed my hand with yer father. He did evil wrong, but not to me."

The easy way in which he says it makes me want to strike him. I do not, however, for I begin to understand his reasoning. I desire to spill Hecate's blood. To learn someone did the task in my place would cheat me of my revenge.

"Why do you help us?"

"Eh?"

"For all the wrong you say my Father did...why then do you help us? Why not abandon us to Hecate?"

Bishop sighs. "Because ye left that first night I laid eyes on ye."

"What—"

"I know ye saw me in the woods durin' the witch gatherin'. Ye damn near gave me away, too, till the Devil's daughter cut in on ye."

The shadow in the woods! It was Bishop!

"I did see you!"

"Aye," Bishop says. "How do ye think the lad knew where to take ye home the next night?"

"You had him follow me?"

"I had him keep ye safe. Knew it took a right strong spirit to turn away from such folk. That's someone worthy of protection in my book." He grins. "The Devil's daughter and others like her deserved their vengeance, I'll grant 'em that. But the rest of ye had naught to do with yer father's sins. Just like me wife had naught to do with mine."

A grim silence settles between us as he looks over Thomas Putnam's words.

"Have you accomplished your own vengeance?" I ask finally. "For the ones who...killed your wife."

His gaze lingers on the open journal. "No."

"But you said—" I pause to weigh my next words carefully. "You said she hanged for a witch."

Bishop stains a page of the journal by placing one of his dirty fingers upon it. "Dr. Campbell asked if we could be trusted," he traces over the words as he reads from Putnam's journal. "An ignorant question, to my mind. Why should we answer anything but aye? Only after we agreed did he inquire if ever we heard tell of Goody Glover," Bishop's voice breaks. "Aye, I said. 'Twas but three year ago they hanged her for a witch in Boston for afflictin' children.

"Dr. Campbell then inquired if we believed in witchcraft, and Goody Glover guilty of bein' one. The hailed *Reverend Cotton Mather*." Bishop spits the name. "Said she were, I recall Parris sayin'. And those four children afflicted too. What else could she be," he looks up from the journal sadly. "But a witch?"

I cover my mouth with my hand. "Goody Glover...she was your wife..."

His face is cloaked in somberness, yet nothing could hide the anger in the old man's voice. "Aye," Bishop says. "I am Patrick Glover."

-seventeen-

BISHOP RESTS THE JOURNAL UPON HIS LAP. "I SPOKE TRUE TO YER father," he says. "A name follows a man. It's why I haven't given mine since learnin' on me poor wife's murder. But if I'm to join her tonight, I'll have it known her husband died avengin' her. Let this Devil's daughter know she's not the only ones who rises from the dead."

He chuckles himself into a small coughing fit.

I assume a man once hanged has no fear of death any longer. I wish I could say the same for me.

"Did he...Priest," I say. "Was that his true name?"

Bishop gives me a cock-eyed look.

I blush at my own question. *Are my affections so obvious? If Bishop senses them at a mere question, surely Priest did whenever I looked upon him.*

"It's all right, lass," Bishop says. "Yer not the first maid to desire an older man. I dare say he cared for ye too—"

"He mentioned me?" I say quickly.

Bishop nods. "In his own way. I believe if ye had been a year or two older, he'd a stolen ye right from under yer father's nose and then off into the wild with both of ye."

Did he consider us eloping on our first ride? Is that why he keeps his silence?

"I wish he could have," I say.

"Augh. If he had done, all the others in this barn'd be dead, lass. Wesley, his muther and father, aye, and yer wee friend too. All of 'em burned and scalped with the others if not for yer warnin'."

No. That is not true. They and I would all be dead if not for *Priest's* sacrifice on the highroad. "Tell me more of him," I bid him.

He snorts and crosses his arms. I have offended him in some way. Perhaps the death of his friend is too fresh in his mind. Only when he sighs do I realize the story I seek is forthcoming.

"I found him a few years after Salem ended," Bishop begins. "While trackin' this Dr. Campbell I'd learned so much about. One mornin', huntin' me breakfast, I saw a risin' smoke afar off. Thought to ride away from it at the first, but then I heard the Almighty whisper to me, 'Twas help ye been naggin' Me for and it's help I be sendin' ye now. If ye've not the courage to ride further, don't be prayin' for Me favor ne'er again, ye ungrateful bastard.'"

His warm telling makes me smile. "And so you rode on and found him."

"Augh," he tuts. "Heavens, no."

He sports with me. I lean forward to look him full in the face. "But, you must have done."

"Lass," he says not unkindly. "I'd heard of raidin' parties nearby. I didn't want to run afoul of 'em, ye see. Better to tuck tail and run the other way, thought I."

"But you found me in the woods," I say. "The savages did not frighten you then."

He chuckles and tips his weather-beaten hat to me. "I think ye for puttin' me up on high esteem. But, if ye recall it rightly, the lad fought 'em. I only took ye by the hand and led ye away. Tuck tailed and ran there too, didn't I?" he asks with a wry grin.

"Alas," he continues before I can speak. "The Almighty knew I'd run. He sent the natives to catch me not a mile away. They pulled me from me horse and stripped me shirt off. 'Twas then they saw this."

I watch him unbutton the top of his shirt to reveal a wooden rosary that lay against his fuzzy chest like a fallen tree in tall grass. He rubs the long end of it between his fingers.

"One bid the others stop then," Bishop says. "They picked me off the ground, bound me hands, and led me through the woods toward the smoke. Augh, I were fearful scared. I'd heard it said the natives oft burned their captives alive in offerin' to whatever heathen gods they worship. Thank Christ we arrived in a clearin' ere I had long to ponder it. A whole tribe, I saw. All surroundin' what remained of a cabin.

"The rains from the night before must've put out the fire, but the smoke hung off the leftovers. The main of it still stood, mind ye, but only by the grace a the Almighty. I saw the cabin door'd been flung off its hinges and the blackness inside seemed an open pit into Hell itself. And, then, a brave spat out." He chuckles. "His limbs cut and bleedin', he wailed like a woman as he ran back to the others. So afeared I thought the Devil hisself put the fear in him."

Bishop seems to forget I sit with him. He sets his gaze on the far wall, almost as though he can see through it.

"They carried me through the crowd," he continues. "Dragged me before the chief to speak a few words. There I saw not only the one brave feared. It grabbed hold on me then, too." He looks down at the rosary. "One of 'em put a blade in my hand. Shoved me toward the cabin."

"What did you do?" I ask.

"Not much I could do." he says. "They lifted their tomahawks and I knew 'twas into the cabin with me, or be sent through the fire to meet the Almighty again. So, I gathered up me courage and walked toward it. I saw marks upon the house. Fresh blood stains covered the shattered windows, and arrows stuck in the wood beside 'em. Ashen rags and hair, black as crow feathers, littered the stoop. A native raid, thought I, or so it seemed." Bishop snorts. "But what demon lay inside to drive 'em off? I halted at the doorstep and made the sign a the holy cross. Then, in I went."

I rub my shoulders to free them of the chill. "What did you see?"

"Nuthin'," he says. "Until the Almighty saw fit to grant me some wee vision. 'Twas then I saw the bodies..." he says, gnawing his lip. "Women and children, all."

His fingers slip from merely rubbing the rosary. Now he clutches it whole. A part of me wishes I had not asked for this story. Still, I cannot bring myself to stop him.

"I saw bits a bead and bone spread over the floor—either from the battle within, or the braves outside pickin' the leavin's off the bodies. I couldn't be sure. I blessed their corpses with the Lord's prayer. When I opened me eyes, a pair stared right back at me from 'cross the room."

Bishop wipes a tear from his eye. "I saw him in the corner, hunched over a slain squaw and his naked skin painted black with soot. Augh, a more feral beast I ne'er looked upon. His stained tomahawk in hand and three slain Wabanaki braves before him. He almost looked a painter who'd spilt his stores all over the floor."

I can picture him in my mind's eye. The grim set of his jaw locked for battle. His blade at the ready for any who meant to make him stir.

"Did he speak to you then?" I ask.

Bishop shakes his head. "I weren't wonton to join the dead braves. I dared not venture further. Two days I sat there with him. The natives sent braves inside only once more." He chuckles. "The lad rose faster than a bleedin' serpent at the sight of 'em. He didn't sit again until the natives left."

He clears his throat of the built up phlegm. "The third morn, I woke to the sound a wood splittin'. I hurried outside. Most the natives had gone, but they left a few scouts to report what happened."

"What sound? What did they labor at?"

"Preparin'." Bishop rests his head against the hay. "The lad walked amongst 'em unafeared to fell the trees he wanted. All day he spent hewin' the lumber to fashion the pyre for his muther. He finished near nightfall. The brave I'd seen run away approached him with a jar, oil that smelled something sweet. The lad made to exchange his axe for it, but, to their everlastin' credit, the natives wouldn't take it.

"The lad said something in a native tongue then. I gathered they lay the ill between 'em to rest. He cleaned his muther's body with the oil. Kissed her forehead. Then he spoke to the braves again. Together, they helped him lift her body upon the pyre ere night fell. That night, they set fire to it. Danced round it, wailin' and singin' in words me ears couldn't understand. Me heart knew the meanin' though. And the lad...he did not dance. He stood there all night, starin' into the flames."

Bishop hangs his head. "When I awoke the next morn, the natives had gone. I couldn't know then the stories they'd tell on him circled their camps already. Ye see, natives know what white men long forgot. There's power in a name. It's why the natives won't give one until ye've earned it."

"And Priest...he earned one?"

"Aye, that he did." Bishop answers. "The natives are a strange lot. Lord knows I'll not pretend to understand 'em. In Ireland, ye kill a man, his brother comes to kill ye, and so on it goes till the end a days. The natives are different there. The lad taught me that. Them ones he killed, it made the lad a brave hisself, in their eyes. For what mere boy could kill so many a their kin? They wanted him on their side, ye see."

"His name," I ask. "What name did they give him?"

Bishop grins. "Black Pilgrim."

A fearsome name, I think. Befitting. "They must have respected him greatly then," I say. "Did they name him so because of the soot on his body?"

Bishop shrugs. "Some say aye. Others believed he wielded some dark magic to blend with the shadows. To them it must've seemed so, for a boy to kill three braves. Indeed, once he cleaned of the soot, I saw he couldn't be more than twelve year old in body. In his face, a man already."

I smile, picturing him just so.

"'Twas then I told 'em my purpose," Bishop says. "Said I quested for vengeance and if he traveled with me, I'd help him find his own. He wouldn't speak yet though, only nod. I asked if he knew which tribe killed his family. I gathered not the ones what left, else he wouldn't have made peace with 'em."

"Hecate..." I say. "She and her witches did it, didn't they?"

Bishop strokes his dirtied beard. "No. His quarrel with her wouldn't come till years later."

"Then who?"

"The same men who wanted his father dead," Bishop says. He opens the journal again and flips through the pages with a dogged smile. "If only he coulda' seen these pages, lass. The lad woulda had a right fit a laughter readin' on his father."

"Priest's father?" I say. "He and Thomas Putnam knew each other?"

"Oh, aye. And knew each other well," he says. "It's all right here in this journal a his. Putnam had him accused for witchery and clapped in irons."

I cannot believe it. The origins of Priest's lineage are in the journal I have been reading? The pages contained treasures indeed, but I too blind to see. "Pray, who was he?"

Bishop rests the journal upon his lap. "Have ye not looked upon the blade the lad gave ye? His father's blade, I remind ye."

"No, why would—"

"Look at it now, lass," he motions to my apron. "Look at it close."

I take Priest's long dagger from my apron. It looks dull in the moonlight as I turn its blade. Near the hilt, I see faint letters etched. I hold it higher toward better light, and read the name aloud. "Captain John Alden, Jr."

Bishop holds up the journal. "Guess that bastard, Putnam, decided to leave out the part where his enemy escaped from prison."

"You mean Putnam did not exact his revenge?"

"Not on Captain Alden. Some other *friend*," Bishop winks at me. "Visited him at jail. It's said this stranger left him a key. It's also said the wily old man told Captain Alden he'd best be off into hidin' ere they could stretch his neck."

"You knew him..."

"Aye," Bishop says with a twinkle in his gray eyes. "A good man. Understood everything came from his bein' an Alden. Called the girls a bunch a jugglin' wenches, he did. Little did I know then I'd meet his bastard son not a year later. Aye, and come to raise him up as me own."

"Putnam called Captain Alden a savage lover and a traitor," I say.

Bishop sucks his teeth. "Aye, many in Salem called him so. The natives though, they claimed him a good man to 'em. Ye see, lass, a traitor to one man's a hero to another. Listen not to what Putnam says. It's hard to figure where the lies stop and truth begins with that lot.

"Trust me, lass. The Alden's be a special breed. Why, the lad's grandfather, the first John Alden, came over on the Mayflower. It's said the stubborn bastard wished to be the first to set foot on Plymouth Rock." Bishop grins. "He knew what the British King and his court wanted to do with these colonies and its native people. It's why the Aldens came here...to stop 'em from makin' it so. The Alden's have been a thorn to those pullin' the strings ever since."

"So Priest..." I say. "He was an Alden."

"Aye, that would've been his Christian name, if he weren't a bastard born to some squaw the Captain loved," Bishop says. "He ne'er went by such a name though. Years later, Captain Alden told me he knew his son'd be hunted the same as he if anyone learned the truth. It's why he had the lad raised amongst the natives. To learn their ways that he might better protect 'em someday."

"Protect the savages?" I say. "But they are the ones who prey upon the weak! The raids, the scalping, the—"

"Still buried neck deep in fear and shite, are ye lass?" Bishop asks. "Ye think every native wants to kill ye? They don't. The natives are just like us, er—better, if the bastard were to be listened to. Always said he found more decency amongst their lot then any of ours."

"They're hardly decent. I heard what the Tuscaroras did."

"Aye. *Heard*, but didn't *see*." Bishop sits up. "Why are we in this barn tonight, lass?"

He means to trick me. I cannot see how he hopes to win this argument though. "Hecate, her witches, and those savages you now defend come to take it from us. Aye, and our lives with it."

"So ye mean to fight 'em because they come to take what's yers."

"Aye."

"And ye lived here first."

My blood boils at his condescension. "I was born here, sir. My Father paid a fair price for this land—"

"I'm not blamin' yer father for buyin' such fine land, mind ye, only sayin' he paid for it in blood money."

"Speak no more of your riddles to me," I say. "Tell me what you mean to say and speak it true."

"The only question ye need ask when solving a mystery... who profits?"

My throat feels dry. "M-my father."

"It's true yer father was greedy, aye," says Bishop. "But this tale goes a wee bit deeper than a man earning monies in Salem sellin' remedies to the Devil's powder. Me poor wife's murder, the Salem trials...who gained most from it?"

"Putnam—"

Bishop shakes his head. "For a time mayhap, but he and

his family wound up dead, didn't they? Same with his partner, Dr. Griggs." Bishop points to the journal. "And Putnam wrote Dr. Campbell, yer father, disappeared in the night. Why would he run from all that profit if he were truly the man what devised the plan?"

"I don't know."

"I said before yer father was smarter than Putnam and the rest. I reckon he knew what came next for the part he played in Salem. That yer father understood what happens to all poppets when a puppeteer finishes his show."

Then my understanding dawns after all Bishop's riddles and questions. "They all go back in the box..."

"Silent as can be with no one to pull their strings and say otherwise, no?" Bishop chuckles. "I reckon yer father knew his good fortune in Salem wouldn't last. That those who sent him would eventually send another to silence him. Tie up the loose ends, as it were."

"Who?"

Bishop snorts. "Executioners wear black hoods to hide their faces, but there's always someone willin' to share their secrets if ye part with a wee bit a coin. I found such a man in Boston when I asked after who gave me poor wife the final shove."

He pauses to give me back the journal. "Putnam were many things," he says. "But stupid he weren't. His estimate someone placed William Stoughton to head the court in Salem was wise indeed. All I spoke with about Stoughton claimed him naught but a wild dog for the Mathers."

Even in the low light I can see him grimace.

"The Mathers turned Stoughton loose on Salem." Bishop continues. "Made sure to voice their disapproval with his actions, sure, but don't be fooled, lass. It's them what appointed him." He sneers. "How else could one explain the hailed Cotton Mather's presence at Martha Carrier's hangin'? The same Mather who condemned me wife for a witch."

"So Reverend Cotton Mather is the Warlock..." I say. "But why? What could he profit from such horrible acts?"

"If witches labor for the Devil," says Bishop. "Then what can be said about the man who stomps them out but he be doin' the Almighty's good work?"

"A hero..."

Bishop nods. "And his name etched in history for all time as such."

"But how do you know for certain?" I ask.

"I teased the confession from their dog's mouth ere I dispatched him to Hell." Bishop says grimly. "Mather sent Stoughton to finish the task yer father started in Salem. With his dog dead and dust, I warrant he set this Devil's daughter on us now."

I hear footsteps behind me. "William Stoughton is dead."

I turn round to see Mother. How long has she been there, hidden amongst the hay bales?

Mother glares at Bishop. "He died almost eleven years ago... not long after the precious Captain Alden you speak so highly of."

"Aye, he did," says Bishop. "And what a happy little bit of vengeance that were for me when I put my axe through his skull."

Mother looks away from him. "Come, Sarah." She pulls the shoulder of my dress. "This man means to fill your head with lies."

"Mother, you know of these men also?"

Mother hesitates. "Only from what little your Father spoke of."

"Then ye'll know there's much to fear from such learned men." Bishop stands. "Yer husband surely knew it. Why else did he lead ye all this way south, tucked away and hidden from pryin' eyes?"

Mother does not have an answer for him.

I hear the quick footsteps of someone running toward us. My body immediately tenses and does not relax until I see only Andrew Martin standing before us. I gather his labored breathing comes not from running so hard.

"Mr. Bishop, sir," Andrew whispers. "They're here..."

-eighteen-

I RUN BEHIND BISHOP TOWARD THE HAYLOFT OPENING, CAREfully avoiding the bit of moonlight that would give our shadows. We reach the barn wall and crouch inside the hayloft door.

Andrew points to the cornfield. "There," he says. "Do you see them?"

"Aye," Bishop says quietly.

I feel a knee in my back.

"Pray," Mother says in a hushed, but interested, tone. "Where?"

Bishop gives her an odd look. "Hidin' in the rows," he grunts. "Watch the stalk tips..."

I do as he suggests. The tips move so slow it would seem but a light breeze blows them. That is until I notice some of the stalks bend and move in ways others do not.

"How many are there?" I ask.

"I count six," Andrew says.

"Ten," Bishop says matter-of-factly. He backs away from the edge and claps Andrew on the shoulder. "Right, lad. Go ready Wesley and his folks."

Andrew hesitates. "Your pardon, but I do not believe they will fight, sir. Mrs. Greene is sore affrighted."

"She'll fight," Bishop says. "Put a shovel in her hand, or whatever ye can find. When she's starin' death in the face, my thinkin' is she'll swing it."

Andrew nods and leaves us.

To my surprise, George leaves his post also. "Where are you going?" I whisper to him.

George pays me no mind.

Bishop moves to take Andrew's position. "Not to worry, lass. They'll be back."

Something about his wording seems odd to me. The Greene family is not far from us. Why would I worry? A nagging feeling I have missed something follows me as Bishop's gaze turns back to the corn.

Anyone hiding inside the field has since stopped their progression. Now it seems only innocent rows of corn instead of a murderous trap.

The nagging feeling returns, this time nudging me in the shoulder. The coldness of it cuts through even the thick layer of my gown. I reach to rub it away, only to feel the barrel of a rifle.

"Can ye shoot, lass?"

I take hold of the seeming black wand, one of Father's rifles, with my good hand. Its weight comforts me as I check to ensure it loaded like he taught me several year ago. I shall have to balance it on my bad wrist to aim though. I wish I could have taken practice with doing so earlier.

"Sarah!" Mother hisses. "You should not have your father's rifle. He will be most displeased when he returns from the village."

"Yer husband's dead," Bishop says coldly. "Yer daughters and son are still here. Do what ye can to save 'em."

Mother claps her hands over her ears. Shaking her head, she disappears toward the back of the barn once more. I think to go to her, but seeing Wesley approach gives me pause. His parents and Emma are not far behind.

Emma hugs a pitchfork to her chest. Mrs. Greene does likewise with her shovel.

"Mr. Greene," Bishop says, "take the far wall. Mrs. Greene, why don't ye and the lass stand by the ladder hole. Kill anyone pokin' their heads up through it."

Each do as they are bidden, save for Wesley. "You think those boys better men than I?" he asks Bishop. "Braver, mayhap?"

"No," says Bishop. "I think they listened on my plans while ye ran away with yer lady love."

I do not understand their disagreement until I hear a soft clacking of wood on wood below us. *The witches!* They have opened the side door and mean to slip in without us knowing. I move from my position.

Bishop stops me. "It's yer brother and the Martin lad." He points below us.

Outside the barn, George and Andrew crawl through the pigsty's muck and manure. Both stop behind the trough. Andrew rolls to his back and looks up at us.

"What are they doing?" My hushed voice sounds panicked. *Bishop sends boys outside with naught but a trough to shield them?*

"They're waitin'," Bishop says.

Wesley clenches my shoulder. "Look!"

A single torchbearer, on foot and stumbling, runs toward our home. "*Help!*"

The voice is recognizable. I struggle to put a name or face to it.

Wesley does not. "That's Benjamin King..."

"Sarah! George!"

"How did he escape the church?" I wonder aloud.

"We must help him," Wesley says.

Bishop grabs him. "Wait..."

"Sarah!" Benjamin continues to yell. "Help!"

We wait in watchful silence.

Benjamin reaches our home and frantically bangs upon the door. "Sarah! Mrs. Kelly? Anyone, please! Let me in!"

Wesley attempts to shove away from Bishop. "We must help him!" he whispers.

Bishop pulls Wesley close enough to kiss him. "Wait..." he whispers roughly.

A board creaks from the opposite side as Mr. Greene shifts uneasily. "The boy is terrified, Mr. Bishop," he says. "Might not one of us go to calm him?"

"Aye," Wesley says. "Let me. He has ever been my best friend."

Why then did he not join us at the church? Rather than spark a disagreement, I turn my attention back to watch my home.

Benjamin has abandoned his hopes of entering through the door, opting instead to move from window to window. He peers inside each whilst holding his torch close to better see. I notice he also glances over his shoulder toward the corn. With new resolve, he turns back to the windows and strikes the shutters.

"Sarah! Sarah, please!"

Wesley struggles in Bishop's grip beside me. "I care not what you say, I am go—"

His voice and body go lax.

Figures cloaked in black emerge from the cornfield. Indian braves painted for war accompany them alongside white fur traders. Even from afar, I recognize Hecate, cloaked once more in her violet garb and standing taller than the others. She strides across my family's yard toward Benjamin with an honor guard flanking her.

"He will be killed," Wesley whispers. "We must do something, Bishop."

And then I understand it. How Benjamin escaped the church when no one else did. "*Bait,*" I whisper. "She uses him as bait to learn where we are."

I know I have the right of it when Hecate and her escort stop ten yards from our barn. "Well?" she says.

Does she have so little care for our defense that she now speaks loud enough for us to overhear?

No. She believes we are inside our home. For why would we attempt to fortify such a large barn with so few defenders? I lean closer to Bishop to peer down at their gathering.

The witches and highwaymen surround Benjamin. Their bodies tremble for lack of Devil's powder.

Benjamin's torch shakes too. The light of it helps me to see his forehead is bloodied. It looks as if someone scalping him were halted. His torch also serves to light the faces of those around him.

I wish he did not have it. I nearly scream when I see Ruth and Charlotte amongst the crowd.

Charlotte's once beautiful skin is now pocked and freshly blooded, picked at no doubt during her fits of affliction. Patches of Ruth's hair has been ripped out. Now, she has bald spots. Their shoulders jerk. Heads twitch. Both pace around Benjamin with the other followers like a pack of hungry wolves.

Benjamin tries to keep his gaze on them, but there are too many for him to keep track of. "Th-they are not h-here," he says.

Hecate steps closer, cranes her neck to better see him. She lifts his chin that he might look into her face. "Oh, but they are."

As if signaled, Ruth leaps forward from amidst the circling crowd. With a quick jerk on Benjamin's hair, she yanks his head back to bare his throat. She lays it open ere Benjamin can cry out and lets his body fall.

I shut my eyes. Bite my knuckle to not scream. I am nearly knocked over when Bishop moves.

"No, lad," he says.

I open my eyes. He and Wesley struggle over a rifle.

Bishop will not relent. "If ye shoot her now, ye give us away," he says. "Wait!"

I reach out to touch Wesley. "Please. Do as he says."

Tears and anger cloud Wesley's face as he releases his hold on the rifle.

A piercing whistle comes from outside. *Hecate...*

I see a small army of witches and highwaymen stream out of the cornfield like a thick plague of locusts. I recognize a few of the girls from the first gathering Hecate attended. Their once mirthful faces now beset with deadly determination. They carry long daggers with carved bone hilts. Their male companions have bows and long daggers.

Hecate waits for them to gather around her. Setting her gaze on our cabin, she loudly commands them. "Bring her to me."

Most of the crowd disperses without question. Ruth, Charlotte, and a few men remain at Hecate's side. Hecate glances toward the road.

In the far distance, an even larger group approaches from the road with near twenty torches lit. Some are so high it can only mean they are mounted.

I turn and see the horror plain in Wesley's face.

"Bishop," I whisper. "How will we withstand such an army?"

He does not answer.

I see movement from the corner of my eye, Andrew waving at us from below.

He and George held their position despite being so near to Benjamin's plight they might well have been spotted. Yet even I, knowing where they hide, find it difficult to see them through the muck and manure they covered themselves in.

Bishop shakes his head no.

Andrew ceases his wave. He lays his hand flat against his chest. George has not once looked up. He lies on his stomach, his gaze focused the cabin.

"What are you planning?" I ask Bishop.

"Come on, come on," is his quiet answer.

The witches and highwaymen descend on my house. A few run around the back. A pair of Indian braves climb Father's cherry tree as easily as squirrels. A moment later, they leap from its branches and land upon the roof. Both scurry sure-footed toward our chimney.

"Come out, come out," the witches chant.

Others cackle and bang upon the boarded windows.

"Give us Sarah and you may all go free!"

The witch on the ground throws up a rope to the men on the roof. They catch it and tow buckets up. I watch them pour the contents down the chimney.

Smoke instantly billows out of the cracks in the cabin's defenses.

The witches shriek and stab their daggers at the wooden planks to pry them free, their laughter turned hateful. "We're coming for you, Sarah Campbell!"

Bishop raises a hand beside me.

I hear a clattering of rocks. A spark of light from below catches my eye. *George...*

He strikes his blade to flint, aiming the sparks toward the ground.

Hecate's head turns at the sound.

I will him to hurry.

The flint is struck once more. Again, the spark does not catch.

Hecate steps away from her honor guard. She hones on the swine trough.

George raises his blade high. He slams it down upon the flint.

It sparks, catches aflame.

A line of fire zooms across the ground bound directly for our cabin.

I see George and Andrew leap to their feet. Both hurry for the barn.

Too late, Hecate gathers what happens. I see her mouth open to scream, but it is not heard. She dives toward the trough.

In a single moment, the cabin Father built explodes in a giant fireball. The percussion of it rocks even our barn. Most raiding the cabin are sent flying to their deaths. Wood and brick shrapnel cut down the others.

The powder kegs Bishop brought with him this morning... This is what they were for! He has saved us!

"Ah-ha!" Bishop rises. "Take that ye spiteful harpies!"

Then I hear Hecate's scream even above her minions in the throes of death.

She rises from behind the trough, her royal garb stained in slop and pig manure. She glares up at us.

A shiver runs down my spine.

Mr. Greene takes a shot at her. He misses, fumbles to reload.

Hecate vanishes to the opposite side of the barn and out of our sights.

I hear a banging in the floor behind me.

"Don't shoot!" George calls from below. "It is only us!"

I hurry to the trapdoor. "Move away," I say to Mrs. Greene and Emma. "Let them up. Let them up!"

I push her and Emma away and open the door. My brother grins at me from the ladder. "I did that for Father."

I move out of the way so he might climb it. Andrew is not far behind him. I move to close the door the moment they reach our landing, and see Hecate reach the ladder.

She climbs.

I slam the door closed and stand upon it. "Quickly!" I say. "We must bar this door with something heav—"

Hecate pounds upon the wood I stand upon. "Curse you!" she screams, her voice muffled as she strikes the door again.

"Sarah, move!" Emma says.

I look at my feet at the sound of sawing. Hecate's blade juts up and down between the small bits of plank like a needle moves through thread. I step aside to watch the blade's movement. It moves in a pattern of elimination through the cracks. I anticipate the next one. As soon as the blade emerges, I kick the side of it, breaking it from the hilt.

Hecate shrieks. She uses her inhuman strength to raise the door I stand upon an inch in the air. To my surprise, Emma jabs at Hecate's face with the pitchfork.

"Die, die!" Emma screams with her eyes closed.

Hecate wilts beneath the sudden attack. The door falls back into place.

I hear gunfire.

Mr. Greene, Bishop, and Wesley taking turns with their shots at the hayloft opening.

"Sarah!" George calls. He and Andrew work together to roll a hay bale the size of Hickory toward me. I move out of the way as they tip it end over end on top of the trapdoor. "There," he says. "Now they cannot lift it. Stay here!"

George snatches the rifle out of my hand.

"What are you doing?" I ask.

He does not stop to answer. Both he and Andrew run to the other men. In quick exchanges, my brother and his friend reload the rifles, then hand them to Bishop and Wesley to fire.

Outside the hayloft opening, I see the larger army of torches and riders not far from the barn. I hear drums pounding, war cries, and witches cackling, all amidst the constant firing line of my defenders.

Emma's face is pale. Her white knuckles cling to the pitchfork's handle. "Sarah! You are alive."

"Aye," I say. "Thanks to you."

"Come out, Chosen One!" Hecate screams rise below us. "Come out, Sarah Campbell! Come *crawling* to me on your knees and belly!"

Emma yelps.

I place my hands about her cheeks. "Emma." I stare into her terrified face. "We will fend them off! Stay here, as George said. I go to take my rifle back. I will return!"

Emma nods at me. Already, she is on the verge of tears.

I leave her side and run to the wall.

"Arrows!" Bishop calls.

All of them turn from the opening. I too throw myself against the wall in time to hear the volley whizz by, the arrows thudding behind me in the wooden beams. I peek through the slats.

A caravan of witches has arrived, accompanied by more highwaymen. All rush our barn.

I notice several carry long ladders.

"We'll be overrun!" Mr. Greene shouts above the din.

Bishop kicks the first of them away. "Quit yer wailin' and shove 'em off!"

George and Andrew jump in to help. For every ladder they repel, I see more landing. There is a clatter liken to horses galloping above me. The wrens and owls in the rafters leave their perches, all rushing to escape in a flurry of feathers and screeches.

I look upward. Faintly feel dust settling upon my cheeks.

"Bishop!" I yell. "They are on the roof!"

Moses and Hickory whinny and kick at the wooden doors of their stables below us. The cows bang against the side of their pen in hopes of finding an exit. And always, the witches cackle at our plight whilst the men shout victory cries.

Emma screams. I turn to see the trapdoor rising and falling, even with the added weight. All whilst she and Mrs. Greene swat and stab at every face that appears. I mean to run for them.

Wesley halts me. "No," he says. "Stay beside me!"

Without warning, three shadows swing inside the barn from the rooftop. One of them comes between Wesley and me, kicking me to the ground. The musky smell reeks of unwashed man.

I roll to my side.

Wesley struggles with the screaming warrior atop him. His face turns purple.

The brave stabs at him with a bone-hilted dagger.

Even with both hands wrapped around the brave's wrist, I see Wesley losing.

I reach for the long dagger Priest gave me and spring forward. With my good hand, I sheathe its blade through the brave's neck.

He jerks at the blow. His elbow catches the side of my face, knocking me astray.

I hurry to find my feet. It matters little.

The brave twitches in death not inches from me.

"Sarah," Wesley sputters blood. His face is covered in it, and I cannot discern whether it is his own, or the brave I slew.

Chaos surrounds me.

I see Mr. Greene and Bishop, both locked in their own battles with white men. Bishop ducks a swipe meant to cleave his neck and kicks his opponent out the hayloft opening with surprising ferocity for a man as old as he.

Our individual battles have given the attackers outside the barn time to regroup. I hear more ladders upon the hayloft opening.

George and Andrew hurry toward each new one, both hacking at the oncomers—George with a scythe, Andrew with his axe.

A rifle fires near my ear. My head rings with the sound. For a moment, I fear I'm made deaf by it. I turn to see Wesley's rifle smoking.

He shot the witch fighting his father in the head.

Mr. Greene lies on the floor, gasping for air.

Bishop limps back into the fray. He pulls Mr. Greene up by the lapels of his shirt. "On yer feet! We don't stop till they do!"

Wesley leaves my side to aid his father. He screams at the

sight of another witch climbing a ladder and slams the butt of his rifle into her chest. Kicking the ladder away, Wesley turns his rifle to shoot down at the massing crowd.

"There ye are, lad," Bishop says. "Use the anger!"

"*Arrows!*" George yells. He ducks over to the wall even as they soar past.

This second volley is different...these arrows are aflame.

-nineteen-

MOST OF THE ARROWS LAND AMONGST THE BOARDS AND ARE EASILY stamped out. A few strike home amidst the hay bales and catch aflame with a whooshing sound. The heat from them hits me in a blazing wave.

Black smoke fills the air.

Vaguely, I see George and Andrew rush about to throw buckets of water that Bishop had the foresight to store away. I wave my hands about in an attempt to clear the smoke. Again, I hear the scurrying of feet above me on the roof.

"Sarah!"

Rebecca! Oh, but where is she?

"I am here!" I call out in answer to her cries. I drop to my knees below the smoke line and crawl toward the direction of her voice.

"They're inside!" George shouts. "We can't hold them!"

The sounds of struggling and battle entrap me. I see the trapdoor flung open, the hay bale securing it now burned away. Emma is on her back. Her pitchfork out of reach, she kicks at a man dressed in animal pelts to keep him from reaching our level.

Mrs. Greene shouts and swings her shovel at his head. The shout gives her away though. The man ducks it at the last. He grabs hold of the shovel. With a sharp yank, he pulls it and her toward the opening. Mrs. Greene pitches forward.

Helpless, I watch her fall through the opening and the man with her.

"Noooooo!" her cry echoes down the thirty-foot shaft of air.

"Frances!" I hear Mr. Greene yell.

I scramble forward to help Emma fend off any others who might make the climb. Mr. Greene and I reach the opening at the same time.

Far below, I see Mrs. Greene's limbs contorted and broken. She lies atop the now dead man that yanked her below, moaning. "Da—vid..."

Several hooded witches reach her. One of them looks up at us expectantly. "Time to play..." she says with a ragged voice.

The others cackle. All produce long knives from their cloaks.

"Don't harm her!" Mr. Greene sounds like a wounded animal.

The witches' shoulders tremble. "Give us Sarah Campbell," one says. "And your wife goes free."

"David..." Mrs. Greene says weakly.

"Give us Sarah—" the witch says, digging the point of her blade into Mrs. Greene's bicep. Mrs. Greene cries out at the sight of her own blood being drawn. "And you all go free!"

The witch raises her knife in anticipation of our answer.

I look into the face of Mr. Greene. See he wrestles with what to do.

He grabs me roughly by the shoulder ere I have the sense to back away.

I shove away from him. Make it a few extra feet from the hole ere he grabs me again.

"No!" I cry. "Please, Mr. Greene—"

He drags me toward the hole.

I kick his shin and am released again. I turn to run.

He grabs me by the hair. Yanks me back.

"No!" I shout.

Mr. Greene lifts me under my arms to keep my feet from the floor and carries me back to the black hole.

I let my body go limp in hope my full weight will burden him till help arrives. It does little good, even when I try to squirm away like a worm upon a hook.

"Wesley!" I yell. "Wesley, help!"

It is too late, though. Wesley cannot hear my shouts above the din.

I look down the hole.

The witches wait for me. Their knives sway as they do.

I only pray the fall kills me before they can.

"I'm sorry, Sarah," Mr. Greene says. "Truly, I a—Ahh!"

Suddenly, I am released.

The witches scream. I hear a thumping sound, akin to a sack of meal hitting the ground, and then no more from the witches.

Emma hovers over me. She helps me to my feet. "Oh, Sarah... what have I done?"

Below us on the ground floor, Mr. Greene lies dead with Emma's pitchfork stuck in his back. Two witches lie trapped under his body, crushed by the weight of his fall. Where the other disappeared to, I cannot say.

"Emma..." I say. "Y-you saved me."

As if unaware of her actions, she hesitates before nodding. "Aye."

"Well," a husky voice in the darkness says. "Look who found her courage..."

A shovel swings out of the black. It strikes Emma in the back of the head.

I hear her neck snap with a loud pop.

She crumples to the floor like one of Rebecca's poppets tossed limply aside.

"Emma!" I scream.

Her killer lets the shovel drop with a clang ere she steps from the shadows.

Charlotte...

Her bloodshot eyes are the last things I see before she pounces. The force of her attack bears me to the ground.

"Sarah!"

Wesley's voice...he has seen what is happening. If only I can hold her off. "Charlotte..." I say. "We are f-friends."

"No," she snarls. "I am a sister of the night!"

Heavy boots run to me. "Get away from her!" Wesley yells.

Charlotte releases her hold on me. She wheels to face her new target.

I see Wesley raise his rifle toward her. "I will kill you, Charlotte Bailey."

Charlotte cackles. "My moon sister does not believe you."

"Wha—" he gasps.

I scream as he falls to his knees, a dagger protruding through his chest.

"Wesley!"

A raven-haired girl steps from behind him. "There truly is nothing so delicious as a sister's kiss in the moonlight," Ruth says gaily.

Charlotte pulls a bone-hilted dagger from her apron. "Should we kiss him again, sister?"

Wesley breathes wheezily. By the sound of it, Ruth punctured his lung. She kicks him to the ground. Laughs when he attempts to crawl away.

I dive at Ruth without thinking. She raises her blade too late. I grab at it with my good hand. Pound it against the boards until she releases it. I see Charlotte's approach out of the corner of my eye. I roll away as she aims a kick at my ribs. She instead connects with Ruth.

I climb to my feet as Ruth curls in a ball to catch her breath.

Charlotte sneers. "You will come with us, Sarah—"

Her gaze set on me, she does not see Wesley still lives, nor his reach for her leg.

"The Warlock means to have you," Charlotte continues. "If Hecate doesn't scalp you first."

Wesley's hand is an inch from her.

"Neither will have me," I say defiantly. "Nor will you live to see it."

Wesley grabs her ankles and pulls. She falls to the floor, her face smacking the boards. I hear her nose shatter in a sickening crunch.

"Sar-ah," Wesley sputters. "I l-love y-you."

It is not until this moment I see how close he is to the black hole. Charlotte starts to rise. Blood pours from her now twisted nose.

Before I can say otherwise, Wesley grabs her left leg with both hands. He rolls his body toward the hole and pitches over the side.

His weight drags Charlotte with him. She screams at the realization. Her hands claw at the boards, but find no purchase.

In an instant, both are gone.

"Wesley!"

I know I am too late, even as I crawl toward it.

Please don't be dead. I pray. *Please don't be dead.*

I look down.

Charlotte's neck is bent unnaturally beneath her body. Thankfully, her bloodied gown covers Wesley's face. I am not sure I could bear to see him dead too. Not when so many others—

A sudden, searing pain shoots through my arm. I scream.

"You killed my moon sister!"

I feel my own blood flowing freely as Ruth plucks the dagger from my body. I roll away.

Ruth follows. She raises her blade to strike again. Swings it down.

The blow does not fall upon me.

A blade whistles from amidst the smoke and severs her forearm.

Ruth falls, screaming and clutching at the bloodied stump where her hand existed not a moment ago.

Andrew appears with his axe in hand. "For Mother!" He kicks her in the face, and raises the axe again. "And Father!"

I look away ere he swings it, but I cannot shut out her shrieks of pain.

The axe whistles again. "For Henry!" Again it whistles. "And Mary!"

I cannot contain my tears. They sting against my face even more than the pain in my arm. I curl into a ball and rock whilst covering my ears. I am convinced naught will ever still Ruth's cries.

"Andrew!" Ruth shouts. "I am y-your s-sist—"

"No," Andrew says, his voice shaking. "You are a shade."

His blade whistles a final time, and silences Ruth forever.

A moment later, I feel the warmth of a human touch. "Sarah," Andrew says quietly. "Sarah?"

"N-no," I sputter. I feel his arms about me. I think to shake him loose, but do not. His comforting embraces reminds me of Priest's upon the road. *If only I might stay here...*

"Wh-why," Andrew says, more to himself than me. "Why have the drums stopped?"

I open my eyes and see Andrew bleeds also, an arrow in his shoulder. His jacket is torn, slashed by a savage blade no doubt. Smoke yet lingers. I gather the barn is not afire, else we would be suffocating in it. A few ashes glow near the hayloft opening. A lean figure rushes to stamp them out. *George.*

"Good lad," Bishop groans somewhere in the shadows. "Ye done right well."

Andrew helps me to my feet. Only when I am steadied does he rejoin George by the hayloft opening. Bishop staggers into the moonlight to join them.

Are we few all that remain?

To my right lies Emma's body. Even in death, her blue eyes look as though she might cry at any moment. My own tears well again. I fight them off. Rather than go to her, I hurry to the trapdoor and close it. Then, I drag her body over top of it. Mayhap her weight will at least slow any new attackers from breaching our landing.

My eyes fall upon a poppet, its hair long since singed away. *Rebecca!* Where is she? Surely she is with Mother!

I rush to the furthest corner of the barn. There, I find a new horror.

Mother's face is blank. She does not stir at my approach. It would almost seem she sleeps peacefully. That is if one did not notice her left wrist opened. The hidden dagger she kept is still tightly clenched in her right hand, almost like she fears Indians will steal her away even from death's grip.

Oddly, I have no tears left to cry. Hate overwhelms me at her cowardice. *How could she do this? How, when so many others died this night fighting to live? How could she abandon us?*

"R-Rebecca," I force myself to say. "Rebecca, are you here?"

There is no reply.

I remind my legs to move, and step closer to Mother's corpse. She cannot hurt me now, I tell them. For a moment, I believe I will have to move her body to search amongst the hay. Fear of what I might discover keeps me back. "Rebecca, answer me," I say. "Pray, tell me you are hiding."

My sister answers, but not from the hay.

"*Sarah!*"

Her voice calls from behind me...outside the barn...

I limp toward the hayloft opening. Bishop halts me ere I keep going and pitch over the side. Below us, I see at least twenty in Hecate's army still live. Torches light their angry faces, their dark mistress...and my sister.

Rebecca struggles in Hecate's grip. "Sarah!"

Hecate holds the dagger at Rebecca's neck close. She grins up at me. "Come down, Sarah. We mean to do you a great honor."

Even in the dark, I feel her penetrating gaze.

"If not—" Hecate raises the dagger to Rebecca's scalp. "I make good on the promise I made last eve."

"Sarah..." Rebecca cries.

Hecate's minions laugh at my expense. Their humor is short-lived, however.

"The tongue of the Devil's daughter?" Bishop yells. "Sounds like a right fine prize to me!"

He casts me roughly aside into my brother's arms. Dropping

his rifle, he turns upon the ledge with surprising dexterity. Then, he descends the sole remaining ladder.

"Wait!" George cries.

Bishop does not heed him.

I crawl to the edge of the barn just as Bishop reaches the bottom.

He strides unflinchingly toward Hecate. Loosens a dagger and tomahawk from his belt. "Unhand her, ye spiteful wench!"

"I know your voice." Hecate laughs. "Patrick Glover, is it? How did you come to join this ragged lot?"

"Don't matter." Bishop answers. "Ye won't live to tell the tale, unless ye be preachin' to the Devil hisself. So, come on with ye," He waves her toward him. "For it's Hell I mean to send ye too."

Hecate shoves my sister into the care of another. "Very well. Tell my Lord Father I said hello."

Without warning, Hecate takes a torch from a witch and flings it at Bishop.

Bishop spins to dodge it. He raises his dagger upon completing the revolution and only barely deflects her dagger from slicing his skull. Bishop dips his blade, pitching Hecate forward. He catches her in the face with an elbow.

Hecate stumbles.

I watch Bishop press his advantage, but the witches move to block him. They step in front of their fallen leader and beat Bishop with the flats of their daggers. He swings wildly to force them back. They relent, but their distraction gives Hecate time to find her feet.

"Clever, old man," she says. "But have you any more tricks?"

Bishop hacks and spits. "I've the luck a the Irish on me side.

And an Irishman ne'er has need for trickery, unlike blatherin' wenches."

"Shall I show you the power of wenches, sir?" Hecate turns her hateful stare on me, then her followers. "Bring her to me."

As one, a group of Hecate's witches and highwaymen rush the ladders to climb.

George pulls me back from the ledge. He and Andrew form a human shield in front of me.

"What are you two doing?" I say. "Ready the rifles!"

"We are out of powder," Andrew says.

So this is our last stand. Clenching Priest's dagger, I push my two protectors aside to stand between them.

George nods at me. Andrew swings his axe in practice.

"Up, up, up!" I hear Hecate urge. "Back on your feet, old man!"

I see and hear the tops of the ladders shake as our attackers climb. My heart quivers with each tap of the wood. I look at the dagger in my hand. It has already served me well this night. I pray it serves a bit longer.

"Remember what Bishop said," George says. "Keep back from the ledge, else they pitch us down."

I do not have time to answer. The first group of witches seems to fly up and over the edge, even as several men swing down from the roof. Then I am rushing forward, screaming at them as they scream back at me. The battle is a nightmare come alive. I see a witch's blackened teeth ere I bury the blade in her chest and yank it free.

Beside me, George ducks a blow meant for his head. He sweeps his attacker behind the knee and brings his foe to the floor. With a vicious kick, my brother smashes his foe's temple like an overripe melon.

I see my next attacker too late. She raises her dagger then her head whips back as a dog gone to the edge of its leash. A long dagger sprouts from her chest.

I shudder at her gurgling. The hooded witch who did the killing slings her aside.

"Move!"

The witch raises a tomahawk and flings it. I feel the rush of wind as it grazes past my ear before finding a home in the skull of another witch come up behind me. My savior pushes past me, wrenches the tomahawk free only to slay another hooded sister ere she can kill George.

I hear the last attacker die behind me as Andrew wins his own battle.

George crawls backward to escape. He pauses when our savior offers to help him stand. My brother's face pales. "You..."

The witch removes its hood. His face is blackened with soot. A palm print of blood stretches over his nose, the painted fingers over his eyes and forehead. I understand it now how his enemies would think him a demon.

"Priest..." I say. "How did you—"

Reaching for his ribs, he groans and collapses to a knee. Blood covers his hand when he takes it away. He looks at me and sighs.

"Oh, Priest," I fall upon him, clinging to his neck, rubbing my cheek against his. "I thought you dead!"

He gently rubs the back of my head. Then, he tugs it. Pulls it taut.

"Ow," I say. I try to pull away.

He will not permit it.

"You're hurting me..." I say.

A cold blade presses against the back of my neck. The cut occurs in one quick slice. I fall forward. A wet sensation trickles down my neck. I put my fingers to it. It feels warm and sticky.

Blood...My blood! I wheel about.

Priest holds my long locks in his hand. Wincing, he looks at George, then Andrew. "Keep her safe," he says gruffly.

He dons his hood anew and strides for the hayloft ledge, still clutching at his ribs.

"Where are you going?" I say.

He reaches the edge. Victoriously raises the fist holding my hair. "*YEYEYEYEAH!*"

I recoil at how alike he sounds to a savage war cry.

They take up his call.

I watch Priest turn upon the ledge and start his descent.

"No, Sarah!" George restrains me from rushing to Priest. "He said to stay here!"

I shove my brother off. I slink in the shadows toward the hayloft opening. George and Andrew are not far behind. Reaching the wall, I peer between the slats at the battle below.

Hecate has left Bishop to her minions. She stands at the forefront of her now smaller army, awaiting Priest's return with my presumed scalp.

I see Bishop struggle to keep his feet, even as the circling group darts in and out when Bishop's back is to them. Witches slice at his legs. Men smack him in the head with their bows. Their combined laughter meant to disorient him.

Bishop jumps as one startled each time they cry out.

"He cannot last much longer," George whispers.

"Look!" Andrew points.

Priest approaches Hecate. He kneels before her, offers the trophy of my hair.

Hecate motions him to rise.

Priest does so, and stabs her in the stomach.

"Aaaaah!" Hecate wails.

Priest wrenches my sister away from her captor. He pushes Rebecca safely behind him ere drawing the tomahawk with his free hand. He removes his hood and shouts another war cry.

With their mistress dead, the remainder of her army flees to the cornfield.

George gasps beside me. "Bishop!"

The few remaining witches have pressed their advantage.

Bishop, forced to a knee, strains to keep his blade locked with one of their axes.

Priest wastes no time. He throws his tomahawk at another witch's skull, splitting it in two. I watch him rush in. He uses his arms like a club, batting down a third witch's arm, disarming her. He butts his head into hers.

The witch stumbles away, fleeing for the corn.

"Kill her," both George and Andrew say at once.

Priest does not. I watch him help Bishop to stand.

It is over. It must be over.

Then I see a shadow rise shakily.

Her movement slow, but sure, Hecate lifts an Indian bow. Fumbles to notch an arrow.

I look ahead to what will be her aim.

Priest...

I push away from the wall. Go deep inside the barn. I halt near the trapdoor and Emma's body. Ahead of me, the full hunter's moon brightly shines outside the open hayloft door; a hulking orb meant to light my path.

With sweaty hands, I reach into my apron. My fingers clench over the dagger Captain Alden gifted his son. Gifted Priest.

I pull it out, thinking back on the stag he killed. How he surprised and killed it without leaving a mark. I sprint forward as fast as my wounded legs can carry me. I never halt. Not even as I approach the edge into nothingness.

George sees me. He leaves the wall to stop me. "Sarah, no!"

My foot touches the edge. I push off, launching into naught but air.

A giddy shiver runs through me. My feet blindly kick in search of anything solid, but find no purchase. Twenty feet from the ground, I look below me.

Hecate has notched her arrow.

At ten feet, I raise the dagger over my head.

Hecate hesitates, seems to sense her demise. She looks over her shoulder at the last. Her fatal mistake is to not turn her gaze toward Heaven.

Earth rushes up to greet me. I blindly swing the dagger down with all the strength I can muster. Pain, far beyond which should be possible for anyone to experience, quakes my entire body. I feel my legs shoot straight up into my chest.

Then my world goes dark.

-twenty-

My eyes flutter open to sunlight. The scent of trees surrounds me. A fire crackles not far away. A horse whinnies and shuffles. The world spins with light. I raise my arm to shield it. Red pain shoots up to my shoulder. "Oh..." I groan.

"Sarah!"

Two figures rush to me. Their faces are fuzzy, but I recognize my sister's voice. Rebecca places her warm cheek upon mine, both made wet by our combined tears.

"Sarah," she says. "You are alive!"

"Aye." I pull her close and let my lips linger on her forehead. "I would not leave you."

The figure behind her clears his throat. "Rule number one, lass—"

"Bishop..." I say.

He chuckles good-naturedly. "—Don't...get...attached. Course I might not be alive if'n ye hadn't...but then, no." he reconsiders. "Mayhap I wouldn't a been there at all if not for ye...blast it, I don't know."

My sight clears. I lay in a wagon. Surely the soreness in my back is liken to those strung upon a torturer's rack. My attempt to sit up does not go well. My right arm, bound and hung in a sling about my neck, will not support me.

Neither will my legs work. At first, I fear my fall has crippled me, yet I feel a deep soreness still resides in them.

I toss the quilts covering me aside. Stiff branches, running the length of my legs, tightly prevent me from bending my knees.

"Easy, lass," Bishop says, rubbing my arm and helping me to a sitting position. He leans heavily on a long stick, I assume a crutch. A black patch covers his right eye. Even it cannot hide all the sliver scars the witches marked him with. Despite it all, he seems happy enough to see me awake.

"Ye won't be skippin' about anytime soon. The lads told me what ye did," he scoffs. "A right brave thing. Mad, to be sure—" His eyebrows raise. "—but brave. Don't believe the Queen Wench ever saw ye comin'. Plum near took her head off, ye did. Death from Heaven, as it were." He chuckles. "Why, the story'd only be finer ifn' a broomstick came down with ye."

His own joke sends him into a coughing fit. He leans back to hack the phlegm from his throat and spit it away.

His humor is not lost on me, but I cannot share it now. Not with the knowledge so many others died to make it so. With my good hand pulling at the side rail, I slowly scoot to the edge of the wagon.

"She is dead then?" I ask. "Hecate, er, Abigail Will—"

He nods. "Aye. She won't be risin' to stir trouble no more. I dare say ye be lucky both yer legs didn't shoot straight out yer arse when ye landed atop her. They'll heal in time, but I'll warrant ye gimp a bit more than I the rest a yer days."

Strange. I do not feel sated with the news she is dead, nor that I killed her. In fact, I feel nothing. With a heavy sigh, I take in my surroundings.

The wagon I sit in lay at the middle of a small camp. The

purplish brown bodies of squirrels and rabbits, stripped of their skin and gutted, rest upon a spit over the fire with Mother's cookware piled beside it.

Rebecca hops into the wagon with me. "We thought you would die of a fever, Sarah." She hugs me again, buries her face into my good shoulder. "That is what Mother died of."

Bishop rests a gloved hand upon my forearm ere I can speak. He shakes his head. "Aye," he says. "We weren't wonton of losin' ye both to ailment."

So he shields her with one of his lies. I rub my sister's back. Kiss the top of her head. Father may have believed a lie remains such, no matter the goodly intent, but I cannot share the sentiment. Better Rebecca grow believing Mother died of a fever rather than be plagued with the same crippling fear that brought Mother to make her own end.

"How long did the fever hold me?" I ask.

"Nigh on three day now," Bishop says. "It broke in the night. Thank God for it. We've a need to be off soon."

"Off?"

Wrinkles form upon Bishop's forehead. "Aye. They'll be others lookin' for us. Why do ye think we're out here in the woods and not yer family's barn?"

"But you said Hecate—"

"Calm yerself, lass," he says. "The crows and worms have fed on her rottin' corpse these past few days."

"You did not bury her?"

Bishop clucks his tongue. "No..."

I pull Rebecca closer. "But what of the others? Emma? The Greene family, Wes—" His name sticks on my tongue. "Surely, you buried them."

Bishop shakes his head. "I gave 'em each the Lord's blessin' ere we left."

I lean upon the railing, tears already welling. "How could you...how could you not bury them?"

"It's a right hard thing to understand," Bishop says. "But it needed done. Ye've no more to fear from Abigail Williams. It's those set her upon us we've to think on now."

A lump forms in my throat. "The Mathers..."

Bishop nods. "They and others servin' 'em most like. The church burnin', murders at the Bailey and Martin homesteads; those sorta things bring questions. Why, folk from the next town over saw the smoke from yer own house and came to check on ye that very mornin'. We barely had time to cart ye and the supplies away."

"But the bodies—"

"Stayed where they fell."

I think to argue my point to him. Then I see *him.*

He leans against an elm tree, his dark gaze never leaving me. With his arms defiantly crossed, I would almost believe him angry if not for his dimples.

Bishop glances over his shoulder. When he turns to look back at me he grins like a dog discovering a bone. "Come, lass." He pulls Rebecca out of the wagon. "Let's rally the lads and check the traps one last time ere we're off."

He lightly sets her upon the ground. Rebecca does not bother to look back as she runs deeper into the woods. Her fearlessness gives me hope our troubles are over, for now, despite Bishop's claims others may soon hunt for us. I feel a tap upon my leg.

Bishop winks at me. "Don't have too much fun now."

He laughs himself into a coughing fit as he stumbles away

after my sister. Only when I can no longer hear his laughter does Priest approach me.

My heart quickens. *What do I say to him?*

His shirt unbuttoned, I see his ribs are bound by black cloth, no doubt torn and bandaged from one of the witch cloaks. Each step makes him wince. Still, he comes on.

I take a deep breath. *Truly, what do two people say to one another after both proved themselves willing to die for the other?*

Priest sweeps all my concerns away. No sooner does he reach the wagon and I open my mouth to speak, than he places his rough hands about my cheeks. Pulls me close. His grip is firm, lips soft.

I exhale. Wrap my good arm about his neck. Now it is I pulling him closer. I hear him groan, but I care not for his pain. My only thought is to not let this moment go. I run my fingers up the back of his scalp. Scratch at his skin like I mean to scalp him with my nails.

The sudden, glorious movement makes my head swoon so fast I am the first to break away. I open my eyes and stare into his.

"You..." I say. "You are an Alden."

I regret the words the minute I speak them. *This is what I chose to say to him? This man who risked his life for me more than once, and I can only speak to I know his Christian name?*

He does not laugh at me, however; only looks upon me with surprising tenderness. He nods.

"What is your name?" I beg of him. "I must know."

He twirls a lock of my hair on his finger. "Priest," he says so softly it is almost a whisper.

"No," I say. "I wish to know the name given you at birth. Not what Bishop named you, nor the natives—"

A shadow crosses his face.

"—I wish to know your true name. The one your mother gave you."

I may as well have asked the rocks and trees to speak. They would give the same answer. I judge my question makes him wrestle with some inner demon by his harsh gaze, but I do not fear him now in the way I once did during our moonlight ride.

Priest looks away from me toward the trees.

He is a wild thing, like unto a bear, or wolf, I have the arrogance to believe I might tame.

Father taught me wild things are best set free ere their spirit be slain.

I reach out, touch his cheek to draw his attention back to me.

His deep brown eyes question me; equal parts anger and sadness.

"Priest," I say quietly. "Your name is Priest."

He stares back at me. Says nothing and everything at once.

I lean forward. Kiss him again.

His lips caress my own in such a way I feel it even down to my toes. Though slower, it does not lack for passion. Only when I hear the voices of George, Andrew, and Bishop approaching does Priest break away.

Seeing me, George smiles. He does not wave, however. Nor does he call out for me as he once would have. In one hand he holds a rifle, in the other a line of trout. Something about him is different. He walks taller now, more sure of himself. Then it strikes me.

George is a man now.

Andrew Martin carries Rebecca atop his shoulders. She laughs as he walks beneath some of the lower branches, forcing her to duck under them.

George reaches us first. He lifts the line of fish over the side and places it in the wagon. "Did Bishop tell you?"

"Tell me what?"

"We're leaving today. Now," he says. "We only waited for you to waken."

Indeed, already the others waste no time in collecting their things from around the camp.

The thought of leaving frightens me. All my fears disappear when Priest catches my eye and I see his dimples. "All of us?" I ask.

"Aye," Bishop calls. "Unless ye'd rather stay in Winford. God knows ye'll have the whole town to yerself now the rest of 'em be dead."

No. I could not stay. The ghosts of all those we knew will forever haunt me here. I have no lurking desire to relive their faces, nor tell the story of how Winford came to fall to any newcomers. "But where will we go?"

Bishop carries Mother's china to the wagon. "Well, speakin' for meself, I've had enough a yer damnable colonies." He places the china beside me and winks at me. "Tell me true, lass...what do ye think a leprechauns?"

"I-I do not know—"

He leaves my side then, and walks alongside the wagon toward the head of it. "The little people are a fearsome, trickerous sort, or so me father claimed," Bishop says as he climbs into the driver's seat. "I've a mind to catch me one a the wee bastards ere a banshee comes to carry me to Heaven."

Rebecca runs to the front of the wagon. "Hurry, hurry!" She wills Andrew toward her.

I watch him lift her up to sit beside Bishop. The old man

welcomes her with a warm embrace. Rebecca laughs and scoots closer to him so she is beneath his protective arm.

I turn back to watch Priest swing astride his stallion.

The noble steed nods its head in approval at having its master back.

"Right, lads," Bishop cracks the reins. "Let's shove off!"

I feel the wagon move beneath me, and hear Bishop clear his throat ere he begins to sing.

Come, fair lass, just you and me.
We're bound for them colonies, far o'er the sea...
'Augh, no,' she said. 'Ye stubborn ol' fool.
I've heard o' those lands, and them savages cruel.'
So the Lord sent me a bastard I came to name Priest.
Ugly as sin, and a stubborn ol' beast.
'Come, lad,' says I, 'We'll hunt us some witches!'
All o'er we went, and by God, killed us them bitches!

He laughs himself into a coughing fit then. A laugh quickly joined by my brother and sister.

Priest grins at me.

I close my eyes, fixing the two dimples gracing his dirtied face in my mind. Then, I allow the sounds of hooves and the creaking wagon to lull me into peaceful sleep.

Salem witch trials 1692 - 1693

"Witches" executed - (hanged)

Bridget Bishop
George Burroughs
Martha Carrier
Martha Corey
Mary Easty
Sarah Good
Elizabeth Howe
George Jacobs, Sr.
Susannah Martin
Rebecca Nurse
Alice Parker
Mary Parker
John Proctor
Ann Pudeator
Wilmott Redd
Margaret Scott
Samuel Wardwell
Sarah Wildes
John Willard

*Giles Corey – (pressed to death)

"Afflicted" accusers – (core group)

Elizabeth Hubbard
Mercy Lewis
Ann Putnam Jr.
Susannah Sheldon
Martha Sprague
Sarah Vibber
Mary Walcott
Mary Warren
Abigail Williams

Acknowledgments

The Salem trials have held my interest since I first learned of them in grade school. However, my initial knowledge merely scratched the surface when compared to the exhaustive research others have compiled.

For any interested in non-fiction regarding the trials, I highly recommend Mary Beth Norton's *In The Devil's Snare: The Salem Witch Crisis of 1692,* psychologist Linnda Caporael's *Science* article linking the behaviors of Salem accusers to that of ergotism, and *Salem Possessed: The Social Origins of Witchcraft,* by Paul Boyer and Stephen Nissenbaum. Also, my hearty thanks to the University of Virginia for their *Salem Witch Trials Documentary Archive and Transcription Project,* and the University of Missouri-Kansas City School of Law's extensive online database.

Additional thanks to the Salem Witch Museum, the History Channel, Discovery Channel, Smithsonian Magazine, National Geographic, and Gail L. Schumann of the American Phytopathological Society, for their related works.

In regards to this novel, I could not have done without my coven: Annetta Ribken, Jennifer Wingard, Valerie Bellamy, and Greg Sidelnik. Thank you all for lending me your many talents and knowledge.

For Whit, Gene, Sarah, Tyler, and my speed-reader, Amber. My humble thanks for the wise counsel you each have given me.

To my parents, siblings, and the countless family and friends who have followed my crazy antics all this way, my thanks for your continued patience and support, or for faking it at least. I remain none the wiser if it's all been just an act.

My condolences to the victims and families of the Salem trials, and my prayers such a tragedy never again occurs.

Last, but never least, to you, dear reader. Thanks for not allowing Hecate to scare you off.

About the Author

Salem's Vengeance is Aaron Galvin's second novel.

His debut, *Salted*, a YA urban fantasy, continues to receive critical acclaim for its unique take on mermaids and selkies.

Aaron is also an accomplished actor, screenwriter, and film producer. He has worked on Hollywood blockbusters (*The Dark Knight*, *Flags of Our Fathers*), starred in dozens of indie films, and he co-wrote/executive produced the 2013 award-winning comedic feature film, *Wedding Bells & Shotgun Shells*.

Aaron is a proud member of SCBWI and currently lives in Southern California with his wife and daughter.

Find out more about Aaron Galvin and the Salt Series:
Website: *www.aarongalvin.com*
Salted fanpage: *www.facebook.com/saltseries*
Author fanpage: *http://goo.gl/cvNhgD*
Twitter: *twitter.com/aarongalvin5*

Now, here's a sample chapter of book one in
Aaron Galvin's *Salt Series*

Available for purchase at most online retailers

LENNY

LENNY DOLAN NEVER ASKED FOR A SALTED LIFE. NO ONE SMART ever did.

But unlike those poor wretches stolen from the surface and dragged into the depths, Lenny didn't have anything with which to compare his Salt existence. Born in the realm beneath the waves, he knew of no other life until his owner raised him up and gave him a profession.

None of Lenny's fellow catchers bothered to stir when he woke screaming from a night terror, two hours past. Each recognized the cries associated with guilt's icy stabs and the shaded memories of those they hauled back into lives of Salt slavery.

Lenny shivered in his hammock crafted of worn trawler nets. *Fear is for runnas not catchas. Don't run from it. Become it.*

He tossed the molded blanket aside and swung his stunted legs free of the bedding. Lenny winced at the cold onslaught when his bare feet grazed the cavern floor. He did not pull away. Once his feet numbed, he slunk through the maze of sleeping bodies.

Lenny had grown quite good at slinking over the years, admittedly not hard for one of his stature. He tested the hinges of the rotted driftwood door. It threatened to fall off but held. He thanked the Ancients for their mercy and slipped out of the shack.

Morn had not yet graced Crayfish Cavern. Some might have risked a torch to ward off the near absolute dark and light their way to the docks. Lenny did not. Doing so would only attract unwanted attention from whichever taskmaster had drawn the early watch. Not to mention the accompanying ten lashes for being outside of quarters without leave. Instead, he used the glittering stalactites, high in the stony ceiling, to guide him. Like countless glittering stars, they winked at him as if to warn they kept watch where taskmasters' eyes could not follow. Declan Dolan had taught his son the use of them as a pup. They had yet to fail him.

Lenny caught a dank smell in the air, rife with the blended stench of body odor, vomit, and excrement. He recognized it for a fresh slave crop come down the Gasping Hole. Not for the first time, he wondered why the taskmasters didn't have the newest catches cleaned upon their arrival. Soon enough the lucky amongst them would earn a Selkie suit. The others...

He snorted the scent away and continued on. Even now, with no one to see, he avoided the boardwalk. Bad habits led to accidents and Lenny sought no more of those. He waddled alongside the boardwalk, trading the slave stink for that of seaweed hung to dry from the tops of six-foot racks.

Barrels lined the dock, each of them brimming with fresh ocean crops—Atlantic cod and haddock, littleneck clams, mussels, and oysters. All awaited surface delivery for the Boston fish markets.

Lenny's stomach grumbled at the sights and smells of the fresh and untouched food. He hurried past, lest temptation overpower his sensibilities, not stopping until he reached the oldest dock. Its wooden beams remained in drastic need of a repair that would never come. He hopscotched over the barren spaces toward the dock edge, leaned over the side to look down.

The cavern ceiling gave the ocean waters an eerie, greenish glow. Three-foot waves struck the thick, barnacle-encrusted pillars. Lenny felt a giddy rush as they shook the rickety wooden pier. The receding tide beckoned him come hunt, then another series of waves rushed to shake the pier anew.

Lenny reached behind his shoulders for the soft and fuzzy hood draped down his backside. Smoky grey and adorned with white circles of varying sizes, it hung from what Drybacks would say resembled a one-piece wetsuit. Donning the hood, he pictured the Salted form given to him—a tiny Ringed Seal.

Lenny's transformation began.

He felt the hood elongate, covering his face, blinding him. His sleeves and leggings tickled past his bare feet and hands, warming them. The sealskin grew further, cocooning his legs into a single tail. He knelt and lay prostrate before his upper body weight toppled him. He felt his feet splay sideways, toes curling to form two hind flippers.

His already pudgy stomach bulged and grew into a fat, seal belly. The white circles of his former hood scattered across his back like a light touch meant to tickle. They shifted in size—some grew to the size of dish plates, others shrank to the size of coins.

He felt his sleeves cover and tighten against his human hands like mittens. They morphed into fore flippers and sprouted nails from tiny digits at the end. His nose and mouth grew into a cat-like muzzle. Whiskers burst from his cheeks. His ears retracted to leave two holes on either side of his seal head.

Lenny opened his seal eyes as the transformation from human to seal completed. He dove into the near freezing North Atlantic water headfirst. The water should feel frigid, he knew, but his seal body's blubbery layer kept the cold at bay.

A school of cod drifted nearby. Lenny gave chase. One he nipped in his mouth before the doomed fish recognized him for a threat. The others he swam down, hooking them with claws sharp enough to hack through glacier ice.

The school unnaturally changed direction.

Lenny halted mid-swim. With a shift of his head, he spun to face whatever predator stalked him now. He saw a chimney of bubbles churn below frothy white circles near the surface where he entered not moments ago. *Looks like I'm not the only hunta this mornin'.*

He caught the scent of his owner's seahorses on the current. The thought occurred to him one might have escaped, but their stable door beneath the docks remained tightly latched.

His seal instincts suggested he surface and head for shore. Lenny dove deeper.

Slap!

The noise came from the surface; a sea otter, floating on its back, used its tail like a paddle to propel it forward.

Endrees. Lenny realized his mistake too late.

A grey shadow with light rings across its back sped up from the depths. Its skull collided with his stomach stealing his breath away.

Lenny swiped at the other Ringed Seal.

His opponent batted away the weak attempt. It weaved behind, collared him by the nape with its pincer-like jaws.

Felt like an early mornin' swim, huh? a man's hard voice growled in Lenny's mind like one of his own thoughts. *Against the rules and five lashes for a first offense. How many times ya done this now? Eight?*

Ya've only caught me eight, Lenny directed his thoughts to the other seal.

Eight times too many.

The sea otter dove to their depth and swam circles around the two seals.

Get away from me, Endrees, said Lenny to the otter.

It replied with a series of trills. Then it flipped to its back and swam alongside him, just out of reach.

Endrees, Lenny's captor spoke. *Go to shore.*

The otter stuck out its tongue but obeyed the command and swam away.

Good riddance, Lenny said. *Ya oughta drown that sea rat.*

The other seal bit down harder. With a quick tug, it dragged Lenny inland. *A catcha watches...waits in the shadows to make sure the goin's safe. Otherwise he's the one bein' caught. Ya supposed to have at least two ways of escape. Ya forget that?*

I was in the water, Lenny argued. *There's a thousand different directions I coulda swum.*

If ya got no plan of where to go it don't matta. Ya neva gonna be big Len, so ya gotta be fasta—

—or smarta if ya wanna live, Lenny interrupted. *I haven't forgot.*

The other seal said nothing more as they neared the shoreline shallows.

Lenny poked his head out of the water to learn who his captor had wrangled to release them both. A pair of sausage-sized fingers grabbed his upper seal lip before he could see anything. The fingers yanked up and then swept the entire seal head backward like removing a costumed mask. The seal head changed to an average hood again before draping down Lenny's backside.

He felt his seal claws retract into fingers as the flippers melted back into sleeves. His tail split in two, the remains of it shrinking up and against his ankles. Lenny shivered, now without the seal's blubber to shield him. He glanced up to see who had released him.

Paulo Varela, a bred-and-born product of slave owner selection. The crayfish tattoo on his neck marked him as belonging to August Collins. Its claws seemed to reach for his jaws as he yawned. His normally dark-gold Selkie coat glistened black, now soaked by ocean water. Paulo wiped the last bits of sleep from his eyes. "Heya, Len. Did you have to get up so early?"

Lenny ignored him, just as he ignored Endrees hissing at him from atop a nearby boulder. He waded up the stony shore as Paulo went deeper to release the other Selkie.

"Don't walk away from me, son," the captor's voice transitioned from thought to spoken word.

Lenny turned around.

A grizzled, middle-aged dwarf had replaced his seal opponent. The little man stood no taller than Paulo's waistline and, like Lenny, wore the smoke-grey suit with embroidered white circles marking him as a Ringed Seal. His hardened, lumpy face appeared marred by a drunken chiseler who had left the numerous scars for sport, and the corners of his hazel eyes wrinkled into crow's feet the longer he stared at Lenny.

Declan Dolan pointed at his son. "How many times ya gotta see others whipped before ya smarten up, boy?"

"Pop," Lenny said. "We're catchas—"

"That don't make ya no betta than those bound for the Block," Declan said. "Ya still a slave! Master Collins can do with ya what he wants. That includes sellin' ya."

Paulo snorted. "August would never do that. Lenny's the only thing that keeps you from running."

"Oh, yeah?" Declan said. "So what if Master Collins decides the lash isn't keepin' his catchas on the straight and narrow? Maybe he takes one of Lenny's ears to remind him how important it is for slaves to listen. Better yet, Paulie, what if he takes ours to make sure *we* keep Lenny followin' the rules? How'd that be?"

Paulo instinctively reached for his ears and massaged the crystal-studded earrings.

"Sorry, Pop," Lenny said. "It won't happen again."

"Mistakes and apologies don't keep ya safe in the Salt, boys. No more than they will on land," Declan said. "Now come on, the both of ya. Ya been called up."

Lenny straightened. "Did someone run off in the night?"

Both young catchers looked to Declan for confirmation. Neither received an answer. The elder Dolan limped alongside the boardwalk with his pet otter close on his heels.

Lenny noticed Paulo's earrings twinkle just before the thought transmission came through. *We're going out.*